DON'T LEAVE ME, FRENCH FRIES

FRENCH FRIES

A Novel By Christopher Abbott

Don't Leave Me, French Fries
By Christopher Abbott

Cover and layout design by Marc Foelsch.
Printed in the United States of America.

ISBN-13: 978-1978452190

DON'T LEAVE ME, FRENCH FRIES

A Novel By Christopher Abbott

DEDICATION:

To my friends from Watson's who have waited patiently...oh, these many years... in hopes they would live long enough to see the reality of my words find their way to the page. Without my wife of fifty years, who continues to show me the meaning of true love, and you guys, there would be no story: Janie, Whitehead, Cooper, Bliz, Elaine, Weatherby, Bancher, Beverly, Pam, Sam, Gary, Donna, Bob. You know who you are. There are two types of people in the world: entitled or indebted. I remain the latter, forever.

SPECIAL THANKS:

Many thanks to my early readers & editors: Diane Horan, Jane Abbott, Jaimee Reinertsen, Scott Abbott, Michael Gerhardt, Jefferson at First Editing, Jeannie Ketchum, Beverly Presti, Ken Cooper, Florence Cooper, Opi and Kirsten Leckszas, Austine Howard, and Peg and Ed Harshaw. Thanks to Marc Foelsch for design & layout, to Ocean City Historical Museum for help researching historical events, and to the medical team at the Hospital at University of Pennsylvania for your skill and care throughout my brain surgery and recovery.

PROLOGUE

Like the song says, "Oh, what a lady! What a night!" I danced down the beach on that warm August night like Gene Kelly in *Singin' in the Rain,* except I had no umbrella, no rain, no orchestra floating music through the evening air… just me and my euphoria stepping on moon beams along the edge of the sea. Oh, don't get me wrong, there was music all right, but the sound could not be heard beyond my own skin. If love were a dance, I would have danced myself to the very edge of forever. I was in a hypnotic daze, weaving unsteadily along a pathway of sparkling sand while a magic carpet of light seduced me to come on board for a ride.

There is a definite moment in a man's life when he knows, without question, that he loves and is loved by a woman. This was that moment.

The last thing I remember was a slow downward spiral onto the beach, and then I blacked out. When I opened my eyes and looked up, stars filled my vision, dancing in celestial circles. I couldn't move from where I had crash-landed. I just lay dormant, focusing on the embrace of the sand that still held warmth from the day's lingering heat. It felt like a deep, penetrating hot massage on my back. Only my bathing suit separated me from being one with nature. I guess I'd lost my shirt in the dunes at the south end of the island sometime in the misty hours of a rapidly vanishing night. How on earth could I be expected to remember simple details like where my clothes were at this particular juncture? I felt naked and free. The only thought soaking my highly pickled brain was how much I loved Laura… God, how I loved her.

As I reached out for the beach underneath to steady my quite inebriated body, a wave came rolling on shore, encasing my tanned six-foot frame in a blanket of sand, salt, and a pile of very soggy seaweed. Instinctively, I flipped over in crablike fashion, along the sand just above the water line, and then tried to hoist myself up to a vertical position.

The effort failed miserably. I toppled over, backwards, like an uprooted tree. Pillowing my arms behind my head, I allowed my eyes to absorb the Milky Way as it formed pinwheels of refracted light that pierced my befuddled brain. I struggled to interpret what my eyes were straining to keep steady.

Everything was so foggy, and the beach wouldn't keep still. In my happily drunken state, I tried to relive the last amazing six hours. So I locked my eyes on a star, light years away, to steady a swirling head just long enough to replay the happiest, most outrageous, night of my life.

CHAPTER 1

I couldn't wait to get out of Watson's Restaurant that Sunday in late August. The night seemed endless. Every time I looked at my watch, the minute hand never seemed to move. I felt like there was a rock in the pit of my stomach. I wasn't afraid of anything; it was just nerves from the excitement I could barely keep under wraps, and eight o'clock could not come fast enough. The last two customers stumbled into the restaurant a few minutes before closing. The Currys were old, familiar guests who always made a habit of dining late, and when, like clockwork, they showed up at the door, I made a big fuss over them. They loved the attention, of course, and as maître d', my role was to schmooze the guests, make them welcome, and treat them like royalty, holding court with them as though they were king and queen of Peck's Beach. That night, I could have cared less. It was a good bet my somewhat dismissive attitude and negative body language didn't exactly tip the scales in my favor as the congenial host. My words and actions were robotic, but I did manage to commandeer the best table on the terrace for this most faithful party of two. I quietly instructed the waitress, as she entered from the adjoining Garden Room, to continue the coddling, and I politely took my leave and back peddled my way into the kitchen.

When the Currys finally left the restaurant, I shot out of there like a bolt of lightning. The owners knew I needed to leave right after closing for an important engagement; they just didn't know where and with whom. That little bit of information would have ripped the roof off Watson's like a tornado.

One break in my favor was that the restaurant closed at 8 PM on Sundays, so I gained an hour. Every other night, we closed at 9 PM, and you could put money down on it that some customer would come to the door looking to be fed just as I was about to throw the lock. After these late arrivals were seated, they felt no hurry to eat and run. Quite the opposite. They would study the menu like they were preparing for the bar exam and consume their dinner with the speed of molasses being poured in January. Meanwhile, the poor girl who had been given the job of "late waitress" had to grin and bear the brunt of serving these obtuse diners as though she were just starting her day, all full of sunshine and light. She would smile as though she had just walked down the runway at the Miss America pageant, as though he or she or they were the only guests in the world worth waiting on. This was the definition of a "Watson Waitress," a conveyor of top service, bringing to the table home cooked family food at a reasonable price, a waitress who knew her stuff, one trained to exude confidence and courtesy no matter what situation the customer was able to create.

My exit out the back door was swift. I jumped into my car, and aimed it straight for our little garage apartment, aptly named the "Tarantula's Nest." A second-floor, two-bedroom flat on top of a storage garage behind the gas station at Ninth and Asbury in the heart of town and opposite City Hall. Occupancy: four male college students, of which I was the oldest and, at 25, the only one of legal age.

I ascended the front stairs two at a time, praying that my esteemed roommates would not be back from work yet. Sam shared a room with me, but I knew where he was: in the kitchen at Watson's, closing down the steam tables. He wouldn't get to the apartment until well after nine o'clock. Bruce and Howie were probably not far behind, but knowing them, after they finished up at Hogate's Restaurant on the Bay, they would most likely head across the bridge to The Point, as it was called, to quaff a few cold ones before the sun rose again.

All I wanted was to peel off my suit and tie, throw on cut-offs and a shirt, grab a beach blanket, a bottle of wine, or maybe three, and most important of all…the ring…and then exit as fast as I could. I didn't feel like having to explain to everyone where I was headed for the evening. Besides, I had perfected the art of smoke and mirrors when it pertained to my love life. None of the guys had any idea I was seeing Laura, and that was just how I needed it to remain. We'd be dead in the water if word got out that we were dating. Even though she was 19, Laura was five years my junior and the only child of the owners of Watson's. It would not be a pretty picture if our relationship became public, so we both worked very hard to make sure that did not happen.

Throwing on my clothes, I scooped up what I needed and took my leave of this Hotel Hilton-on-stilts. Like a rabbit on the run, I raced down the front steps and jumped into my Pontiac Lemans convertible all in one smooth motion. Checking the time on the dash, it was nine o'clock, and I only had four blocks to traverse before I was at Watson's. Sunday night in August was a crazy time in town because it was the height of the tourist season. The place reminded me of Times Square on New Year's Eve...the island was packed.

I put the top up as I vacated the apartment driveway. I wasn't about to pull into the restaurant's parking lot on full display in a very identifiable car. I had timed things so that Birch, the parking attendant, would have closed up and left a half-hour before. His pattern was to cut out early Sundays, leaving the entrance chain down until all the employees made their exit. The owner, John David, or JD, as we affectionately called him, would wander out to the parking lot around 10 PM and put the chain up himself. After endless hours in a sweltering kitchen, he would emerge like a hermit crab in need of a larger shell to take a much-needed break, along with catching some fresh night air.

Hooking a left into the parking lot, I made sure to drive straight back to the farthest point. A chain-link fence, which bordered the backend of an empty adjacent lot, made a perfect cover for this clandestine rendezvous. My candy apple red Pontiac was too well known to risk being spotted. I turned off my lights before cutting the engine and sat very still, looking in the direction of the restaurant's rear entrance to see if Laura was coming down the outside stairs that exited the kitchen. There was no sign of anyone around, so I waited impatiently, looking often at my watch. With a shaky right hand, I reached into my left shirt pocket to make sure the ring was still there. I must have checked it twenty times since leaving the Tarantula's Nest. I tried to convince myself to calm down.

What I feared was rejection. All kinds of scenarios raced around in my head, most ending in disaster. I, the eternal optimist, was afraid of crashing and burning just thinking of those four little words, "Will you marry me?" Finally, I saw Laura walking down the back steps, her slender silhouette outlined by the interior lights of the kitchen.

Spotting my car, she ran in quick steps along the fence separating the parking lot from a string of three-story boarding houses. I was in the middle of an adrenalin rush. My heart was pounding like waves against a jetty. How I was ever going to make it through this night was beyond me. Just the sight of Laura made me stop breathing for a few seconds. I was totally unaware of what I was doing, and this was the easy part. Before I realized what was happening, Laura leaned through the window on my side, gave me a quick kiss, and then, doing an end run behind the car, opened the front passenger door and slid in. Without missing a beat, her arms wrapped around my neck just one second ahead of her lips meeting mine. I could feel heat rise up the center of my body. My breathing got a jump start.

"Let's get the hell out of Dodge before your mother finds out you're among the missing." With that, Laura slumped down in the seat, resting her beautiful head with its flowing blonde hair low against my right shoulder while I slipped the car into first gear. Top up and lights out, the convertible glided through the parking lot like a bat at twilight threading its way blindly through the sound of evening traffic.

I fought to keep my emotions in check and focus on the road. Aiming the car south, I made a number of quick turns just in case anyone was following. Paranoia was running high. The southern end of the island was all sand dunes, sea, and stars, just perfect for what I had in mind. Nowhere on Peck's Beach could one be more isolated.

Traffic was light once we got out of midtown. The tourists, better known as "shoobies," had landed in full force, but the further south we drove, the less congestion we encountered until the road became quiet, and we could begin to pick up the sound of the surf riding in on gentle evening breezes. The night air was barely moving by the time we parked the car close to the dunes. Stepping out, we could feel the warmth of the sand underfoot, and without saying a word, we separately reached into the rear seat. I grabbed the blanket, and Laura scooped up the cooler, a familiar routine. We had been here before.

The island came to a point at the south end, forming a triangular stretch of sand dunes for a good two miles or more. It's here that the ocean currents pour through a narrow inlet to the bay separating Peck's Beach from the next island along the barrier chain. The ocean waters and the bay collide in one dramatic upheaval, creating turbulent waves of white foam and sea spray in a symphony of ebb and flow, all while the tide performed its eternal dance along its shores.

We headed toward a familiar path that snaked its way along a portion of protected state land, creating a sanctuary for wildlife inhabiting the coastline. We quickly moved down this sandy path until we were deep into the dunes. The remaining lights from the beach houses slowly lowered behind us, almost as if they were stars setting in a late-night sky. The moon was full, positioned just west of midnight, so we were able to find the interior set of dunes. The wind and wave action over the years had piled fifteen-foot mountains of sand beyond the high tide mark, offering protection from the ocean's capricious ways. It was here that Laura and I tucked ourselves away where no soul could find us. We had the routine down to a science. Like clockwork, the blanket was spread, the wine extracted from the cooler, and glasses quickly filled to the brim with nectar from the gods.

By now, I was convinced Laura knew what I was up to. It was an irrational conclusion on my part. We sat there for a moment, just looking into one another's eyes, saying nothing. Kneeling on the blanket with glasses raised, we took a sip of wine together, and I slowly moved forward, kissing Laura so gently I barely felt her lips. I kissed her again and again. And without missing a beat, we put our drinks on top of the cooler as though on cue. I cuddled her warm, supple body against my chest and looked down into those stunning sapphire blue eyes.

"Stay here in my arms till the moon is long gone, OK?" I whispered. "Don't let this be just another summer romance."

Laura raised her head, placing those soft lips of hers just at the tip of my ear. "I never intended it to be."

A passing cloud cleared the moon, allowing its beams to pour onto her face. Right there, right then, I looked into the eyes and heart of the woman I knew I would love for the rest of my life. That deep-seated assurance was more real than anything I had ever known, dissolving all my fears and anxiety.

I gently pulled back, eyes still focused on her, before it became too late to stop where my body was yearning to take me. I had to quickly reverse gears before I totally lost control, so I could carry out my surprise.

"Laura, it's a perfect night to swim. Come with me down to the water!"

"But Sax, I didn't bring a suit."

"So? Neither did I," as I tore off my shirt and dropped my cutoffs to the ankles. This, of course, left me standing there stripped to the bone except for my boxers.

"You are crazy, Mr. Saxon." With that, Laura jumped up off the blanket and grabbed my hand, and we raced over the dunes like two school kids.

When we got to the water's edge, I spun around in one quick revolution, grabbed her around the waist, and pulled her in tight against my body.

"Now baby, take it off, take it all off," I said, kissing her while trying to smother a laugh at the same time.

"But what if there are people around?" came her half-serious response.

I let loose a laugh that must have reverberated down the beach for miles. "You've got to be kidding. There's not a human in sight, just me and you and nature."

Now Laura started to laugh too, and we stood there, ankle deep in the ocean, looking fairly comical, me in my boxers and her fully clothed, getting soaked by the surf with every incoming wave. Meanwhile, the wine was beginning to work its magic.

It's rare, but once in a great while, usually in late August, when the water is very warm, there's an influx of bioluminescent algae known as noctiluca, or "sea sparkles" in layman terms. Thousands of these tiny creatures can fit in a drop of water, and they sparkle neon blue when agitated, an effect believed to be a defense mechanism to distract predators, who become intimidated by the sudden light. If the night is losing the moon and the surf conditions are ideal, stepping along the edge of the sea causes the sand to light up like fireflies on a June evening. If you're among the favored few, you might catch the waves illuminating, each breaker internally exploding like fireworks on the Fourth of July, aglow with florescent shimmering lights.

This was one of those magical nights, perfect to celebrate and validate what I had in mind. Amid the sparkling sand and glowing waves, I gently let go of Laura, dropped to my knees as the water quietly swirled about, and said, "I've been in love with you since forever, Laura Chandler. I want to spend the rest of my life with you. I want to care for you, protect you, make love to you, raise a family with you, and stay beside you as long as the Lord allows. Will you complete my life? Will you be my wife?"

Before she had time to respond, I took her left hand and slipped the engagement ring, which had been hidden on my pinky, onto her finger. Not a sound came from Laura. Only the ocean was talking. There I was, knees on the floor of the sea, in my skivvies, surrounded by saltwater and florescent algae, and I was positive I was about to be humiliated beyond belief, to be rejected beyond all human endurance. My self-esteem had just tanked big time. Looking up at her, I waited for some sign, some little signal of encouragement, and then I caught it. Fading moonlight lit up tears streaming down Laura's cheeks. She bent down and gently cradled my face in her hands.

"I love you, Christopher Barrett Saxon, more than I love my own life. To not have known you would be to not have life itself. Yes, yes, a million times yes. You crazy, nutty, wonderful man, I'll be your wife, and I'll love you no matter what tomorrow brings."

"Could you repeat that? I want to make sure I'm not dreaming. I could have sworn you just said yes."

I stood up and put two fingers over Laura's mouth, blocking her attempt to say the words again.

"Shhh, I heard you loud and clear the first time. What I'm feeling right now could never be a dream. I'm too alive." As I swept Laura into my arms, I spoke in sounds barely audible above the quiet rumble of the breaking waves. "I'm going to make love to you all night, until you tell me to stop." I carried her back along the same path we had come. There was no resistance, but rather, total surrender.

The universe covered us with a blanket of stars, and the moon took its leave underneath the horizon. The air, damper and a little cooler now, coursed across the shoreline with increasing authority. Nothing in time or space existed beyond this moment.

If Laura said stop, I didn't hear her. If she did, she couldn't have meant it, because we made love long and hard. There are no spoken words, no written language that's able to bring to life what I was feeling, what I was experiencing. To say we were lost in one another doesn't even come close.

If it weren't for a sand crab scampering across my ankle, we would have slept until sunrise. I sat up with a sudden shiver and then quickly looked at my watch. "Oh my God, it's four AM. Laura, honey, wake up. We're in deep caca. We've got to get our bare asses out of here, pronto!"

Not very coherent, Laura mumbled something about how she never wanted to go home again and then slipped back into her dream world. I gathered up the cooler after putting on my shorts and was able to collect Laura in my arms almost in one continuous motion. Gradually, she came to a fair degree of awareness, though the affect of the wine was slow to retreat.

Slightly slurred, she blurted out, "Let me help, Sax."

"I've got it all under control. Just hold onto me, and we'll weave our way back to the car." Weave was the right word. I was not doing a whole lot better than Laura; however, fear became the sobering factor at this juncture. If we were caught dating, forget the fact that we were now engaged, her parents would hang me out to dry. I'd lose my job for starters. That was the practical side of the equation. The emotional side would be losing Laura. With her father, I had an outside chance of living, but her mother? Not a prayer. She'd banish Laura to some private women's college in Europe, just like her own mother did with her. Anything to break up our relationship... The age difference alone was enough for Vivian the Vicious, as I loved to call her, to make sure her only child was untouched by any lover's hands, especially mine.

Sheer panic is the equivalent of ten cups of coffee and creates its own brand of sobriety. I drove away sober as a judge. My head was in spinning mode, but I knew I had to hold things together, think straight, and retrieve my balance. We had done major damage to two bottles of wine plus one bottle of Champagne. It was a miracle I ever woke up, let alone regained the capacity to think on any coherent level. You know you're pretty wasted when you silently give thanks to a sand crab.

Laura slept almost the entire drive back to the restaurant. I made no attempt to rouse her. Sleeping was a good thing under the circumstances. The longer she slept it off, the better chance we'd have. We had rehearsed this scenario on more than one occasion, mentally preparing in advance what we would do if one or the other parent suddenly appeared at the back door of Watson's.

I barely pulled my car into the curb cutout of the parking lot, hit the emergency brake, quickly got out and took down the chain. I took hold of the steering wheel so fast I almost forgot to close my door. I slammed it in first gear, drove over the chain for a second, then cut the engine and coasted, lights off, back to the rear of the lot. All was quiet, too quiet. It was unnerving, yet I didn't have time to analyze feelings. I had to keep things moving.

"Laura," I whispered, "wake up, honey. We're at Watson's now." With a jolt, she sat up straight as an arrow. She had been curled up on the seat, her head partially on my lap, and had not budged once since leaving the beach.

"I'll be OK, my knight in shining whatever. Just point me in the direction of the big W, and I'll be on my way. In fact, just give me a shove, and I'll take to flight like a little seagull, soaring above the earth, engaged in all kinds of fun. Engaged? I'm engaged, did you know that?"

Holy crap, I was in real trouble now. At 25 years of age, I was well above the legal drinking age of 21. But Laura was barely 20, making her the engaged, under aged daughter of JD and Vi, bombed out of her gourd, attempting to fly like a bird... There was no chance I'd survive this... I was dead.

"Laura, look at me, honey," I said, gently using my hand to steady her somewhat wobbling head. "You've got to pull it together. Do you think you can walk to the kitchen door by yourself, or do you want me to hold onto you?"

"NO, no, I'll be fine. Just give me a second to get my balance. I know I can't blow it now, not after all this."

Laura looked down at her hand, the one that sparkled. It caught what little ambient light there was, its facets sparkling just enough to be mesmerizing. Then she started to tear up. "Don't make me go in, Sax. I hate every minute we're separated. Can't we stop this charade and run away and get married?"

Funny thing was, I had been thinking the same thing only minutes ago on the drive back. "You know how much I'd love to do that, but it's not an option, honey, and we both know it. Do you have the key?"

"Sure, it's right here somewhere in my head, I mean, my beach bag. Don't worry, Mother's fast asleep. She doesn't suspect a thing. Nobody's up but us lovebirds anyway... Did I ever tell you how much I love you?"

"You sure have. Now, try to concentrate and focus. We've got to pull this off."

"I better be as quiet as a mouse. Tippy, tippy toes, quiet as a mouse." Laura demonstrated how a mouse would make not a sound, walking on her toes with short, petite ballerina steps.

I'm thinking, This is not going to work. She's going to either fall flat on her face or fall up the outside steps to the kitchen and we'll be shit outta luck. Vivian's bedroom window was on the second floor to the far right of the rear door, but sound travels at night... It was tense, believe me. I gently took Laura's arm and walked her quickly to the rear of the building.

"You OK?"

"I'll be fine, my knight of the realm. Just point me in the right direction."

And so I did. But Laura spun around, kissed me fast and hard, and then graciously, as if she were cold sober and in full control of her faculties, made her way up to the back entrance. I watched as she blew me another kiss... I did the same. Not a sound could be heard when she opened the screen door.... Please, dear God, let her make it to her bedroom undetected.

I navigated a fast retreat to my car, bare feet helping to maintain silence. But the night still had some life in it. I was in a desperate need to unwind. So, I made a quick decision to hit the beach for a very late-night stroll, clutching in one hand my sandals and in the other my euphoria.

It was a wave crashing over my body that did the trick, shocking me into the here and now. The instant replay of the last few hours running non-stop in my head was rudely interrupted by the pause button in my brain. Once again, I found myself ensconced in seawater and sand. I flipped over and struggled to my knees, trying to collect myself, brain not cooperating well.

Suddenly I felt a tremor underneath me like nothing I'd ever felt before. Instinctively my body turned from the ocean and faced the sound roaring toward me. I was so disoriented at first that I wasn't able to make sense out of what I had just barely seen through blurring eyes. Nothing registered, nothing. I was paralyzed, like a deer stunned by headlights from an oncoming car. I couldn't move until I saw the light from the flames encircling Watson's steal away the darkness. And then I ran like a bat out of hell, screaming, "Oh God! No, no!"

The faster I ran, the deeper I seemed to sink into the sand. Everything I loved was in that building. My body was moving in slow motion, each step dragging along the beach as if some weight were holding down my feet. In one fraction of a moment, I imagined my life with no more magical nights, no more dancing on the sand, no more songs to be sung... a life left with only confusion and fear. I was crying so hard I couldn't see where I was headed. I just knew I had to keep moving toward the inferno. Somewhere, engulfed in the sight and sound of all those flames, smoke, and sirens' screams, in one indiscernible second, my mind allowed me to escape to another time and place.

CHAPTER 2

The month was May, the year 1962, the place a little church on the city limits of Philadelphia. My best friend was getting married, and I was the best man. It was an exciting day on two accounts, the wedding and the start of a new summer job for me at Peck's Beach in South Jersey.

The wedding was a happy one, a new beginning for a young couple very much in love. For John Hartle and Noel Key, it was a day they'd been anticipating to be united ever since the groom had come home from the Navy.

John and I were close buddies, having graduated from high school together and then lived as roommates in college. We went way back, sharing lots of good times and wonderful memories over the years.

When it was my turn to toast the bride and groom, I just had to tell of the time John was stationed in Bermuda with the Navy. I knew it would get a laugh, and the story showed that the groom always had my back, especially when I needed him the most.

John asked me to come to visit him when he was stationed on the island, an obvious second choice since Noel was not able to get the time off at the department store where she worked. I, of course, jumped at the chance. But alas, I was only two weeks into a new job in Philly. Not to be discouraged, I went to my boss and asked for the time off. Now, that takes balls. It must have been my charm that did the trick, because, much to my shock, he let me go. I couldn't believe it.

What a week of outrageous fun and frolic we had, packing a month's worth of craziness into seven glorious days. John dressed me up in one of his buddy's Navy Blues and marched me over to the mess hall. I signed in as an officer, wrote down the necessary ID numbers, and proceeded to enjoy a wonderful, and free, breakfast, all at the generosity of the US Navy. I get cold all over when I think back to our not so little escapade. The risk we both took was huge; had we been caught, today I'd be in jail or shot, not to mention the hammer the Navy would have lowered on John's head.

But sadly, all good things must come to an end, and my departure from the island was classic. John and I wasted time all morning on the day I was to leave. Besides not wanting the vacation to end, putting off packing until the last minute, we had not calculated the time it took to get from the boarding house where I was staying to the airport. After I finally made the move to get my ass in gear and pack, I noticed I had only thirty minutes to make the flight. The drive, under normal conditions, was just about an hour, so we were in deep water, surrounded by alligators! We threw all my stuff in my only suitcase and jumped into the car almost in one continuous motion. John knew the way to the airport like the back of his hand, but the traffic was going to be the killer. Bermudians operate under island mentality, so the need to make my flight didn't rank at the top of everyone else's priority list.

We took the back roads, which cover most of the island, but time was not giving us much of a break. Only one choice remained an option...cutting through the golf course to save precious minutes. At this point, we were cruising well beyond the speed limit, and I was terrified we'd be caught by the police any second; lucky for us, there was not an officer in sight. Before I realized what was happening, John had cut off the main road and blitzed through the seventeenth hole of the most famous course on the island. There was no way we weren't going to get hammered by the authorities, but it happened so fast I think the spectators and players alike froze, shocked at the spectacle unfolding in front of them.

In the time it takes to make a hole in one, John traversed that golf course before anyone playing knew what hit them. This little shortcut was a stroke of genius. It brought us out at a point a mile from the airstrip, shaving off a good five minutes of vital time in our quest to beat the clock while driving from Hamilton to the airport.

Pulling up to a screeching halt at the front gate, John yelled, "Jump out now! I'll follow. Check in and go for it." Bermuda's airport in '59 was not the last word in terminal design. It looked like something right out of a classic movie from the early forties... Picture Casablanca... You checked in at the only reservation desk before walking onto the tarmac to board the plane. Security was a word not even remotely connected to air travel.

So far so good, things were looking up. I figured I had defied the odds by showing up alive and, therefore, the rest should be a piece of cake. Arriving more than slightly out of breath, I told the counter clerk I had a ticket for the Pan Am flight to New York; the unbelieving look on his face was priceless.

"Sir, that flight is on the runway, about to take off."

"No, it can't leave! Stop the plane! I've got to get home by tomorrow."

To this day, I don't know why he took pity on me, but he probably did because I looked so anxious and pathetic. Another irresponsible teenage tourist from the States. Without missing a beat, he picked up the phone and called the patiently waiting pilot while I stood there with my mouth open.

"We have a passenger here, sir, and it's vital he does not miss this flight... OK, thanks." With that, the reservation manager turned to me and said, "The plane is being held on the runway. All I need is ID to get you out of the country."

"I don't have any."

"What? You've got to have some kind of ID, a driver's license, birth certificate, something!"

"I'm telling you the truth. I don't! When I left Philly, I brought a new wallet without transferring any papers."

"Well then, I can't let you off the island."

"Good, I didn't want to leave anyway."

By this time. John had arrived on the scene, also out of breath, and he asked, "What's happening ?"

"They won't let me board the plane without ID, which I don't have."

John looked at me like I was out in left field somewhere...which I was. The clerk mirrored John's expression as though on cue while I just stood there looking like the village idiot.

"Look, sir, I'm in the Navy here on the island, and if I can vouch for this guy, will you let him pass through? I'll give you my rank and number, and I do have ID."

Firing back a look at me that could kill, the clerk gave in, and while John was signing his life away, I was running down the hall toward the entrance to the outside gate. I looked back to see the clerk behind me yelling, "Through that door!" pointing to the right as I was about to exit into the men's room.

I burst onto the runway, and as the plane engines roared, I ran up the stairs to the cabin, two steps at a time. The stewardess was standing at the top of the stairs, one hand holding the hatch open and the other trying in vain to keep her hair out of her face. With a move like an octopus, she grabbed my arm, yanked my body into the plane, and slammed the door, sarcastically shouting over the roar of the engines, "I'm so glad you could make it!"

My Bermuda tale, though self-incriminating, was a crowd-pleasing success and got the response I was hoping for. With Champagne glass raised high, I said, "Here's to a marriage with many blessings to come, because John and Noel, now Mr. and Mrs. Hartle, have been a blessing to so many others."

Everyone joined in and lifted their glasses, the music played on, and I graciously took my leave. I wasn't happy about ducking out, but the newlyweds knew how important it was for me to have a job in order to pay for college in the fall. I hadn't been raised with a silver spoon in my mouth; to the contrary, it wasn't even silver plated.

So, I reluctantly said my goodbyes, hopped in my car, and took off... It was already 4 PM.

As I peeled out of the reception driveway, I settled back and relaxed a bit, but running through my mind was a quote from the white rabbit in Alice in Wonderland. "I'm late, I'm late, for a very important date. No time to say 'hello, goodbye,' I'm late, I'm late, I'm late!" I told myself to relax. This isn't the end of the world. Keep the speed a hair above 75 mph because you can't risk a ticket... With big fines and no job...this is not an option.

As I settled into cruising speed, my thoughts flowed back to the Bermuda scene in the airplane, where the stewardess had led me to my seat. The flight was uneventful, thank heavens. My fear of flying and drowning should the flight turn into a cruise did not materialize, though, in actuality, my fear of drowning had valid roots. Once again, my old demon managed to surface as I settled back in my seat.

When I was twelve, two of my buddies and I had gone swimming in the Asteria Hotel's saltwater pool during a vacation at Peck's Beach. It was a vacation I took with my mother and her best friend's tribe every summer in August. And, I might add, it was well-deserved time off for some fun in the sun. My mother, lovingly known as Jane Christopher Saxon, was a single mom who never seemed to catch a break from the time I was nine.

In 1949, Paul Saxon, my father and super sales rep with Quaker Oats Co. out of Philly, accepted a transfer to Decatur, Georgia, the heart of the Deep South. It was a time when you were required to call the police if your maid was going to be on the street past dark, when colored people assumed their place at the back of the elevator or bus, when the KKK burned crosses on Stone Mountain, when our next-door neighbor's maid ate her lunch on the back porch because she wasn't allowed to eat in the house at their table, when, every morning in school, our third grade class would place hands over hearts, say the Pledge of Allegiance to the U. S. flag, and then sing Dixie!

We were considered damn Yankees from up north, not held in high esteem. The Civil War was not over by any means, the evidence of which was to be seen everywhere.

My parents tried their best to blend in, but it was a lost cause. My father got into a terrible fight one night, yelling at and nearly knocking out our next-door neighbor because their maid wasn't allowed to sit at the kitchen table.

My father said, "You have this woman make your lunch every day, but she can't sit down with you at the same table? You make her eat outside on the kitchen deck, rain or shine, just because her skin is different from yours? Unbelievable!"

As my mother did her best to be accepted within the town and by the neighbors, she jumped at the opportunity to accept an invitation to a luncheon at the Ladies Club of Decatur. As a way for the ladies to get to know my mother better, they asked her to share some background about her family and life in general. She gave a quick rundown on when and why we'd moved to Decatur, her husband's job necessitating a transfer from Philadelphia, and then ended with this little gem, almost like a period at the end of a sentence.

"And now I can't wait to visit all the historic southern plantations I've heard so much about."

To which, a southern lady replied, in a drawl as thick as Spanish moss and pronouncing two-syllable words as though they had four, "Well, my dear, we'd be pleased for ya'll to see them except you damn Yankees burnt them down!"

In an effort not to be upstaged, my mother returned the salvo. "Well, I know you southerners have a reputation for moving slowly, but you've had almost a hundred years to build them back!" Needless to say, my mother was never invited back for lunch again... So much for blending in.

My father left on Monday morning, December 12th, on a business trip to Memphis, Tennessee. I remember him standing at the front door, saying goodbye. I don't think he gave me a hug. That very night, when the downstairs wall phone rang, I was startled out of a deep sleep. Looking at the clock on my night table, it showed 2 AM.

I heard my mother's trembling voice ask, "When did it happen?" and I knew from the way she said it that my father was dead. I buried my head in my pillow and cried so hard that if it had not been for my pillow soaking up my tears, I would have drowned. I never heard more of my mother's words, but when I lifted my head, I could hear her crying in her room at the bottom of the steps. I ran down and jumped into her arms as she sat on the edge of the bed....no words spoken, just tears.

Suddenly I was forced, not into "never, never land" but into the land of never again. Gone was the smell of his after shave lotion, seeing him comb his hair, his joy at Christmas playing Santa, sneaking into my room and gently kissing me, all the time thinking I was asleep. Gone, never to be heard again, were my screams of delight at the train set he built while I was sleeping, and his love of surf fishing on our vacations in Florida.

Our lives changed forever with the ring of a phone. My mother lost her husband of ten years and was always grateful she'd married him at such a young age. They met in the summer of 1938 at Peck's Beach on 1st Street. She was a tomboy and volunteered to play touch football when they were short a player. It proved to be the connection that fueled a romance leading to marriage, July 25th, 1939, a year later in New York's "Little Church around the Corner," a city landmark still there today.

My mother was an only child. It nearly killed my grandmother to have her daughter run away and marry. It was an impulsive act she was never able to forgive, then I was born April, 28th, 1940. Rumor had it that my mother had to get married. The gossip mills were working overtime, counting the days, but she was not pregnant when she married. My father and she came back to Philadelphia from NY and lived separately for a number of months, each at their own parents'. When my mother began to throw up, true confession time was inevitable. They were able to find an apartment, so they could start a new life. It wasn't until I was an adult I asked my mother if in fact I was a love child. She looked a little caught off guard by my question. Her response was emphatic, "No. I did not have to get married, but this I will tell you, you were conceived on 1st St beach".

I've always wondered why I've loved Peck's Beach so much? Maybe where you're conceived has some connection to what you ultimately become. Just another of the many unanswerable question we call life.

My mother sold our home in Georgia. We returned to Philadelphia, where she had grown up and where her parents lived. A survivor and fighter, Jane Saxon got a job at $45.00 a week and managed to keep a roof over our heads, but I know there were sleepless nights worrying about how to keep the lights on and food on the table.

But time has a way of marching on, and we made it through the rain, not without a lot of ups and downs, but always with a pile of love for each other, not to mention the love and support we received from family and friends.

The Asteria Hotel had two pools, one fresh and one saltwater. This ten-story, opulent Grande Dame of the boardwalk stood majestically along the beach, dominating everything in its shadow. No building was as tall, and no architecture was as beautiful as its Spanish Mission Revival. The Asteria was the first to build a basement below sea level, complete with pumps to drain any water seepage and tunnels that led to the beach. Wealthy families from Philadelphia's Main Line, New York, and Washington came to be pampered and spoiled for anywhere from a week or maybe the entire summer. The length of vacation was equivalent to the depth of one's assets, and with train service from Philly to Peck's Beach, the man of the house could park his family at the beach while, at the same time, make midweek visits and therefore keep both his wife and employer happy. If truth be told and one were to look close enough, a mistress might be seen hiding out somewhere... To a philanderer, a well planned summer's worth of freedom was a pearl of great price.

Teaming up with my friend Peter, we went swimming in the saltwater pool. We dove in and out of the water like dolphins. I remember pretending we were deep-sea divers such as I'd seen in the movies. I'd hold my breath and dive into the water at the deep end of the pool, imagining we were a thousand leagues under the sea, fighting the villains of the deep. In order to stay down at that depth, we would exhale slowly, lose buoyancy, and sink to the bottom like a rock. Then we'd pretend to do battle with a great white or seek lost treasure inside a Spanish galleon.

Even by letting out breath, I wasn't able to stay underwater as long as I figured, so I devised a method to solve the problem. I went to the diving board again and, jumping off, dove down to the floor of the pool, and grabbed the iron intake grate. By moving along from rung to rung, I was able to stay under without the buoyancy of air in my lungs forcing me to surface prematurely.

As I walked inverted across the grate, hand over hand, the ring on my left finger slipped through the rung, trapping it so I couldn't free my hand. I was seized with uncontrollable panic, the kind that short circuits your brain. I yanked my hand with such force I thought my finger would rip off. I yanked repeatedly, thrashing from side to side. A thousand bubbles carried my unspoken screams to the surface, but none registered the cries of a desperate kid with burning lungs, and no sound was heard as each bubble dissipated among the swimmers having fun on a wonderfully sunny day.

I will never know how it happened, but miraculously, the ring, still on my finger, worked its way through the grate just as my lungs were about to collapse. I shot to the surface, gasping for air. The entire event had gone totally unnoticed. Even now, every time I recall the incident, my chest tightens and a faint feeling of panic tries to surface, but I stuff it down and hide it deep inside.

CHAPTER 3

Glancing down at the clock on the dashboard brought my wandering and heavy thoughts of the past back to the reality that it would take me an hour and a half to drive from Philly to Peck's Beach...which meant I wouldn't make it to Watson's until 5:30 PM, so I pulled into a gas station, one with a visible phone booth, to call the restaurant and relay my ETA. As I was dialing, a panicked thought crossed my mind: Watch the boss answer. With that, the boss answered. "Watson's, JD here." The voice sounded stressed and barely audible through all the background noise, clanging of what sounded like dishes and the din of voices

"Hi, this is Christopher Saxon, and I'm calling to say I'll be a little late, but I'm moving fast." The slight tremble in my voice could not have gone unnoticed.

"Move faster!" And with that terse statement, the conversation terminated, and it was clear the terminator was not happy.

This time, when I peeled out from the gas station, it was like leaving a pit stop at the Indy 500. I was no longer driving the car; I was aiming it. Screw the cops.

The drive down was a blur. My mind was too focused on the road in front of me. I hadn't stepped one foot into Watson's yet, and already I was on the owner's shit list.

Before I knew it, my car was heading over the bridge that connected the mainland with the island of Peck's Beach. The open bay shimmered like a blanket of sparkling diamonds in the late afternoon sun, and I felt an unexplainable calm settle over me.

The car reached the apex of the first of two drawbridges, and my eyes tried to take in all the breathtaking beauty so lavishly laid out before me.

No matter how many times I came over that bridge, as a kid or as an adolescent, it always felt like coming home. There was a sense of belonging, of knowing I was meant to find my home on this island, maybe not now, but a quiet yearning deep within assured me, "Your day will come."

So, on this particular evening, my anxiety was mostly allayed by the mere sight and vastness of the skyline I captured with an unobstructed view from my ragtop. Thirty feet below, there were marsh islands dotting the harbor, white triangle sails catching the wind, and the island of Peck's Beach viewable in full panorama view, north and south, for a good portion of its seven miles. I could even see the ocean from that height, and if I were able, I would have pulled over and watched this amazing unfolding display of nature's extravagant light show as it slowly changed with the fading of the setting sun.

Unfortunately, such luxury was not mine to have. The guy behind me laid on his horn as I drifted into the other lane, bringing me out of my trance. Instantly I was forced to concentrate on the road in front of me, along with getting to Watson's alive.

I remembered very clearly my interview from months before. I was grateful that my good friend Sheila Cook suggested working at Watson's instead of schlepping into Center City, Philly, doing the boring summer job at the American Stores Company I was always complaining about.

"I know for sure they need another busboy. The tips are really good, and I'd put a word in for you. What's there to lose?"

"Thanks, Sheila, not a bad idea genius. Now, suppose I landed the job, could I stay at your mother's boarding house?"

"I don't see why not. Get the job first, and then I'll talk to her."

So, I wrote a letter to the owner, Adrienne Watson and, to my surprise, it won me an interview in early March. On that particular day, I was on time and also a little nervous. Reputation had it that Adrienne was from the old school, so when it came to whom she hired, her standards were way up there... Few made the cut.

Watson's was an authentic Victorian house, built in the late eighteen-hundreds. When I entered the front door, I found myself in the center hall of what must have been a very gracious home at one time. It was late on a March afternoon when I arrived, and the place was barely heated. Lowering gray clouds moved in off the ocean, and the wind was building out of the northeast. I could feel the draft even after I closed the entrance door behind me. From the hall, I could see four of the dining rooms, and with the fading outside light, only a lamp on a table by the spiral staircase shed any illumination on my surroundings. The cold room only exaggerated my uneasiness.

An abrupt voice from upstairs filtered down the steps. "Next person, please."

A young girl came into view as I made my way up the stairs. At first, I thought she'd voiced the command, but she silently nodded as we passed on the steps, her expression devoid of emotion. Catching a hint of hurt in her eyes as we glanced at each other, I sensed she would be crying when she got outside.

Things were not looking up! As I ascended the stairs, I abruptly found myself coming face to face with Adrienne Watson, "The Madame," a name Sheila said the waitresses had called her. Standing there, she looked quite regal and in full command of herself. She was of medium height but with a look of confidence that made her seem taller. Her hair was auburn, obviously dyed, and a heavy hand when applying red lipstick made her look older than her years. She was dressed very casually, and but my first impression was she must have been a beautiful woman in years gone by.

Glancing down at me from the top landing, Adrienne said, "You must be Christopher Saxon."

Having arrived on the top step and standing in close proximity, I looked her straight in her eyes and said, "Yes, I am," while drawing my best, confident self to full height. "But if the food you serve here tastes anything like the expression on that last girl's face, I'm out of here!"

The thought hit me I may have just torpedoed any chance of landing the job with that little quip of mine. My backup plan was to apply to the other restaurants in town, the Chatterbox, Simms on the boardwalk, Plymouth Inn, Hogate's, or Chris's on the bay, but I really didn't want to work any other place except right where I was standing with breath suspended.

Surprisingly, the owner let out a hearty laugh, and I knew that if she found me amusing, I wouldn't be the one descending the stairs devoid of emotion.

As we moved into her living room, I was invited to sit among a heavy décor of Victorian trappings, replete with window drapes made with fabric that would have made Scarlett O'Hara proud and that blocked out the most determined of sun rays. Numerous oil paintings on the wall were by artists unknown to me, but only because I hadn't had the Art Education course yet. At least, that was how I rationalized it.

The interview commenced. It was obvious Adrienne Watson was a woman of substance and means, but a woman whose reign was slipping.

Did I mention we weren't alone in the room? Her maid sat quietly in the corner, just about as old as Adrienne, but with far more serenity in her deep chocolate face. She was not introduced, nor did she speak, but I figured there had to be a reason for her presence. Adrienne, well ensconced among her surroundings, reminded me of Miss Havisham in Dickens's Great Expectations. The room felt like it was waiting for someone to return, someone to come home from a long and painful absence. It was heavy with memories, a freeze-frame in an old movie. I was uncomfortable sitting there, and I worked very hard to prevent my body language from revealing what I was thinking.

The owner started the interview by saying she'd received a very nice letter from Sheila highly recommending me. We discussed details of the busboy job, and then, as quickly as the interview began, it ended with the madame standing up and dismissing me with "What shall we call you?"

"Pardon me?"

"What shall we call you? We already have a Chris on staff. So your name won't do. What is your middle name?"

"Barrett, it's a family name…father's side."

"Well, Brett would work as a nickname, but it doesn't seem to fit you."

There was a long pause, coupled with an expression that signaled she was digging deep for the right name. Then, with sudden delight, she said, "Sax, that's what we'll call you. Sax."

There was no one authorized to challenge her choice. The dark-skinned person in the corner remained silent. Adrienne was obviously satisfied she had solved a minor little problem.

"I can live with that," I said, smiling ever so slightly.

She liked me, she'd named me, and, best of all, Adrienne hired me.

I took the stairs two steps at a time, making a quick left at the bottom into the kitchen through the swinging doors. Huck was there to give me the guided tour of the place. A wonderful old man of color from South Carolina, he was the overseer of Watson's; more to the point, I would come to know Huck was a guardian angel to Adrienne. He was the one who made sure no harm would ever come to Miss Addi, as he liked to say. Devotion was his middle name, and whatever her needs might be, he was there to make sure they were met.

After the success of my interview, I had to call Sheila to let her know what had happened and to thank her so much for recommending me. I practically yelled in the phone, "I got it, I got it! She hired me right there on the spot." Sheila was thrilled and said she'd get her mother to talk to me about staying at their boarding house at Plymouth and Ocean Avenues...two blocks from Watson's.

CHAPTER 4

Watson's...the word brought me back to reality as it came into view at the corner of Ninth and Ocean Ave. I hooked a quick right on Ocean and then a left into the parking lot. It was a good thing I'd had the tour in early spring. I knew exactly where to park and how I was to maneuver through the kitchen once I was inside... False moves were time lost, and I had to get myself into the center hall to meet the head hostess without first seeing JD.

I parked and made a mad dash to the rear door of the kitchen. The scene unfolding on the back landing was classic. Two young dark skinned guys, shooting the breeze in a slow southern drawl, sat opposite each other on step stools, completely oblivious to their surroundings. Amid the aroma of seafood and all things worth frying, and kitchen sounds of chaos emanating through the screen door, they snapped green beans in a large iron pot, laughing as though the world, with all its troubles, was a million miles away.

For a second, I stopped, looked at the screen door, and thought, when I open this door, I have the feeling that life as I've known it will never be the same again. Little did I know how prophetic that would turn out to be.

I was startled when I heard, "So glad you could make it," the sarcastic salutation spoken by the very person I was so hoping would be nowhere in sight, J.D. himself.

That was the second time in my life I'd heard that pithy little saying, but amidst all the craziness in the kitchen, I was too distracted to make the connection with a very distressed stewardess yanking me aboard the Pan Am flight departing Bermuda.

Without missing a beat, JD disappeared before I could utter, "Hello." I dodged a number of objects, both human and machine, and made a beeline for the swinging doors that led to the center hall.

It was just what I had pictured it would look like on the Saturday night of Memorial Day weekend. It was dinner time at the hugely successful Watson's Restaurant in a supremely popular shore resort. Controlled chaos featured waitresses busting out of the kitchen with entrée dishes stacked up their arms and busboys, coming from multiple directions, balancing on one hand trays filled to the brim with dirty dishes, evidence of the remains of what had been only minutes ago a patron's dinner.

I stood there, frozen in place like I'd just seen a ghost, surrounded by total confusion, discovering however, that it was well orchestrated. Above the cacophony of sound, I heard someone ask, "Is Sax here yet?"

This made no connection to my disjointed brain at all, so I continued to take in all the commotion and motion swirling through the center hall. Then it hit me: That's me they're calling!

Weaving around several waitresses in an effort not to dislodge the dinners they were carrying on their arms, I made my way to the front of the hall. On a holiday weekend like this, Watson's makes a beehive look like a lazy day in June. Waitresses cut across the center hall from four connecting dining rooms at various rates of speed. Add in five busboys, then mix in customers arriving, departing, congregating, and cashing out at the front register, and you've got a convergence that rivals a traffic circle during rush hour!

The what-am-I-doing-here thought came rushing to mind, followed by the next thought that almost paralyzed me: If the rest of the place is like this center hall, I won't live to see the night's end. I'll be trampled to death, and no one will notice until they've swept up in the morning.

That bizarre thought would be only slightly off the mark: years of training and conditioning would prove that only the fittest survived at Watson's—the weak were carried out.

And to think, I'd only been there four minutes!

I was disheveled, still dressed in my tux from the wedding, and definitely did not blend in. Besides, I had that lost look on my face, which compounded my inability to fade into the background. At that point, I wished I could disappear into the woodwork!

A very refined lady approached me, her granny glasses balanced on the end of her nose, multiple amounts of menus tucked under her left arm, and a pencil in her right hand writing down notes while she shot a quick glance at me.

Looking over the grannies, with eyebrows raised, she said, "You must be Sax: the wedding, the tux, your message you'd be late."

"Yes, ma'am, I'm Chris, I mean Sax. I'm not used to hearing that name yet."

"Oh, that'll be the easy part, you may be sure, so go down to the 'dungeon,' as the help likes to call it, change clothes, and get back up here immediately. You know where you're headed?"

"Yes, I had the guided tour. Be right back." With that, I turned on my heels and aimed straight for those swinging doors into the kitchen. Once again, the comparison to an airport leapt to mind. I was, so to speak, on the wrong runway, entering the kitchen through the "out" door instead of the "in" door.

The resulting sound shook the building to its foundation, although I never heard it, being knocked out colder than a blue fish lying on a slab of ice. The poor waitress coming from the kitchen into the center hall had been loaded with four precarious dinners balanced on one arm and one held with the other hand.

Arm service is not easily learned; it takes practice, talent, and balance that defies gravity. It's a lost art today, but one that is highly efficient, especially where quick service is essential to profits. It's a waltz, the waitress needing to guide her body and delectable cargo through a maze of obstacles while she weaves as gracefully as possible from the kitchen to her tables of diners. It's the dance that's performed while swerving the hips, upper torso remaining steady, then swiveling the body around steam tables, side stands, and dinner tables, that separates a good waitress from an exceptional one.

And the greatest challenge of all was the maneuvering through swinging doors from the kitchen into the center hall. A waitress couldn't just hit the door head on. She had to first kick it with her foot and then, as it opened, make a choice to go straight through, should the kick have been a good one, or, if the door didn't open all the way, go through butt first. That way, if the door returned too fast, the waitress could block it with her body, dance with her hips, and steady her arms to save the dinners from careening to the floor.

There is, of course, no alternate plan if one is going "in" the "out" door at the same time a waitress is trying to exit the kitchen. When that occurs, it's called "Oh shit!!"

When I regained consciousness, I was draped over the bottom step of the spiral staircase, aided by someone I didn't know. People were all over me, making sure I was all right and helping to clean up the mess. The poor waitress that I'd wiped out was not hurt, thankfully, and had gone back into the kitchen to try to resurrect her dinner orders before her customers died of starvation, not to mention a rapidly diminishing tip!

I sat there on the floor, very confused, and would have crawled on all fours right on out the front door had it not been for Gail. She was a seasoned "Watson Girl," with five years of wait staff experience under her belt, a true veteran of many Watson battles, not to mention the fact that she was a favorite of JD's. Slowly my focus returned, and when it did, my eyes fixed on a face that was making every effort not to laugh hysterically. I was covered in tossed salad, blue cheese dressing, Watson's famous French fries, and various chicken parts, all topped off with ice cream in my hair from a cherry pie à la mode.

"Hey, busboy, that was some entrance or exit you made. I'm not sure which way you were going', but I couldn't have done it better myself." Reconsidering that statement, Gail leaned down close to me and whispered, "Actually, I've done the same thing, but that's another story. If we wind up friends, I'll fill you in on the details. But for now, let's get your soggy ass down to the dungeon, clean you up, and start over. You're a God awful mess. What's your name?"

"Sax."

"Well, Sax, you look like shit." With that, Gail pulled me to my feet. We went into the kitchen, through the correct door this time, as she guided me down to the dungeon, but not before JD saw us. I was learning that somehow, the boss had the ability to watch and hear you no matter where you were or what mistakes you were making in the kitchen. He didn't miss a trick, a fact that would prove to piss me off time and time again.

The look on JD's face was priceless. He just stood there, unshaven, dressed in white pants, dirty white shirt, and white apron, his skin as pale as Casper the Friendly Ghost. I caught the shaking of his head from side to side, his arms folded in total disbelief, and a scathing "look" that screamed, "you asshole." All I wanted to do was disappear. If I could have wiggled my nose and evaporated at that moment, I would have done so instantly.

Gail was quick to pick up the vibes and translate that infamous expression.

"He's seen worse, trust me. It won't be the last time you see that look of his. It's classic JD, so get used to it. He thinks we're all a bunch of idiots."

As I followed Gail downstairs, I noted the dungeon was aptly named, like maybe something akin to the Catacombs of Rome. Homes on the island have no basements or cellars; dig too deep, and you hit water. Most structures are built on cement slabs or pilings. The highest point on Peck's Beach was ten feet above sea level, an unfortunate fact proven to be true after the devastating nor'easter the first weekend in March of the year I got hired.

An eight-inch wet snow fell fifty miles inland, but along the eastern seaboard from Virginia to Rhode Island, heavy rain and near-hurricane-force winds pounded the shoreline for three unrelenting days. Coinciding with a full moon, the tide never really had a chance to work its natural rhythm from high to low. Instead, northeast winds pushed the seawater deep onto the beaches, well over the protective dunes, and then filled the back bays to the point that the water had nowhere to go but rise and flood the island.

The accompanying destruction was unbelievable. Homes were split in half, straight down the middle, like a doll house open at one end so you could see all the interior details: beds made, bathrooms intact, pictures on the walls—a surrealistic scene.

Life out of sync. Sand was piled in streets parking meter deep, as though a blizzard had just blown through. Lives were lost, dreams shattered. People attempted to set their homes on fire in an effort to collect insurance; some got away with it, while others died in the process. The story was duplicated all up and down the coast. Like so many communities, Peck's Beach residents faced the challenge of their lives to rebuild the town and proved they had the resolve to do just that...piece by broken piece. Watson's was among the more fortunate buildings. Other than flooding in the dungeon and the wind damage to the roof, the restaurant weathered the storm well. Its sturdy structure and position above sea level made it a natural haven in which to find refuge in relative safety. Literally several hundred residents huddled behind its walls at the height of the storm. It wasn't the first time, nor would it be the last, that this stately mansion would provide shelter for the displaced.

When entering the front or back door of Watson's, there were seven or eight steps before getting to the first level. This allowed for space underneath the building to be utilized for storage, a work area, or whatever else might be needed to accommodate the business at hand.

And right then, I was the one feeling displaced and in the need of shelter as I entered the low-ceilinged dungeon. It was comprised of a series of rooms containing male and female dressing areas, one small bathroom, and the bakery. It was damp, musty, and poorly lit. Gail left me to fend for myself, her parting words: "See you topside."

As luck would have it, my change of clothes was in a duffle bag, and when the now-infamous hallway crash had occurred, the bag had survived unscathed. I stripped off my tux, which was heavily lathered with all kinds of food stains, and changed into black pants, white shirt, black shoes, and a gold busboy jacket that buttoned up to the collar.

As I was about to ascend the stairs, three waitresses and a busboy came down the steps two at a time, moving fast but managing to introduce themselves on the fly.

"Hi, I'm Bob John. This is Anne, Florence, and Jeanne. Nice job in the center hall. Gave us all a good laugh. Got to sneak a quick smoke. See you later."

And with that, they disappeared into the catacombs, and I was topside, heading for my marching orders from Eleanor, the head hostess in charge.

The rest of the night, thank God, was uneventful. I guess I had done enough damage for one evening. I got the routine down pretty quickly. Speed, at Watson's, was paramount. Slow walkers and workers were run over, dismissed as incompetent, and left for road kill if one didn't move at a pace that implied, "Catch me if you can."

Turnover was essential to making the restaurant profitable, so everything from the kitchen to the take-out window to the parking lot attendant was geared to maximize turnover. Seating capacity was 350 patrons, and on any given night, the restaurant would turn over four to five times. Twenty-nine waitresses and five busboys serving 1500 people in four hours! It was a well-oiled machine, and much of that clockwork precision was the result of JD's unbelievable organization, timing and demand for perfection. Serving those high dinner numbers was due in part to eating quickly then aiming for the boardwalk... Amusement rides, miniature golf, shopping, Shriver's salt water taffy, Johnson's popcorn, Mack & Manco Pizza, Kohr Bros. Thinking about these places transported one to the smells and flavor of the boardwalk, all part of the memories collected over the years. It's what drove the tourists to return, year after year, to recapture their childhood summer days. The entire island was packed with 7 miles of memories.

In order to attain those nightly numbers, a waitress couldn't just wander into the kitchen, stand by the steam table, and wait for her dinners to be put up. No way. Every facet of food production and delivery was well thought out, and all the kitchen crew knew exactly what their job was and how it had to be executed. The place was run like a boot camp. At least, that was how I saw it. The effort and structure was nothing I had ever seen or experienced before.

The dining public never saw the other side of those infamous swinging doors. Good thing, I guess. Waitresses would place their orders by leaving the duplicate guest check at the steam table when they first came into the kitchen. Then, while the entree order was being filled, they would round up the soups, salads, fruit cups, and whatever appetizers were requested and head out to serve customers with the first round of food.

Timing again came into play, and an experienced waitress had it down to the seconds. A misstep here, and she would be "in the weeds" all night. A waitress could have as many as four four-tops as well as a party of six in the Boardwalk Room, referred to by the staff as the Kiddy Corner. This was the room with tables for six to eight people, even nine or ten if we squeezed them in along with high chairs. So, naturally, this was where the big parties wound up, and believe me, working that room was like being sent to the salt mines.

People with lots of "grimmies"—loosely translated to mean pain-in-the-ass kiddies— as I was prone to call them, were notoriously cheap when it came to tips, and this room lived up to its reputation in spades. Young families on vacation, out for an evening of dining and rides on the boardwalk, were not the best at expressing their thanks by leaving a nice gratuity on the table.

That said, working as a waitress at Watson's was the best place in town to make serious money. Volume made up for skimpy tips. Turnover was king. Move them in, get them out; just do it as fast and as pleasantly as you can. And do it with a smile on your face. Somehow it worked. It all came together in a well-orchestrated symphony of kitchen chaos and culinary colors and smells that left the customer wanting more of the same, year after year after year.

It was a recipe for success—with a capital S! And once again, the S belonged solely to J D. All this craziness was completely under his tight-fisted control. Without him, the finely tuned clock known as Watson's would never have been able to keep time. It was his uncanny ability to pull together all the seemingly disoriented elements of the kitchen—almost as though he were directing the making of a major film—bringing all the pieces together just in time to feed the masses...1500 starving shoobies, all of whom were willing to stand in line for what seemed like hours for the chance to dine at the famous Watson's.

And exactly, what is a shoobie? It derives the name from day trippers who came down by train, many seasons in the past, from Philadelphia, and they carried their lunch in a shoe box, having no intention of spending a dime in the town...thus the term shoobie.

My first night at Watson's was over before I knew it. The food factory slowly ground to a halt, and I was one happy camper—and one seriously tired busboy. What a day. Everyone seemed to have their closing side work down to a science. Waitresses and busboys cleaned up the side stations where all the silver, napkins, glasses, and placemats were kept. Once restocked, the waitresses filled the ketchup bottles, sugar bowls, and salt and pepper shakers while the busboys went from room to room flipping chairs upside down and placing them on the tables. These closing tasks were not viewed as "happy hour"; quite the contrary, everyone just wanted to get the hell out of there and go back to their various boarding rooms or to their parents' homes and lick their battle wounds. And if, by chance, you were one of the unfortunate ones chosen to do "ketchups," you were majorly pissed...the punishment being meted out based on inadequate customer service that evening. Why would this seemingly benign task of combining two partially filled bottles into one be so irritating? Because it took forever for the stuff to drain from one to the other, delayed your exit from the "Big W" by a half-hour. Besides, this little exercise required you to balance one bottle on top of the other, neck to neck, and in doing so, you could be guaranteed to screw things up by having the top bottle fall off, thus spilling ketchup on the table, forcing an instant replay, and producing much irritation.

When all was finally done and side work was "inspected" by the head hostess, I descended to the dungeon to change into street clothes. My busboy jacket looked like it had been used to dry dirty dishes. And to think I had put a clean one on halfway through the evening. Everyone had left, so the dungeon was empty.

I threw on my clean clothes, grabbed my tux, and as I was heading to go upstairs, a wonderful cinnamon smell hit me from somewhere in the bowels of the building. I redirected myself and walked down a rather narrow corridor that forced me to stoop a little so I wouldn't hit my head on the low ceiling. One more whack on the skull I did not need tonight. I came to a door slightly ajar, and when I opened it, I was surprised to discover the bakery, clean as a whistle and packed with all kinds of desserts in various forms of production.

I had assumed all the baked goods on the menu were bought elsewhere and imported for consumption by the patrons. Not so. It seems that in the wee small hours each morning, at 3 AM to be precise, Rob the baker would trundle into the bakery below until 9 AM every day. Good thing Rob was vertically challenged; a munchkin only five foot five, he baked his way into heaven as far as I was concerned. These delectable desserts of delight were in large part the reason Watson's was such a hit. I had already indulged in a few stolen cups of custard during my premier performance topside, and I was hooked. But I never guessed the creator of such delectables had been literally right under my feet.

I walked out of Watson's that night feeling comatose, tired, dazed, and somewhat lost, and was sure of nothing except that I had survived an incredible day. How? I have no idea. I just wanted to get in my car and drive to the boarding house where Sheila's mom, Aunt Gladys, as we all called her, was holding a room for me at 704 Plymouth Place. The ride was short; the house was only two blocks away. My room was on the third floor of this old Victorian home. There were about ten rooms to let, with the bathrooms down the hall. I had made it clear I was only staying for two weeks. After that, I was going to move to another boarding house called

The Gnorr's. It had a much larger room than the one at Aunt Gladys's, one with its own bathroom, minus a shower, and on the ground floor, accommodations were barely basic. The shower was outside and not enclosed, so stripping down to bathe was not an option. The one redeeming feature was a private entrance through a side door. Going and coming, no matter what the hour, was essential for me. As I came to learn, Mrs. Gnorr was a lovely Christian lady, one who would not have approved of my lifestyle had she known what was going on. The side door was a blessing in more ways than one.

On this particular maiden voyage workday, I was so glad to crash at Aunt Gladys's place that night. All I wanted at this point was a bed. I don't even remember hitting the pillow. I was down for the count.

When I look back on it, the summer of '62 was somewhat of a blur. So much has happened since then that events during my initial introduction to Watson's have been overshadowed by life's unforeseen surprises.

But the summer of '62 had its lasting effects through the indelible friendships that, in some strange way, bound all of "the gang" together for decades to come. It was also the summer I met Laura.

CHAPTER 5

I had no clue she was only seventeen years old. If a seventeen-year-old can look near my age, be stunning with blonde hair, tan, and eyes as blue as a late September sky, then she completed my checklist for the perfect woman. Did I mention she was the boss's daughter? I thought, If only I were twenty-three, Laura would be nineteen. Should I wait for her to grow up? Timing is everything, and the clock was not on my side. By the time I was twenty-three, my life would have morphed into something totally at odds with what I had in mind right now.

As I emerged from the dungeon, Laura glided passed me, rounding the corner by the pantry, heading for the hall. I made a weak effort to try to catch up with her to introduce myself, but I reconsidered and slowed my pace. From the sound of the swinging doors, I figured Laura was aiming for the second floor. I couldn't be positive about her direction, but one thing I knew for certain, beautiful a girl as she was, I wasn't about to go anywhere near those doors again tonight.

Being the owner's only child has its privileges, so they tell me, the major one being the wherewithal to afford summering in Paris at the age of sixteen. Not bad duty to draw if you're teetering on becoming a young adult in a few years.

Coming from a poor family—no, let me rephrase that—coming from a family that's broke, I had a hard time wrapping my mind around the word privilege.

I think '62 was the last year of our innocence.

The summer was hot and dry. Business was booming in spite of the March disaster because the island residents were determined to remain upbeat, and their positive outlook paid off more than anyone could have imagined.

Watson's proved to be the linchpin by which everything was ultimately bound together for a number of reasons, and especially for all of us who had solidified our friendships with each other.

Life was beautiful. Kennedy held court in Camelot, one year of college was under my belt, and events were moving toward the American Dream. "The Twist" was in, and long skirts were out. Drugs were isolated as an inner-city problem, alcohol and sex were the dominant sins of the day, and rock and roll was here to stay.

We all worked hard and played even harder. Watson's became our central point of contact. It was where we met every night, surviving the cravings of a hungry dining public. We made it through the other side of chaos night after night, and our survival hinged on teamwork.

This teamwork overflowed into our social lives as well. A typical day for our gang was comprised of falling out of bed by 10 AM and then heading straight for sun, sand, surf, and socializing. If it should rain, God forbid, we declared it a health day, one where we'd sleep in until noon, then catch up with laundry as well as general cleaning. There was little toleration for two such days in a row.

We loved the beach and all the craziness that went with it. We got a lot of laughs just observing the day trippers and tourists as they seemed to lay claim to the sand like one would plant a flag of ownership on foreign soil. Proper behavior, once settled down on beach blankets, was a lost art not observed by the masses. So, one day, to entertain ourselves, I decided to write down what we thought was proper "beach etiquette."

When you first arrive on the beach with all your gear, lathered with baby oil and iodine, the equivalent of laying in the sun covered in bacon grease, and there is only one small group within sight as far as the eye can see, don't plant all your "stuff" right next to this family, whose only desire is to have a modicum of relative peace. I mean, you have the entire beach at your disposal. Why on earth would you want to snuggle up to total strangers?

Smoking on the beach is permissible. Now you have increased your own demise by a considerable percentage. If skin cancer doesn't get you, lung cancer will. Three caveats prevail. Always smoke downwind, never put your butts out in the sand... would you snuff out a cigarette on your floor at home? The beach is the rug in the living room of life. Collect butts in a baggie and trash them later... And cigars are always a no-no.

When shaking out your beach towel, make sure you are downwind. Those of us who are relaxing in our sand chairs, absorbing vitamin D, do not want to be sandblasted due to your inability to care which way the wind is blowing.

Lifeguards are not babysitters. They are not in charge of your gaggle of Grimmies. They are too busy watching your teenage daughters.

Wear sandals to the beach... The sand is hot as hell, and no one wants to hear you scream your head off because you're walking on a surface that's the equivalent of burning coals.

We all love music but not when it's so loud that it makes your thighs quiver! Turn it down. Your taste in music does not need to be shared by the entire beach. Buy head phones.

When planting your umbrella in the sand like you just discovered Antarctica, make sure the pole is planted securely in the sand… Failure in this endeavor may cause the umbrella to take off in a stiff wind like a rocket on the Fourth of July, causing the pole to impale the lovely little old lady who is sleeping fifty feet away in stake-like fashion that would put Dracula to shame.

When the tide is inching its way up the beach, build a wall of sand for your neighbor while you're doing the same for yourself… You may make a friend. There's no way you'll win against the approaching sea, but you'll buy time before you have to schlep all your gear twenty-five feet in reverse.

The ice cream man with his obnoxious bell and bellicose voice must go… Teach all children under seven that when the bell tolls, it means there's no ice cream left. This will save you much aggravation and mucho money. Yes, this is suspending the truth a bit, but so is belief in Santa Claus and the Easter Bunny! Children are flexible; they'll adjust.

Never get up from your beach chair to shake hands with a new acquaintance. All greetings are done while sitting or prone… Remember, new people to the beach are on your turf. If they get offended, too bad… Get over yourself.

Beach attire for men: never come to the beach fully clothed. Shoes with socks are so wrong it's not even worth mentioning, and Speedos, unless you've just won an Olympic gold medal in swimming, are forever banned.

For women: bikinis and two-piece swimsuits were designed for the young, the firm, and the curvy…not the old, the saggy, and the flabby. Please, spare us the pain… Contrary to what you may think, you're not invisible.

When having a conversation, talk…don't squawk. If your voice is irritating, have someone else talk while you lip-sync… No one will notice the difference… There's no original thought out there anyway, and peace and quiet will once again reign over the sand.

Sex on the beach is never permissible during daylight hours. This isn't the mile-high club. You're at sea level; different rules apply. One blanket, one person. Two people on one blanket? This leads to moaning, groaning, and humping. Get a room!

Besides, it can lead to "double standard" talk. All the women on the beach will say, "She's a tramp." And all the men will say, "Isn't he lucky!"

We got a kick out of reading back to ourselves what I'd put down on paper, and all agreed we should try to get it published. It would make a fun little book, and as we lay there on the sand, wondering where that creative idea might land us, we heard our transistor radio break forth with this little gem of a song:

When you're in the mood for a dining delight,

Watson's welcomes your appetite.

A meal at Watson's is family fun;

in Peck's Beach, it's number one.

You'll come back to Watson's, as all people do,

for a meal you'll remember, it's Watson's for you.

We all looked at each other, groaning very audibly in unison. The little jingle managed to find us no matter where we were. It was our daily call to action back to the salt mines to face the hungry shoobies.

From the beach, we reluctantly returned to our various boarding houses, changed clothes, and worked from 3:30 to 10:00 PM. After the restaurant closed, we went back to our various places to clean up, change clothes again, and then team up to party at someone's apartment or go dancing and drinking at the Point until the wee hours of the morning. We lived that routine day in and day out. Our shared lives, whether laughing or crying over life at Watson's, were very special times together, and our zany antics were legendary for years to come.

The summer of '62 taught me a lot about the people I worked for and with. As a result, I did more listening than talking. It's amazing what you can learn by keeping your mouth shut. People inadvertently reveal more than they should or ever wanted to. Over time, I got to know JD a little better, though the progress was slow to develop.

JD was married to Vivian, Adrienne's daughter, and had come into the business because Adrienne was losing it mentally. She suffered from deep depression and had been hospitalized several times for shock treatments. At that point, Vivian convinced JD to take over the running of Watson's, letting Addi back off into more of a figurehead roll. Problematically, Addi still wanted control; after all, she was the founder and owner of the establishment and couldn't come to terms with being relegated to playing second fiddle to her son-in-law.

So Addi made herself visible during dinner hours, greeting customers at the door and even working the register for several hours each night. Near closing time, she would have her dinner served on the Porch, usually accompanied by a special friend or prominent guest. If you received an invitation to dine with Adrienne, you knew you had made it into the social registry of Peck's Beach... She seldom ate alone. If not entertaining a guest, Adrienne would dine with Ella, her maid and childhood friend, who, I also came to learn had been the other person in the room during my interview.

But somehow September always manages to make a sudden appearance just when you don't want August to end. I was not looking forward to fall after this summer. There once had been a day when the expectations of burning leaves, crisp, frost-laden nights, and college had gotten my juices flowing, but no longer. I didn't want the summer to end. It had been a reprieve from the hectic winter schedule I had grown so used to living. All of our crazy gang of ten had become very close with one another, and I wasn't prepared to separate quite yet. I really didn't have a choice when it came to September responsibilities; school was essential, and although I knew what my priorities had to be, it didn't make the transition any easier.

The holidays were fast approaching, so I figured I better get a move on and complete the plans for a Christmas party/reunion with all the worker bees at Watson's. I sent out invitations to one hundred of my "most intimate friends," as my mother liked to say, and wouldn't you know, ninety of them accepted. I lived in a two-bedroom apartment on the first floor with my mother in this old stone castle of a house in the burbs of Philly. It had a fireplace in the living room and one in my bedroom, with French doors that opened to connect the two rooms, ideal for accommodating large crowds...great for entertaining...and good thing too, because a heap of people was coming. Fortunately, the kitchen was as big as my bedroom, so the place could readily absorb the masses, so to speak. Besides, most parties wind up in the kitchen anyway, and as it turned out, this wasn't any different.

It proved to be a huge success, going a long way to adding additional cement to an already well-forged bond that held our group tightly hinged together.

What really surprised me most was the RSVP from Adrienne Watson and her friend/companion Harry Blake, the Boardwalk Kettle Fudge king.

Harry was "the king" when it came to boardwalk entrepreneurial ventures! He operated fudge stores in all the beach towns up and down the barrier islands from Cape May to Long Beach Island, plus a successful mail-order business. Harry started with nothing except a vision, worked as a teenager for a candy man in Wildwood, and developed his own recipe for fudge. Then, at eighteen years of age, he opened his first small retail shop on Peck's Beach, adjacent to the Asteria Hotel, and the rest is history, with piles of cash to back it up.

So, when he showed up at the party with Adrienne on his arm, I tried not to show my surprise. I didn't really believe they'd make the drive. Huck had driven them from Peck's Beach in Harry's infamous white Lincoln Town Car. They were more than gracious in the way they mixed it up with an age group well younger than their own. I had never met Harry formally, though I had taken him to his favorite table many times at the restaurant. He liked to dine with Adrienne on the Porch and did so more than once a week.

The gang loved the fact that the owner of Watson's would actually take the time to travel one hundred miles to socialize with a bunch of college crazies. It was a good political move, if nothing else. Everyone at the party who worked for Adrienne felt her presence spoke volumes about her level of caring for her employees, and without saying a word, "the Madame" had made mega-points with every one of us.

CHAPTER 6

The summer of '63 arrived just in time to save the sanity of almost everyone on the Penn State campus, especially mine. I had to travel east to Peck's Beach in late winter at the request of Adrienne.

She wanted to talk to me about a change in job position, and I was anxious to hear her what she had to say. As it turned out, the head hostess had resigned because she and her husband were moving to Florida. Patricia Smith had been at Watson's for twenty years and knew the place like the back of her hand. She could put a Paris Island drill sergeant to shame, so you made sure you never wound up on her "drill" side.

Since I was the oldest of the group, Addi felt I would be the best candidate to learn how to manage the front end of the restaurant. She knew I was an undergraduate at Penn State with plans to go to graduate school for business, so my guess is she banked on me being around for a few years. It was accurate discernment on her part. I was a quick learner, so when the snows of the Nittany Mountains melted into spring, I found myself being trained to take over the full responsibility of managing the entire dining room staff.

The gang all returned that summer to the Big W en masse. I rented an apartment over a gas station garage on 9th Street with three other guys. The girls rented a single house on West Ave, well within walking distance of Watson's. We thought the girls were living large, having a whole home all to themselves while we were crammed into a tiny two-bedroom/one-bath second-floor over the beat-up mechanic's workshop of the corner gas station.

Such are the inequities of life. But once the entire crew reconvened, the good times and laughs came rolling back. The past academic year became a blur, and the only thing visible was the reality of a beautiful summer ahead...sun, sand, surf, and, in our dreams...sex.

June 6th... I remember dates. Not good at remembering your name, but dates—they stick. I went to work in the late morning that Tuesday to do table assignments for the waitresses. I went in through the front entrance, mainly because I had to shoot upstairs to the office. It saved time, as the back entrance into the kitchen was too hectic to maneuver, even at that hour. Humble as my little office was, barely closet-sized, it served its purpose. However, the climb to the third floor seemed to get higher with every round trip!

I could have had my eyes closed and known exactly where I was by the sheer smell of the restaurant: a blend of everything deep fried, baked, steamed, and broiled all rolled into an aroma so unique to Watson's that it wafted through the building like a culinary perfume, invading the very fiber of anything material it took refuge upon... not an offensive smell, but as identifying as a finger print. As I bolted into the center hall, barely paying any attention to my surroundings, I came to a screeching halt. There, at the bottom of the staircase, I saw Ella sitting on the bottom step, her large frame heaving up and down as if she were struggling to breathe through her tears.

I couldn't kneel down in front of her fast enough. "Ella, what's wrong?" There was no response, as though she had disconnected from the reality surrounding her.

"Ella, please tell me what's happened?" I took hold of her trembling hands, and she slowly lifted her face so our eyes connected. The brokenness and devastation I saw was overwhelming.

"Miss Addi is dead!"

"This can't be true," I said in total disbelief. "I just saw her last night. She can't be dead." I sat alongside Ella so I could wrap my arm around her curled-up now fragile body.

"Lawd have mercy, child, I wish I was jus' dreamin', but Miss Addi was asleep in her bed when I comes in to wake her 'cause she usually is up by now and she wanted to make sure she didn't miss a doctor's appointment. I saw two pill bottles on the nightstand, empty, and I was scared to death she might have harmed herself, but I don't know, I was confused... My heart was poundin' somethin' awful. I shook her and said, "Miss Addi, Miss Addi, wake up, but nothin' happened... She was so still. I yelled out for Huck, and he came a runnin'... Guess I sounded pretty desperate. Thank heavens he was there, 'cause he knew what to do. He's upstairs now with JD. I had to leave the room... Just can't take this sad day no more. I know I gotta stay strong for Vi and Laura, but I have no one to hold onto anymore... She gone, Sax. What gonna happen now?"

Just then, the sirens began to wail, and it sounded like they were crying too. I sat there next to Ella, drawing her to my side. It was my feeble effort to give her some sense of comfort and security at a moment laced with total abandonment. My heart really broke for Ella. She was a devoted friend to Addi and a big part of her family. She had never left Addi's side for almost sixty years...always there for her, through the good and the bad, regardless of circumstances crashing in on them. Ella's family was long gone, so she had leaned on Addi for her emotional support. They understood one another for the very reason they shared life together. From childhood days on the family farm to the remaking of themselves on Peck's Beach, no matter what happened to them, they'd been joined by a unique bonding built on trust and unconditional love.

"I just can't understand it. Addi seemed to be doing so well... Do you think she took the wrong medication or something?" I asked.

Ella lifted her head and looked right into my eyes. "Master Sax, I found a note and pills by her bed and gave them to Huck. I don't know nothin' about what it said. I was afraid to read it. Please don't say a word. Huck said he'd give the note to JD but not Vi… Too much to bear at once, and that's God's truth."

The front door flew open, and our private, intimate moment was shattered. I helped Ella gain her balance and walked her into the Garden Room. The paramedics did what they were trained to do and, without missing a beat, were up the stairs and into Addi's bedroom before we even had a chance to sit. Huck came into the Garden Room and cradled Ella in a hug so tight I thought she'd snap in two, tears running down his black face like an open spigot. This man was huge, both in height and width, and you knew right away you never wanted to mess with him. Though old and gray now, one could lay money on it that Huck could beat the shit out of you if push came to shove. And "shove" never showed up—the challenge was never taken despite many a chance by the young bucks in the kitchen. They knew better than to play the "shove" card, so whatever Huck asked for, he got, and without any backtalk from the crew. It was a trait JD was quick to relish.

"Ella, you don't wanna be sittin' here, what with all your tears, and watch them bring Miss Addi down. It's too hard on any soul to bear, so let me take you to my house for a spell, let things calm down a bit." Huck never spoke much. Words were well chosen, sparse at best. When he did speak, you just had to love this man. His eyes would pull you in. His round face and gentle spirit convinced you everything was going to come out all right somehow.

Ella nodded, and Huck took over where I had left off, leading her through the back kitchen doors and out of the building. The paramedics brought Adrienne down the stairs through the center hall. It was a tense and heart crushing scene as the medical team guys took her out the front door and into the ambulance.

I sat there, not quite aware of all that had just taken place. I needed time to let it all soak in, but I didn't want to go back to my apartment. Instead, I got up and went down to the dungeon and told Rob, the pastry baker, what had just taken place. He was as shocked as I was and became visibly upset. Rob had been at Watson's since he was a kid. When the restaurant closed every year in September, he would return to the University of Penn, to his main job as pastry chef, just like Popcorn, my favorite deep fryer, and several other cooks. University life simmered down in the summer months, so working at the Big W meshed well for these men and kept them employed throughout the year.

After sitting in the dungeon with Rob and trying, without much success, to put together what had just taken place, I told him things would eventually settle down and, hopefully, all this turmoil would calm itself. I left him sitting alone on one of the benches the waitresses used to change clothes, looking as though someone had hit him in the stomach. I felt bad, but I had to go topside to make calls to the staff with the sad news.

Vi and Laura entered the kitchen through the back door, unaware of what was taking place. I was on the phone, the one JD often used in his makeshift office, and I could tell by the way both were talking that they had no clue of Addi's death. I turned around, trying really hard not to show any emotion, when suddenly JD appeared. He motioned to me to take Laura aside as he took Vi by the hand.

"Sax, take Laura into the Beach Room, and I'll have Popcorn bring you both some breakfast. Vi, come with me, need to talk."

"John, what's wrong? You're worrying me."

He didn't answer, but I did what I was asked, leading Laura into the dining room through the swinging doors. We sat at a nice deuce, and after a few moments, one of Popcorn's favorite specialties arrived…a pile of pancakes that would put Aunt Jemima to shame. I had lost my appetite completely, but Laura sure hadn't. She had no trouble quickly reducing that stack of freshly flipped delicious discs, and I didn't have the guts to tell her about her grandmother.

Laura was becoming quite a beautiful young lady. She was unaware that I was really seeing her for the first time. She had suddenly grown up since last summer. There was a different level of maturity, a more adult way she expressed herself. We talked about the past year, her high school experience, her friends, and the way she was looking forward to the summer ahead.

Vi walked up to the table just as we were getting into some fun conversation. I was trying to keep things light, not wanting to show how sad I felt for the family. I don't think Laura was able to see through the mask I was sporting, or if she did, she didn't let on. Our conversation was upbeat until Vi said, "Laura, I need to talk to you in private, honey."

I quickly stood up and said, "I'll go and finish the work schedule," and took my leave. Vi sat down next to Laura, taking her hand. It was evident she had been crying; her eyes were bloodshot and puffy, giving away the pain she must be feeling. The kitchen door shut behind me, and the words "I've got something really hard to say" were suddenly lost amidst the growing din of daily restaurant prepping.

I didn't see Vi for the rest of the day. The word spread quickly about Addi's death, with lots of speculation about how and why it had happened. Everyone had a theory, an opinion…but the truth remained a holdout.

When I was finished with the work schedule, I went back to the Beach Room, not expecting to see Laura where I had left her, but there she was, just staring at nothing at all, alone. I approached her quietly, and when she saw me, she started to cry. And of course, I was pulled in emotionally. The one thing I can't stand is seeing a girl cry. I sat down quickly and put my arm around her. She let me hold her close, crying softly and whispering something so quiet it was not discernible. I said I was there for her and that I couldn't imagine the shock and loss she was feeling.

Laura was very close to her grandmother. Since Laura had been her only grandchild, Addi had felt free to spoil Laura whenever she wanted to. This, of course, had caused Vi a great deal of consternation from time to time. Vi was a tough and demanding mother, expecting discipline and self-control from Laura, attributes that Vi had a great deal of trouble maintaining herself. Teenagers don't often think about the consequences of their actions, wanting to be independent while at the same time needing to feel secure in knowing they are loved, even though their parents won't let them do whatever it is that may harm or even kill them. Vi was totally aware of the genes that ran through the blood of her only child. She worked hard to control her daughter's every move, a parental tactic that seldom proved effective. The tighter Vi held control, the greater the struggle to get out from under it. If anyone had the will and determination to actually break free and become her own person, Laura did.

Addi experienced with Laura what she missed with her own daughter, gaining a second chance to reconnect on an emotional level that was so lacking with Vi. Addi never really had the chance to know Vi's father. What would Greg have been like as a man? A teenager's one-night romance never had time to evolve into a mature relationship. What would Greg have been like as a father? The questions would never be answered.

Addi's death was really traumatic. The shock was just setting in. Laura, needing time to process all of it, left the Beach Room. I knew she was grateful I was there to give a small bit of comfort and support to her, but the one she needed most was her mother, and Vi was not available on the level Laura sought. In all her young life, it seemed to all of us who observed them, that Laura was never able to rely on her mother to understand her the way Addi had.

The funeral was massive. The entire island must have shown up to pay their respects. I drove Gail and Sam in my convertible, the rest of the gang following in separate cars along with the kitchen crew, some of whom had been employed by Adrienne Watson for over thirty years. One of them, Dennis, the head chef and a native of Charleston, South Carolina, came north every summer to work at Watson's, never missing a season in twenty-five years. Son of a preacher man, Dennis had an undying faith. He knew where he was headed if the Grim Reaper showed up unannounced, and he wasn't shy about sharing the Good News with anyone who was willing to listen. I loved hearing him expound scripture. And when he was winding down I couldn't help but get a picture of him picking boiled chicken apart in an effort to assist in getting chicken crochets made. When it comes time, just fry me up and cast the ashes somewhere meaningful. I won't be there, so who the hell cares where I wind up? The beach might be a nice place to scatter my remains about. After all, that's where I had my beginnings. But to come to a viewing and file by a casket filled with the pasty, painted remains of what was once a living human being is not very uplifting, especially for those who pathetically trundle dutifully by the deceased in agonizingly slow motion.

The receiving line consisted of Vi, JD, Laura, and Ella. The casket was open, and her beloved dog, a miniature French Poodle called Puddles, was also with her. Evidently, Addi had put in her will that the dog must join her upon her death. A visible shock registered on people's faces as they filed by to give their last respects. There they were, the two of them, side by side in a peaceful pose. I half-expected Addi to sit up and Puddles to bark!

Vi showed no emotion at all, her eyes looking empty and her body moving robotically on command as though she were being controlled by someone far away to ensure she performed according to social norms.

JD stood between Vi and Laura, doing the job he was expected to do, supporting his grieving wife in this most difficult of situations. What they didn't know was he knew the truth about what had actually taken place in Addi's bedroom.

On a solemn promise never to reveal, I came to know that when Huck came to Ella's aid, realizing Addi was dead, he'd quickly removed the pills and the note she'd left on her night table. Then Huck hid them. He loved Addi and didn't want people to think poorly of her. But he didn't take into account the guilt he'd feel, so he confessed to what he'd done to JD.

Feelings of genuine compassion for Vi overcame JD. He pulled her closer to himself, but Vi didn't even pick up on it. She continued greeting the next person in line, robotically as before, and quietly crying in an embrace with an old friend of Addi's. JD was not looking forward to revealing the true story to Vi, because it would cause additional hurt and abandonment issues on top of her already devastated emotions.

We all sat five or six rows back from the open casket, the pews in front being roped off for family and close friends. A darling old couple whom I knew from way back in Philly and had just warmly greeted on the way in made their way into the row right in front of us. It was obvious by the way they walked and acted, by the canes they carried and the hearing aids they wore, that they were well on the far side of eighty.

It was a few minutes after they had settled into place that the old codger leaned his head in toward his wife and said in a voice loud enough to wake the dead, "Have you seen Adrienne?"

We couldn't miss hearing the question, and I was dying to find out the answer.

Her reply, as she turned her head close to his ear, was: "Adrienne who? Our daughter Adrienne? She's not coming."

With hand gestures to match a baseball ump's "safe" at home plate, he yelled, "Horizontal Adrienne!"

All three of us tried with all we had within us not to laugh. We managed to stuff the urge until our faces turned red, and then we lost it, and the tears came in torrents. We stifled the laughter the best we could, but the sound just could not be squelched. Thankfully, it sounded like we were crying, and we were very grateful the immediate family had not yet been seated.

As heads turned and we got looks that killed, it was hard to swallow the laughter. Gratefully, the pipe organ bailed us out with the opening song, "Because He lives," saving us from an embarrassing scene. The service commenced, no thanks to us.

There's only a tear that separates laughing and crying. It was well with our souls that we had both. Life has to go on.

And life did go on at Watson's, despite the sadness over the loss of its founder. The restaurant reopened after a two-day period of mourning. J.D. took complete command, never really missing a beat. I've never had a real handle on his relationship with his mother-in-law. I know both were the owners of strong personalities and were known to lock heads from time to time. But I think they respected one another, especially when it came to their faith, a shared experience in the latter years.

JD was drafted, so to speak, to rescue Watson's from falling to pieces from lack of strong managerial direction. Adrienne, who periodically battled bouts of deep depression, had to be hospitalized for shock treatments. At the time I came to the restaurant, JD had been in command for two years, having left his former job as head of acquisitions for the prestigious Chandler Hotel chain.

Now that Adrienne was gone, JD was free to shape the restaurant to reflect his vision, bringing Watson's into the 20th Century. Times were changing; the nation was heading for an unbelievable shift in direction , both politically and socially.

Public dress became more casual. Dressing up was no longer required for an evening stroll along the boardwalk, or for dinner at Watson's. Gone were high heels for ladies, not a totally bad adjustment in fashion since once on the boardwalk, ladies would have to put rubber discs on each heel to prevent it from getting stuck between the boards, ripping the heel off the shoe. Men's ties were discarded in favor of a collared shirt but slightly open at the neck.. People were more discerning in their choice of food quality and cuisine. Air conditioning was a staple in many fine restaurants of the day, but Adrienne had opposed it. She'd once asked customers to vote on whether they wanted air conditioning or the cool ocean breezes. The "breezes" won the day but proved to be extremely unreliable. However, Adrienne held her ground, it was best to please the customer. Forget the fact that not only the temperature in the kitchen could reach the one-hundred-plus range with little effort, but that the dining rooms suffered as well.

Since it was June, it was somewhat easier to run the restaurant in the aftermath of such a sad funeral. The staff was not at full capacity, and the crowds of vacationers had not yet landed in full force. JD and Vi could tend to all the legal matters facing them, not to mention the emotional ones, and not be quite as pressured to handle all the many details after such a personal loss.

Vi turned to an old ally to ease her pain, prescription drugs. But drugs aside, she was more visible in the restaurant after her mother's death. She only played "hostess" periodically, causing an anxiety-producing event whenever she would surface. I could be well into managing the chaos of the evening when, out of nowhere, Vivian would be standing at the center hall entrance, menus in hand, looking for direction from me to hand off starving patrons for her to seat. She was not cut out for the job. Vivian's very presence caused uneasiness among the staff, who were quick to deflect her air of superiority as she helped the "little people," stooping to their level occasionally to give needed assistance. I learned early on to work around her whenever she showed up.

Ella was another story, the total opposite of Vivian, and a person I wanted to understand. And when she showed up every night to eat dinner alone on the Porch, I couldn't wait to talk to her. It was a routine she had developed with Adrienne that went back years. The two would always sit down for dinner together, no matter where they were or what they were doing. The only exception to this particular party of two would be if Addi had a prominent dinner guest from out of town or a meeting to attend.

Dinner took priority, mostly for the chance to stay connected with each other and share the day's events—the highs, the lows, and everything in between. The food was just an added bonus.

I was so used to seeing the duo dining together each night that it was a shock when I began seeing Ella at the table alone. I supposed it must be like the loss of a twin, your other half cut off, leaving you adrift in your own thoughts, unable to share.

When the evening would begin to wind down and the line of patrons dissipated, I would have dinner served to me on the Porch. After a week of observing Ella, I asked her one night if I could join her for dinner. Fortunately for me, I wasn't turned down. One evening turned into two, and two turned into many, many more; those were probably the best dinner reservations I ever made.

At first, Ella's dinner engagements with me were just that and nothing more. We were polite in our conversation, but everything discussed was surface stuff, the weather, business that night at the restaurant. As time moved on, I began to gain Ella's confidence. I was trying to pump her for information or gossip about Adrienne's life or, for that matter, about Watson's. It wasn't really necessary, because eventually the conversations progressed in that direction on their own anyway.

Ella was a woman of strong character with roots that went back to the plantation era. Her grandfather was a slave who managed to slip north during the Civil War thanks to the underground railroad. His son, Ezra, and wife, Sarah, birthed six children before Ella came along. A Baptist preacher most fierce, Ezra proclaimed the good news...Christ crucified, buried, resurrected from the dead, and rose on the third day. This was his message, and he preached it wherever he happened to place his feet on terra firma, whether in a tent in Virginia or a church in Pennsylvania. People would come up to Ella and say, " I hear your father is quite a powerful preacher." Her response, "You know it too?"

"Ella, how did you come to know Addi?" I finally found the courage to ask her.

"Well, child, turns out my father had a wandering eye. I'm, what do people say, a love child. Seems his lady friend was about to bring into the light the darkness that lived on the other side of all that fancy preachin'. Sometimes Jesus is better shown than spoken about. I was put into an orphanage, and no one knew the better. When all was lost, Miss Emily, Addi's mama, found me workin' my little fingers to the bone at a small tea room. She talked to the owner, who was as tough as nails, persuading him to let her take me home for a spell. It didn't take much fancy talkin' before he let me go, so she brought me home to help cook and clean. Eventually, she was able to convince the orphanage to let me stay until they found me a home. I don't think they tried too hard, and that was fine with Miss Emily. She was the first person I can ever remember lovin' me. She gave me a clean bed and a full stomach. I was seven, and so was Addi.

"Then, on a night I will never forget, Addi's father came home drunk and angry. Money was low, and Addi innocently asked him for money to buy something, and he went crazy. She started to cry, and he hit her, yelling awful things at her. As he was about to hit again, I came down the living room stairs from her bedroom just as Addi's father's fist was about to come down. I put myself between them both and took the hit. I stood my ground and said, 'It's the bottle makin' you do this. Please, please, dear Jesus, don't let Mr. Tom hit my sister again.' The scene was a bad one. Mr. Tom suddenly sobered up, realizing what he'd done...dropped to his knees, grabbed us both, and cried out he was so sorry. Miss Emily by now, had entered the room after closing down the tea room and couldn't believe what she was seeing. Addi had a cut above her eye, and I had a swollen left cheek. We were like sisters ever since."

Night after night, Ella and I came to trust each other, sharing our lives on a personal level that allowed her to express how special her dear friend Adrienne had been to her—as well as the deep loss she felt. So our conversations turned genuinely open and honest during those nightly dinners on the Porch.

I can still hear her voice and see her sweet face, sitting by the window at her favorite table as she began to reveal a story that I never thought I'd hear, and she never thought she'd tell.

CHAPTER 7

Adrienne Wynne was born an only child to a middle-class family in New Hope, PA, in the year 1900. Her father, Thomas, was a carpenter by trade and a functional alcoholic by vocation.

Thomas Wynne was a direct descendant of Thomas Wynne, the seventeenth-century physician to William Penn. He married his neighbor's daughter, Emily, when they were in their teens, setting up a carpenter shop in the garage of his parents home. Having no money left from starting a new business venture forced them to live at home until finances allowed an escape to greener pastures.

Over time, Thomas slowly drank his way into an alcoholic abyss, with dire consequences for his family. Life at home was tough. His bitterness over serving in the Spanish-American War of 1898 only exaggerated the pain he felt from the reign of death surrounding him on the battlefield. A love affair with the bottle is never an isolated event. It doesn't happen on its own; underneath lies the source of the disease, but Thomas never wanted to face his demons... Denial dominated.

Emily's parents died in a house fire when she was very young, and she was raised by a paternal aunt. That tragic event and its repercussions were life-changing and affected not only how she viewed the world around her, but, more directly, how she raised her only child, Adrienne. No one was there to watch her back. She was all alone. She knew firsthand what it was like not to be in control of your own life with no choice about who gets to oversee that life.

Emily opened a tea room in New Hope on the first floor of their three-story Victorian home, a calculated business move for self-preservation in the face of a husband whose income could not be counted on. Adrienne's mother was a dominant figure in all respects. She controlled her daughter, her business, her life, and the people around her, all but Thomas. In later generations people would describe Emily as an enabler, cleaning up after her husband's mistakes, but at the time it was simply called saving the family's good name. He worked hard and brought money in from his cabinetry work with one caveat...the money went to support the wrong thing... the bottle. Emily was brought to her knees many a night, asking the Lord to open Thomas's heart so he'd be able to see the deep need in his life for God's love and healing power. Emily never knew which Thomas would show up at dinner, the loving man she married or the demon emerging from the booze.

Emily taught Adrienne the business along with Ella, who was now their maid and cook. New Hope was a quaint town hugging the Delaware River, thirty miles north of Philadelphia and just south of where George Washington made his famous crossing. As it turned out, it was an ideal place for a small tea room to flourish, and flourish it did.

Thomas Wynne was a Navy man within every sinew of his bony body. He loved the sea, and every chance he got, he'd take the family to vacation at the shore to fish and sail. It was the one thing that Adrienne couldn't wait to do every summer for two reasons: first, she loved the sea almost as much as her father did and, second, she wanted the chance to spend time alone with him. Their love for the sea was a shared experience, and it proved a valuable way to make some attempt to connect with each other. So it was to the southern coast of New Jersey, to Peck's Beach they consistently revisited each year. It got its name from a 1700 whaler, John Peck. He would use the barrier island for storage of freshly caught whales. Before him the Indians used it for a fishing camp and cattle grazing. It was an ideal place for both, full of grasses, sea life, cedar trees and no inhabitants, except an occasional mainlander coming for a picnic or to hunt. It was there on the sand, down by the sea, that Adrienne's life would change in a way only dreams make happen.

The recently built Asteria Hotel on the Island was the Wynne family destination in the summer of 1917, and for Adrienne, the anticipation of staying in such a beautiful "mansion," as she liked to call it, increased with every passing day. Built in the Spanish Mission Revival style, the Asteria's architecture design became popular, and the style was duplicated in other buildings in the town. The grand hotel entrance, complete with marble floors, two-story-high wall paintings of beach and boardwalk scenes, and a crystal chandelier ballroom, all converged to create a feeling of luxury being lavished upon you so that you never wanted to leave your surroundings.

With its many guest rooms and boutique shops to accommodate house guests, the Asteria was also constructed with what became known as "the catacombs"...a unique design with a basement below the water level. Equipped with water pumps, the catacombs served many purposes over the years, most notably during prohibition, when the Eighteenth Amendment restricted the sale of liquor. The catacombs became a speakeasy, where guests would have a drink at the bar. They'd come down the back stairs in their formal attire, change into a bathing suit or casual wear, and then walk to the beach through the tunnel that led under the boardwalk from the catacombs. When sunbathing was over, guests would return the same way, change back into formal attire, and reappear in the hotel lobby as if by magic.

Several years before the completion of his lifelong dream of building the finest hotel on the coast, the founder was walking on the beach one moonlit night, and in the distance, he could barely make out the image of a man holding a lantern and throwing objects into the sea... At first, he thought they were shells being tossed into the waves, but upon closer inspection, he saw they were starfish.

With each flick of his wrist, the man would hurl the starfish into the night sky. As he did, the light from the moon illuminated each one and, as they fell back into the sea, they looked like shooting stars falling to earth.

So, to get a better sense of what was happening, the owner walked up closer and asked, "What are you doing?" to which the man replied, " I'm throwing starfish back into the sea."

The owner said, "But there are so many here on the sand. You can't possibly hope to save them all."

"No, I surely would be at a loss to save all of them, for there are hundreds at my feet. But this I know to be true: I can't save them all, but I can save a few."

The developer never forgot that encounter, impressed by the notion that it was possible to make an impact, small though it may be, upon the world around you. He went home that evening knowing he had found a name for his new hotel...Asteria, the "falling star," Greek Goddess of mythology...a name that would serve to remind him of the night he met the "Star Thrower."

The hotel turned out to be such fun for Adrienne. She loved staying there. It was like a palace out of a fairy tale, and it made her feel like a princess. She dreamed of owning such a castle on the sand, as she referred to it, and she fantasized about her prince coming on a white stallion and taking her away to a land filled with passion and charm beyond her wildest imaginings.

The summer of 1917 was the summer the prince showed up, only he didn't arrive on a white horse; he sailed in on his thirty-five-foot schooner. Greg DeVries was his name, the son of the owner of the Asteria Hotel. Adrienne's father was an old Navy buddy of Greg's father, so Thomas arranged to take his daughter sailing with the DeVries family.

Sailing, they did, every day for a week. Beautiful weather only added to the fun and challenge of moderate winds and following seas. Greg and Addi hit it off from the start, he being just a year older. They seemed to converse with such ease on a number of subjects: she said she wished she weren't an only child; he said he might as well be one, as his fraternal twin brother had been banished from the family for not fighting in the war. As it turned out, each daily sailing adventure couldn't come fast enough for either one.

Then, at the end of the week, came the final and perfect day. The sparsely clouded sky became a canopy of color that reflected off the bay and, like an artist with a broad brush, painted the water below with shimmering hues of lavender, turquoise, and violet.

Both fathers were reliving the good old Navy days and hardly noticed the magnetic attraction taking place right under their noses. When the schooner docked, it was just before sunset. Addi and Greg sat together on the upper deck, drinking in the changing light display as the sun's orange ball of fire found a resting place just behind the far reaches of the bay. The afterglow was magnificent. The evening clouds had begun to streak in from the west, allowing the setting sun, now well out of sight, to cast its fading rays on a ceiling of gathering ice-crystal clouds. Turquoise and lavender gave way to fuchsia and scarlet, setting the entire sky aflame with color. The world must be aflame, for it looked like the heavens were about to explode.

Greg and Addi were speechless as they sat there in total silence, their fathers having left the boat to go into the yacht club. Even the water, soaking in the fiery reflection, was totally calm, as if it was afraid to move lest a simple ripple would destroy the painting the Creator was slowly crafting. You couldn't script it better, and just like a poem written to a lover, this scene ended with a kiss, one that had no intention of stopping right there. In fact, just the opposite was true.

"Will you meet me later tonight on the beach?"

"How can I? My parents will never let me out after dark, and never alone."

"Sneak out after they've gone to bed. They'll never know. Besides, I know a secret elevator that leads to a tunnel no one knows about." And then Greg whispered his plan to set her free.

Adrienne's room was separate from her parents as well as Ella's. Captain Wynne, as he loved to be called, had reserved three adjoining hotel rooms. The accommodations were beautiful, and every morning, all of them would have breakfast in the Star Room, and then dine every evening in the Grand Victoria Ball Room.

Greg's plan worked like a military maneuver, right down to the minute. Adrienne slipped out when she knew the coast was clear. Lying silently and still in bed had seemed an eternity. She analyzed every sound she heard, hoping her parents and Ella were on the deeper side of their dreams. She found herself driven by an unfamiliar stirring within her body, one she had never known before, and even if her escape was aborted by her parents, she was prepared to run to meet Greg...to hell with the consequences.

This was really crazy; it didn't make any sense at all. Hadn't she just met Greg only 8 days ago? Yet the connection they'd made on the boat had made it seem like they'd been picking up where they had left off, almost as though they had known each other at some other time in some other place. Did Greg feel the same way? Here she was, taking a risk that he would, in fact, be waiting for her as planned. What a fool she'd be if he was a no-show.

Adrienne followed Greg's directions just as he had laid them out. "Take the service elevator down to the lowest level," he had said. "Turn right and go through the door to a narrow hall that leads to the back servants' entrance to the hotel. At this hour, all will be quiet. The staff is a skeleton crew once past midnight, so it should be safe. The door at the end of the tunnel lets you out onto the beach, where no one will see you. Head straight for the sea, and you'll hear a song you'll know very well. Don't be afraid, go with your instincts, and let me prove I can be trusted."

The door closed quietly behind her, and then she ran over the sand like a seagull about to take flight and then she recognized the song "Love Will Find a Way," and she followed the sound. It was as dark as night can get. The moon was nowhere to be found; even the sea was empty of the slightest reflection. Only the distant stars held proof of light.

The song fell silent from the Victrola Greg had set up on the beach to surprise Addi. A sudden shudder rippled through her body, but it never had time to turn into fear. As she walked over the sand in blind expectation, she heard Greg's voice.

"Over here, inside the cabana," he said, and with one motion, Greg's hand took hold of hers, pulling her into the hut. Before Adrienne could catch her breath, Greg brought her body tight up against his, kissing her with a passion that ignited feelings within her she wasn't prepared to experience.

In the seclusion of the cabana, in the depth of night, a false sense of security wrapped around their naked bodies like a blanket, and they made love, twice...her first sexual encounter.

It was 3 AM when they left the cabana. The realization of what they had just experienced and the consequences if they were ever discovered suddenly overwhelmed them. But there were no regrets, and they knew there never would be. Greg held Adrienne tight as they made their way back through the tunnel into the hotel's basement.

He stopped suddenly right before letting her go. " This is not a one-night stand, Addi. Please believe me when I say you are the first girl I've ever made love to and you'll be the last."

"I do believe you, Greg. I've risked it all for you, my reputation, my self-worth, my virginity, and know this. I'd give it all up again. You've captured my heart, but I surrendered it gladly."

Greg leaned down and kissed her gently. "It's a secret trust I will never break. You captured me too the moment we locked eyes on each other. I can't explain the feelings. I just know, as sure as I know my own name, I've never felt this kind of feeling for anyone before. It's not your beauty, and it's not the sex. It's something far more than that. There aren't words for it, so 'I'm falling in love with you' will have to do. I'll get a note to you so I can see you once more before you leave."

Adrienne went back to her suite, floating on air as she slipped silently beneath the covers of her empty bed. If only Greg were here to hold me close, wrapped in his arms, just like he did only minutes ago. She closed her eyes and imagined a beautiful scene where her prince came riding in to carry her away into a world of endless beauty and love, where they would live in happiness forever and ever. But her imagination gave way to sleep, so she never knew how her fantasy ended.

The next day, no note appeared. And the following day, the family's vacation ended. Before she was able to find Greg, Adrienne packed her bags with the family and headed for New Hope. It was the longest ride home imaginable for her... Her heart ached. She was not prepared to face reality as their car pulled away from the hotel.

Several weeks later, she received a letter from Greg saying that as a West Point graduate, he would be commissioned to go to Europe to fight "the war to end all wars." He wrote how much he loved her, that nothing would ever be the same in his life after falling so hard for her. She knew he had just graduated from West Point but had not expected him to champion the call to make the world safe for democracy. Europe was in the thick of all-out war, old allies once again willing to pay the ultimate price with lives and treasure to dominate the continent. The cost was monumental, and America was joining her allies in an effort to bring the battles of WWI to a swift close.

Adrienne was so desperate to see Greg she decided to confide in Ella, revealing the details of their romance and all that took place that night in the cabana. Greg's departure to Europe was swift. No more letters arrived. The silence was deafening.

That year...1917...tragedy struck without warning. Adrienne's parents fell ill with the great influenza outbreak, the Spanish Flu. Both were hit hard and fell victim to the epidemic, despite every effort by Adrienne and Ella to save them. Miraculously, Adrienne and Ella escape the plague that killed twenty-five million people worldwide. In a period of only three months, the pandemic circled the globe, leaving a trail of death in almost every known country. If one survived, one was among the blessed. Pregnant women and the elderly were the segment of the population that felt the full force of the disease and suffered the highest death tolls.

Adrienne and Ella never forgot the horror of witnessing endless horse-drawn carts rolling past their house, bearing the bodies of neighbors, friends, and the shadow people of the world. The sound of the "death carts" could be heard long before they were seen, and the fear it caused was paralyzing to the soul. Would we be next? The thought was ever present and dominated how everyday activities were to be lived. Life was dependent on obsessively avoiding crowds, washing every piece of clothing that might have come in contact with another person, wiping down surfaces with disinfectants.

Adrienne never had time to mourn the loss of her parents. Survival trumped grief, and somehow, Death passed them by. Was it a miracle, a kind of Passover...blood over the doorway?? Adrienne didn't know and wasn't even asking the question. It was the lucky draw of the cards, the roll of the dice. She only knew she wasn't dead, and the reasons eluded her. But Ella asked the question, and every night, when she went down on her knees to pray at her bedside, she always gave thanks to the Miracle Worker, the God who answered her when she'd knocked at His door so many years ago.

At seventeen years of age, Adrienne was left an orphan with a tea room to run. Where and to whom could she turn for help? There was no family left on either side. There was a sudden realization she was out there all alone. No one was about to rescue her. If she were to survive, it would be due to her belief in herself, her strength, her wit, her ability to seize the moment and run with it and to hell with the consequences. She'd deal with tomorrow's problems when they came, and they were guaranteed to come. But for right now, it wasn't tomorrow; it was today, and Adrienne never liked to mortgage the moment…but, rather, face it and get it done. Don't leave a "balance due." Pay it in full today!

Adrienne knew the food business inside and out… She was highly confident on that point and the knowledge she could totally depend on Ella. Together, they made a formidable team. The combination was unstoppable if they kept their focus and blocked out the fear that came creeping in "on cat's feet" every night she climbed into bed. Then the morning returned on the crest of a rising sun. Slowly darkness was dispelled by the light, and the birthing of a new day shouted, "There's hope!"

The Christmas of '17 was about as lonely as one can ever experience, and it would have been ten times worse had it not been for Ella. She made sure life went on no matter what the circumstances, so she set the scene for the holidays in great detail. The house was decorated just like it always was, and the Christmas turkey was served with all the trimmings. The table was set for two now, but the way Ella embraced the holidays made the empty place settings almost tolerable.

In the soft light of candles illuminating this festive dinner, Adrienne looked over at Ella and quietly said, "Ella, next year this time, you'll have to set an extra plate."

Ella looked startled. "Lordy be, child, you mean you've finally heard from that doughboy? Adrienne couldn't help herself and let go a hardy laugh at Ella's use of the WW1 nickname for USA service men in France.

"Well, no, not a word has arrived from France, but I have heard from Greg in a most profound way… I'm going to have his baby!"

Ella jumped up from the table, ran to the other end, and hugged Adrienne with such force she almost knocked them both on the floor. They held onto each other like they were drowning, small rivers of water poured down their cheeks, each tear a mixture of joy and heartache. They both knew how life was going to change, that major decisions had to be addressed and quickly. But for now, they just shared a very precious moment as inseparable friends, one filled with all kinds of mixed emotions but with a heart where no judgment could be found.

Adrienne and Ella spent the holidays planning the future: where to go, what to do. It was overwhelming, even under normal circumstances, but now the life of a child had come abruptly into the equation, and suddenly the future had become unbelievably complicated.

"We can't stay here, Ella. We've got to move somewhere where no one knows us. You know what people will say, what they think but don't say? I refuse to have our child born starting out life under the title of 'bastard.' That label sickens me. Greg and I love each other, and when he returns, we'll get married and live together in a place where he can build a career. And believe me, it won't be here."

Ella listened with care, always weighing her words to give the best counsel as gently as she could.

"Bless you, child, you know I'm with you all the way. I'll be supportin' your decision to move no matter where. Just be sure you're doing this 'cause it's best for you and your child and not 'cause people are driving you out of town by their hatred and prejudges. You knows my feelings about runnin' away. May seems like a new place leaves all your problems behind, but child, this here miseries is gonna be hanging on your heart no matters where we be settlin'."

A letter finally arrived from Greg, giving Adrienne a chance to write back, since previously she had not had his overseas address. Greg told her how much he loved her, and in a flood of tears, she penned a beautiful letter in return, telling him all about his baby she was carrying.

In his return letter, which took many weeks, Greg wrote he was stunned by the news of a baby on the way...unequivocally positive it would be a boy...and shared his concern about the heavy burden he had left on her shoulders. He promised to make things right, supporting her in every way when he returned home. But the letter carried an undertone of quiet resignation. He expressed his deep concern for his safety, as millions were being slaughtered in the trenches and the odds were heavily stacked against his survival. He told her not to say anything to his family about the baby, that he'd take care of the situation when he came home. He was due for leave in a month.

"But darling, if I should not return, make sure Samuel DeVries knows of the birth of his grandchild."

Adrienne wrote that she knew deep in her heart he would come back to her, that they'd live out their lives together in a place unknown to them now, but where they could find happiness and joy they'd never known so far. She told him of her plans to go to Peck's Beach to determine if the town would be a place they could relocate during the war years.

The letters stopped coming...but the baby had other ideas. Vivian was born in May of '18 at home with the skilled confidence and gifted hands of a midwife, ably assisted by Ella, who felt it a blessing from God to witness the first breath of a new life arriving into the world. It was a happy day, and Adrienne came through the birthing process as though this were her third child. Throughout Addi's pregnancy, Ella had been able to cover up the fact that a baby was on the way. Farm life offered some privacy by nature of being outside the main town's gossip realm. She told everyone that Addi was away and had married right after her parents died, and then her husband had gone off to war in Europe. The scheme seemed to work.

Vivian let out a scream the moment her tiny body hit the cool air in the bedroom, all seven pounds of her. She was determined to have the world know she had made her entrance. A similar scream was heard loud and clear over the many years to come by those who crossed her path. She was destined to make her presence known.

The bold print of the Newtown Daily Ledger broadcast the news on the fourth page: "Gregory DeVries, West Point Captain, died at the Battle of Marne." The article went on to say he was the son of the owner of the Asteria Hotel on Peck's Beach and had valiantly fallen on a grenade, saving the lives of three comrades.

How much pain can one human take? How much loss until one breaks in fragmented pieces like crystal dropped on a tile floor? When you lose what feels like your other half, death becomes a welcomed friend, if only you could follow through and die as well, but you can't.

Adrienne mourned in silence, crying herself to sleep every night with only Ella to share her loss. Weeks went by, and then, one day, she woke up to realize life had to go on. She had a baby who would need a family, a mother to love and care for her. Suddenly her situation became clear. Sell the business, pack their bags, and move the baby and Ella to Peck's Beach, a new beginning. Start over and leave behind the old losses and hurts and write a new chapter in life, one that would force them to look toward the future and not wallow in the past ever again. And that was exactly what she did.

A heavy rain was let loose from low-skirting clouds as Adrienne and Ella pulled up in front of the Asteria Hotel. The ride down had been uneventful, and conversation had been clipped...spoken in short sentences, none of which begged a response. Both women were absorbed in their own thoughts.

The doorman came to their rescue by shielding them from the rain-soaked wind with a large umbrella, quickly moving them away from the open portico and into the main lobby of the building. Adrienne had forgotten how beautiful this hotel was, how really elegant its architectural design was and how gracious the staff. What wonderful memories these walls conjured up as she and Ella made their way to the front desk.

Adrienne's thoughts were flying in a million directions when she heard the desk manager ask, "May I help you?" Ella, meanwhile, had stepped aside, letting Adrienne handle the business affairs with the concierge. The hotel had always fascinated Ella, so she moved in slow steps, eyes wide open, taking in all the décor and interesting guests that surrounded her.

"Why, yes. My name is Adrienne Watson, and I'm here with my maid to check in for two weeks."

"Thank you, madam. I'll be glad to help you. If you could wait just one moment, I'll be right back to take care of you."

With that, the desk clerk moved several paces to his left and continued a conversation with a woman who was in obvious mourning dress. A quick glance told Adrienne the woman must be a widow from the war, and immediately her heart ached for the emotional torment the woman must be going through. Adrienne's own emotions were not even close to healing, and she had a very strong urge to reach out to the widow and ask what kind of sorrow she was bearing.

The clerk dismissed the woman with a simple "Thank you, Mrs. DeVries" and turned to resume his interaction with Adrienne.

"You are in suite 710, facing the ocean," he said, and handing her the keys he added, "It's a pleasure having you as our guest. Please enjoy your stay."

The confusion registered on Adrienne's face was so visible that the clerk looked perplexed. "Is there something wrong, Madame?"

The woman in question had by now moved away from the counter, and Adrienne, trying to compose herself, responded, "Everything is quite lovely, thank you. I was just wondering if the lady you were talking to is the owner's daughter?"

"Oh no, Madame, that's Captain Greg DeVries's widow, the owner's daughter-in-law." Shaking his head, eyes cast down as though he were looking for something lost on the floor, he said in an almost inaudible whisper, "Killed in action in France; very sad, very, very sad indeed."

Adrienne went numb, not hearing any words beyond Greg DeVries's widow. Her knees began to buckle, and her heart pounded with a murderous force. Like a sleepwalker, Adrienne moved in a daze from the counter to the elevator, proceeded by the bellhop and luggage. She would later have no memory of taking the keys off the counter or of seeing Ella run over to her just in time to hold her up.

A week later, a letter arrived from the front lines in Europe, postmarked several months prior and forwarded from New Hope to the Asteria Hotel. It was from Greg, and in it, he confessed to Adrienne what he had done. When he first met Adrienne, he was already engaged to a girl who was a longtime family friend. It was the social and political thing to do…joining money and class in a marriage both families had preordained. But once he met Adrienne, he realized what a loveless pairing he was being anchored to. He did not want to go through with the marriage but lacked the guts to stop it.

Greg openly admitted in the letter that he would always love Adrienne, that never in a million years could he have ever seen coming what was about to hit him the day he'd first laid eyes on the most beautiful woman in the world. He begged Adrienne to forgive him, to not live with hatred in her heart as retribution for his weakness in lacking the courage to cut off the engagement and run into the arms of the woman he needed more than life itself. But he could not be disgraced by a divorce; honor and duty trumped love. Adrienne never revealed to Greg's father that her daughter existed, and as years went by, Vivian was always led to believe her grandparents on both sides had died from the pandemic flu of '17–18.

CHAPTER 8

The waitress came to take our dessert order, and Ella's story came to a quick end. I just sat there with my mouth wide open, thinking, You can't leave me hangin', Ella. Ah, but she could, and she did. I didn't want to push the subject too hard. Ella, for some reason, was able to confide in me, and I in no way wanted to break that trust. The summer had many more dinners for two in its future, so I jumped in and changed the subject. It proved to be a good move. There was a look of relief on Ella's face, and she laughed out loud when I relived one of the waitress's latest evening tales of a woman who, when ordering the fried chicken, requested the back legs! I thought Ella would fall off her chair. She had a wonderful laugh that seemed to roll up from the depths of her soul, and when it hit the surface, it was so contagious you laughed harder than she did. The entire room stopped talking while Ella and I dissolved in tears at the thought of a chicken with four legs. I know she blushed under that beautiful black skin of hers, but who could tell.

In the past, Ella had spent much of her time picking up the pieces after Addi's daughter, and she still did. Vivian considered Ella part of the family and knew her mother would have wanted her to provide for Ella. In return, Ella made sure things were maintained and in good working order. Vivian benefited greatly from the deal as well. Ella was loyal to a fault, but Vivian was no Adrienne, not even close. She was high-maintenance, very demanding, and unfortunately, Ella was the undeserving recipient, in other words, she was stuck with the fuzzy end of the lollipop!

As a result, our dinners together on the Porch were infrequent. Vivian would hostess occasionally or cashier once in a while, but not with any consistency. She never invited me to join her to dine… Quite the opposite. She'd eat alone. Every so often, she'd invite Ella to join her, but that was rare. Ella remained upstairs in Vivian's apartment, doing whatever she did to make Vivian happy, or spent time on the third floor, in her own small living quarters.

So Ella's tales had to be spun in fits and starts, while I had to learn patience. It was like a TV series that leaves you hanging until the next week. I knew the story was only just beginning, and yet somehow I knew it was going to be worth waiting for the next installment.

Whenever we crossed paths, as we often did in the mornings when I came into the restaurant to work on the waitress schedule, we'd give each other a smile and sometimes a little hug. In subtle ways, we connected, gradually forming an unspoken bond that over the years came to be a thing of great value.

Though the summer of '63 began on a very down note, the balance was just the opposite. It was a hoot. Sam, Howie, Bruce, and I rented a garage apartment on top of an old auto repair garage at 9th Street and Asbury Avenue. You ascended fourteen steps and entered directly into the living room; the eat-in kitchen was to the right. One really detailed look at the kitchen, and you wanted to cry. It had no redeeming features. Wallpapered with a floral design that appeared as if it had fossilized into the plaster, the metal cabinets and linoleum floor screamed, "Help me!" Walking straight from the entrance placed you in the bathroom. Turn right or left and you stumbled into one of the two bedrooms. That was it. No more amenities. It was a dump, no doubt about it, but it was home for the summer, and I use the word "home" loosely.

This would become the Tarantula's Nest, a name Gail had christened it with, and she'd also given us the gift of a wonderful guest register, designed and hand painted by her as only she knew how to do. A "first in her class" art graduate from Syracuse University, Gail had just landed a job with Hallmark Cards in Kansas City. She was to start in September at $125 per week, and we thought that was a fortune.

The name was apropos. It became a magnet for the seemingly poor and homeless college students Bruce and Howie scraped up to rescue...those who had no place to crash after they'd quaffed too many beers at the Point, necessitating a pad to sleep it off. You could always judge how drunk one of these pathetic characters was when throwing up on himself while sleeping did not arouse him. Though it was not a nightly occurrence, it happened more often than one would have liked.

Sam and I shared a room and fortunately for us, we were fairly neat when it came to keeping our clothes organized and our bed made. The room was nine by ten feet, so we're not talking spacious. As space was of the essence, we lived like we were aboard a small boat... Everything had its place.

Bruce and Howie, on the other hand, were the total opposite of Sam and me. They too had a room of the same size, but that's where the resemblance stopped. The word "slobs" leapt to mind... Actually, that's kind. These two were beyond description. Their bed was never made, the sheets never cleaned, for the entire summer. No joke. The sheets were yellow by the time September rolled around, because of their dual purpose. Not only were they used to cover the mattress at night, but they magically became beach blankets in the daytime. The word "clean" was not part of our roommates' vocabulary, despite the fact that the apartment was directly across the street from a laundromat!

Howie and Bruce would come into our nicely ordered room after we had changed our sheets and gently rub their hands over the surface of the bed as though they were caressing the breasts of some voluptuous lover, cooing like adolescents.

It was pathetic to see, and we loved it. This too could have been their lot, but they chose the path that led south of white trash. Nothing was going to change them, at least not in the world as they saw it, so they lived vicariously, which enabled them to enjoy the finer things of life even if they were not attainable within the confines of our little apartment atop a grungy garage.

Sam and I did try our best to reform Bruce and Howie, on occasion, but to no avail. Both were lost causes. One evening, I came home to our second floor shack only to be shocked to see Bruce trying his best to cook dinner, a noble attempt for sure. A buddy had given him two live lobsters, which he proceeded to put in a big pot of cold water and then turned on the heat. The hotter the water, the livelier the lobsters became. Bruce lifted off the lid to check on their progress, and the poor lobsters leaped out of that pot like they were shot out of a cannon. You can't make this stuff up; it was hysterical. He screamed like a girl while I lost it, laughing my ass off, yelling, "You don't cook lobster that way, you idiot. You're killing them in slow motion. Boil the water first and then drop them in...instant death. How would you like it if someone slowly boiled you to death?"

By then, the creatures of the sea were bright red and dead...so much for dinner. I lost my appetite.

One night, we even took the owners of the yellow sheets over to the laundromat in hopes that seeing people washing their clothes and linens might induce them to take the plunge...wash a few thing just to get the hang of it. Unfortunately, rather than wash their clothes, Bruce put Howie in the commercial dryer, closed the door, inserted a dime, and watched him tumble around for the next five minutes like a hamster in a cage. Needless to say, the entire laundry audience was spellbound. Thank heavens there was no encore... Howie was too dizzy to even stand up after his ten-cent ride to nowhere. And to think both these guys came from very prominent Main Line Philadelphia families.

Unfortunately, "Butterworth," as we called him, and Howie worked day shift in the kitchen at Watson's, so they were free as birds all night long. This invariably led to troubles, troubles, troubles. All summer long, as the days passed by, directional and street signs of all types became increasingly visible in the apartment. At first, a one way sign and then a no parking sign decorated the walls, and no one thought anything about it. Slowly, the signs seemed to multiply to the point that every vertical space in the place was covered with some kind of verbiage written on wood, metal, plastic, or fabric. It didn't matter... Butterworth thought it was fun and, more importantly, a challenge to beat Howie by collecting the most signs by Labor Day... It was Labor Day Eve.

I think the score was tied at twenty to twenty when, that night, while well under the influence of the "happy liquid," Howie decided to steal what he called the "pièce de résistance," the corner drugstore's outside penny scale, chained to the cement and probably weighing a hundred pounds. How he managed to break it loose is a mystery to this day, but he cut it free somehow and dragged it across the street and up the stairs to the Tarantula's Nest. It's possible he could have pulled the caper off and won the unofficial contest had it not been for the fact the drugstore was adjacent to City Hall and the police station.

As Howie made his grand entrance into the apartment at three in the morning, heavily laden with the penny-loaded evidence, what he failed to take into account was the entourage of PBPD blue in hot pursuit. Howie stumbled in through the door, dropped the scale with a force that could wake the dead, and also awakened the sleeping...Sam and me. It was a miracle the scale didn't crash through the floor, as the construction of the apartment had always been questionable. Any big wind caused the place to sway like a boat at anchor in high seas. No telling what damage a scale could do. I lay there in bed, wide awake, not moving an inch. As I listened, I heard major troubles brewing. A number of "holy shits" rumbled rapidly through the air and swiftly under our door, obviously not the "scale thief's" voice. I heard lots of commotion and then Howie saying to the cops in slurred words: "These signs were all here when we rented the place osiffer." Try as he might, there was no chance the proper pronunciation of the word officer was ever going to leave his mouth.

Trying not to laugh, I thought, Let's see you get out of this one, oh man of the dirty sheets. The cops didn't buy Howie's excuse for one second. More muffled sounds, more protesting, and then the sound of heavy feet approached our door. I remained frozen… This was a scene I had no interest in becoming part of, so I prayed the door wouldn't open. Sam slept through the entire fiasco and never woke up. The cops, for some reason, did not enter our bedroom; they entered the two idiots' bedroom instead. I heard Butterworth say he had nothing to do with the sign caper and Howie say that was not true. We now had a turncoat in our presence, and it was not going down well with Butterworth. I could hear the cops dragging both of them out and off to jail for an overnight stay.

Suddenly it got very quiet, so I woke Sam. He thought it was morning and began to tell me of a crazy dream he'd had about somebody coming into our place and stealing all the signs.

"Go back to sleep, Sam!"

Since I was the only one of the group who was over twenty-one, I figured I'd better play the den father, so I got out of bed to try to save their sorry asses. I threw on shorts, shirt, and sandals and literally shot across the street to the city jail. The police were not in a forgiving mood, and I was told both guys were there to stay overnight "to prove a point" and to face bail in the morning.

The judge held court at 9 AM sharp, so I was present in the room when they brought the two sad-looking creatures in and sat them down. Fortunately for them, the judge exercised reasonable mercy on their souls, exacting a punishment of three days civic duty, which meant cleaning the streets with the city work crew. He demanded the immediate removal of all signs in the apartment. Bail was set at $100 each, which I told the judge I'd post. Once freed, they'd owe me big time.

I went to work later that day and told JD the story. He just gave me that look of his. The one that says, "Those idiots," and then I said I bailed out their butts mainly because they were friends but also because I knew it would leave him short-handed in the kitchen.

With that devilish smile of his, he said, "Well, you're a better man than I, and thanks. But don't worry, I'll get you your money back. I'll pile extra work hours on them, and the only one way sign they'll be seeing will be pointed right back to Watson's."

When Butterworth and Howie came through the kitchen doors, they looked like they had been run through the wringer and not put in the dryer. What jerks.

So JD exacted a toll of greater price, in hours as well as work, on both, their penitence being assigned to the salt mine: ie, dishwasher detail. A pig on a farm had better living quarters, and may even lead a better life. For five hours and counting, dish detail involved being surrounded by human garbage of every flavor and smell. Speed was essential when it came to dishes. If you couldn't keep up with the high volume being dropped off at lightning rate, one became Lucille Ball at the chocolate factory, never catching up as the conveyor belt kept moving at an ever-increasing speed so that eventually the dishes began to slide off the racks and crash to the floor. This was absolutely not acceptable, and JD took a dim view if one got that far "into the weeds."

As it happened, the night Howie and Butterworth were working off their bail money at the "garbage dump," a storm hit hard. Lightning cut the electric off for three hours, and to make matters worse, there was a full moon and a high tide right in the middle of rush hour, 7:30 PM. This combination of events spelled trouble with a capital T. The island of Peck's Beach did not handle things well when heavy rain plus a full moon and a high tide converged all at once. The water had nowhere to run off. The streets' old drainpipes backed up as the tidal waters rose, resulting in major flooding.

The restaurant was jammed, it was pouring buckets outside, and all the people waiting along the sidewalk had to be ushered into the center hall. This was a mathematical impossibility, as there were far too many people to fit inside. Accommodating waitresses were doing their best to maneuver through the masses to get to and from the kitchen. I put some customers upstairs in the hall and some along the side of the building under the steel awning, and for those who were weak and weary, I made sure busboys came to their rescue with chairs. Kind of reminded me of a cattle chute. But Watson's customers were loyal to the bitter end; waiting in line was all part of the scene, and they loved it. The owners loved it too…a line was the best advertisement a restaurant could ever have. It didn't cost anything but was the ultimate in PR. If people were willing to line up for an hour in spite of the elements, then dinner must be worth the wait.

"The line," as it became known, was a nightly show for ten weeks in the summer. It started at 4:30 and didn't end until 9 PM, although some nights, the restaurant stayed open just to make sure those at the very end of "the line" made it in for dinner.

In the middle of as wild a night at the big W I can ever remember, Gail came charging out of the kitchen like a bull, yelling, "Sax, Sax", loud enough to carry over the noise of patrons eating in the dark with no air conditioning.

I turned around and yelled back, "What's wrong?" making a move toward the people still waiting in line.

Gail stopped me and said, "It's Charles, he passed out on the floor behind the steam table."

Hearing that, I almost ran into the kitchen…I loved that mystery guy…no one seemed to know much about his past except that he was a loyal employee, returning every year coming from University of Pennsylvania during their summer break since the mid 1950's..

It was shocking seeing him on the floor and so pale. I dropped to the floor, making sure he was still breathing, which thankfully he was. The boss and Popcorn, his buddy and deep fry cook, ran to bring him water. My first assessment was he passed out from heat exhaustion, kitchen temperature was 110. So I said "Charles, you are the whitest black skinned person I know. This would normally make him laugh, but, nothing...no response, so I got right by his ear and said, "Don't leave me, French fries, please not now...we need you and we'll be in serious weeds if we don't have you on the steam table line, this night of all nights. One eye slowly opened then the other followed by a big smile crossing his face.

Popcorn, JD and I got him to his feet and JD force him outside to breathe in some cool air and drink lots of water. As soon a he felt revived, Charles was back at the steam table, once again talking to the food.

The electricity came back on around 8:30 PM, and when we saw what the lights revealed, we were hoping they would go off again! The restaurant looked like it had been hit by a bomb. Howie and Butterworth were buried behind mountains of dishes and garbage, barely visible, and every inch of the kitchen floor was covered with water...slippery as an ice rink. The three steam tables were in a state of chaos, with pieces of food and grease everywhere. Cutting off electricity meant all cooking was done by gas. The fryers were out of commission, as was anything dependent on electric power. Food in the pantry was melting at a rapid rate, and the kitchen temperature was still inching above 110 degrees. The fact the kitchen crew didn't walk out on the job spoke well to their devotion to JD. How we fed a thousand people that night was both a miracle and nightmare.

The summer went by way too fast. I only saw Laura once during the entire summer, and that was at the beginning of the season. She had gone to Europe, to the South of France according to restaurant gossip. Evidently, it was a gift from her parents as part of her sweet sixteen surprise party, and Ella had gone as Laura's chaperone. Dinners for two on the Porch disappeared.

I remember well and with great clarity seeing Laura in mid-June. I happened to leave early one day to go home to Philly and found her in the parking lot of the restaurant, looking lost and bewildered. She was standing by her new car, trying to figure out how to change a flat tire. It was still hard to believe she was only sixteen.

I walked over, shaking my head. "Ah, a damsel in distress."

Laura gave me one of those looks that reminded me of her father. But that was where the comparison stopped. Those eyes of hers were like magnets: once locked into them, I wasn't able to even glance at anything else but her.

Then she said, "Oh, my hero, you've come to rescue me." She had no idea how much I wanted that to be true.

"Well, no, this hero is not going to rescue you. He's going to teach you how to rescue yourself."

And with that, I began to unlock the secrets of changing a tire…a mystery I would learn that women are loathe to solve, since knowing the secret means they have to tackle the task by themselves. Much better to plead ignorance.

Laura was a fast learner. Kneeling down on the ground alongside of me. She listened intently while I instructed her where to place the car jack under the frame of the car. Then, showing her how to take off the lug nuts, I took my hands and covered them over hers so I could help create more torque on the star wrench. The lug nuts were on very tight. Laura didn't have the strength to spin them free on her own. I was so close to her now that the fragrance coming from her neck and shoulders was enough to make my thighs quiver. That coupled with a quick glance down her cleavage, and I found myself feeling like Samson. Suddenly my strength was ebbing, slowly melting away.

After I helped her take the tire off and put the spare on, I had her tighten the lug nuts, again with my combined force to make sure they weren't about to come loose.

"There you go. You've now changed your first flat tire."

There was a slight look of satisfaction on that beautiful face of hers. "It's a good feeling, and thank you very much, but in the future, isn't there something like road service available if I need it?"

"So, you always plan to have a flat near a phone to call for road service or your 'hero'?" I asked, pointing at myself.

"You got me there," she replied, and we both laughed. "That was pretty dumb reasoning, wasn't it."

"Yep, but should you be lucky enough to be near a phone, feel free to call this 'hero.' He'd be glad to come to your rescue anytime," I said with a big smile, wishing someday to actually get that call.

I kept thinking, Why, oh why, is this girl not eighteen or nineteen?? Her beauty was captivating. For a fraction of a moment, I let my eyes lock once again onto hers and hang there just a second too long. I wanted to divert them…didn't want my feelings to be exposed like I knew they must have been, but it was too late now. I started to blush… I could feel the heat rush to my face, so I quickly stood up, and Laura did the same. In an instant, the moment was lost, but I never forgot it.

Laura thanked me again for "rescuing" her, jumped into her car, and drove out of the lot. I stood there, watching her go. Then, just as she got to the end of the driveway, she turned, looked back, and waved. I did the same and shot off a smile. I caught those eyes of hers again and was never so grateful for a flat tire in my life!

CHAPTER 9

The summer of '64 came rolling in like the tide, right on schedule and none too soon. Campus life was getting to me; I needed a break, big time. Looking forward to working again at Watson's and hooking up with my old friends was just what the doctor ordered. We'd all kept in touch with each other over the winter, but time restraints and distance always seemed to cut into our good intentions, so the gang had a lot of catching up to do when we reunited on Peck's Beach. And we did "catching up" well. Time that had passed was just that, only time... it didn't distance us...we picked up right where we had left off, not missing a beat.

I would have rented the Tarantula's Nest again with Sam except for two not-so-minor points. Point one: Howie and Butterworth were no-shows this season. JD didn't want them back for obvious reasons. Point two: the city had condemned the garage apartment. Can't understand why. So a somewhat-new cast of characters teamed up and rented a third-floor walk-up at 868 1st Street, one of the old classic homes so familiar on Peck's Beach. Built in the twenties, its design reflected the architecture of the times: large wrap around porches with solid wood construction, interior entrance that serviced all floors, and magnificent wood trim detail throughout each unit.

Officially, the lease called for no more than six people, but we managed to squeeze in a number a good bit larger than six. Our friends came and went all summer like the tide, so unless one were to "case the joint" and track the people as they arrived and departed, there would be no way in hell to tally up the number of guests who actually slept at our special penthouse. A guest register and schedule was mounted on the wall with a fixed fee payable by all who entered. Redefining the concept of a bed and breakfast, it was bed, breakfast, lunch, and, unlike any other establishment known as a B&B, dinner, all wrapped into a nice little package at bargain prices. Throw in a location half a block from the beach, and you've got heaven!

In the 60's, residents living on Peck's Beach, and tourists as well, were still prisoners to the blue laws. The town was dry, with no booze and amusements, and sporting and corporate events were closed on Sundays. The founding fathers had made sure the Sabbath was obeyed to the letter of the law.

Sam and I joined forces with Cooper, our recently married cohort Peg Cooper. She and her new husband, David Ray, shared living space with us at our third floor apartment. I had reconnected with Peg at Charlie's Bar and Grill in Somers Point one Saturday in May. We'd met there after we'd had our usual interview with JD concerning the upcoming summer. Peg had married her high school sweetheart, David, the year before, and they both planned to finish their senior year at Ursinus College in PA. Although money was paramount, dollars earned at Watson's were not going to make any of us rich, that was for sure. The waitresses made the big bucks. Both management, of which I was one, and the hostesses drew the short end of the salary stick. Being maître d' came with a lot of responsibility, coupled with overseeing the work schedule of thirty-five waitresses plus six busboys. One quickly realized the job description exceeded the pay scale...an early lesson in financial wisdom, that if you want to make real money in this life, never work for anyone else.

None of us had a spare dime to speak of, so renting rooms at this three-bedroom "rooftop penthouse" proved to be a stroke of financial genius, even if it failed miserably to meet everyone's expectations as to how to live together in harmony for sixteen weeks. Life was crazy at the 868 1st Street apartment , but it was a barrel of fun. With the beach being a stone's throw from our back door, needless to say, our "guest house" was filled to overflowing most of the summer. Board money from our many "friends," newly acquired and old, made it possible for the four of us to live rent free from May to September.

And a wild summer it was. Peg and David were the only legal adults, so to speak, meaning they signed the lease. The landlord did not want a bunch of kids renting for the season. That was amusing, as, on reflection, we were all kids, but having a married couple in the mix gave us an air of respectability along with some level of normalcy. All of this was a charade; if the landlord had lived on the premises, we'd have been kicked out before we'd even unpacked.

Our place at 868 1st Street rivaled Watson's for food output and sheer number of patrons…guests don't pay, patrons do, and we weren't afraid to charge. We entertained like royalty, though with a decidedly smaller budget and no sign of silverware or fine china. Party time was anytime, and party we did. Beer, wine, burgers on the grill…there was a small deck off the living room where the designated chef of the evening could see part of the ocean while he or she cooked whatever sartorial surprises were in store. We called it "Sliver View." It wasn't much, but it was all we had.

Gail, Elaine, Sam, and I were the four musketeers. My friendship with Gail had grown out of my ungraceful entrance into the Watson Hall of Fame…the night of my first "on the job" training. Elaine was a waitress at Watson's and Gail's best friend. They grew up together, and '64 was the last year of college for both. So, as a foursome, we rendezvoused most nights at Gail's family home to play bridge until midnight or after, and then we'd hop in the car and dance till dawn at the Dunes, a nightclub nestled in the wetlands between Somers Point and Longport. All bars closed at 2AM at the Point, as it was known, and since no one was ever ready to call it a night, we would all trundle over to the Dunes, where you could drink and dance till dawn…and did we ever…the Locomotion, the Twist, the Frug…you name it, we did it.

After dancing our feet off all night, we'd somehow manage to get up, head for the beach, and fall on our blankets around 11 AM, grab some Z's in various depths of unconsciousness, throw down a quick sandwich, either brought or bought, and then split the scene to take a shower, dress, and be at work by 3 PM. We had this daily routine down to the minute, and it was a ritual repeated every day but one…our day off. What happened then? We spent the entire day at the beach and then partied all night. In other words, same church, different pew.

Strikingly absent from Watson's as a patron was Harry Blake. After Adrienne's death the year before, Harry was not to be seen, either at the funeral or at Watson's, and Vivian was very cold at any mention of his name. I had become very familiar with the people who were loyal customers, so Harry's absence was glaring, at least to me. I was accustomed to seating him later in the evenings, often bringing an employee with him as a way to say, "Thanks for your loyalty."

And occasionally he'd have a date on his arm. When I innocently brought my observation to the attention of Vivian one night, she bore a steely gaze right through me.

"That man is a persona non grata. He's not welcome here, so don't seat him if he shows up some night, which I seriously doubt."

And I seriously hoped he wouldn't show either, since I didn't relish the scene it might cause, aside from the embarrassment of telling a former close friend of Adrienne's that he was not welcome. Once on the bad side with Vi, it gave her free license to spread her venom, the dose equal to the degree of the offense. Not a good place to find yourself.

Earlier that summer, Ella came down from upstairs and requested to dine on the Porch. It was late for her, about 8:00 PM, but I was able to seat her at her favorite table…the one she and Addi always shared. Her surprise invitation to join her caught me off guard. Of course I said yes. We ate and talked, and then, over dessert, Ella opened up again, spinning her Watson tales like a web, each silk-like thread intricately designed to capture you before it's too late to escape. I was caught, trapped and mesmerized all at once, and I loved it.

CHAPTER 10

Adrienne had money in her purse when she arrived on Peck's Beach in 1920. It wasn't a fortune, but enough to keep her afloat for about a year if she managed it well. She sold the farm with little regret, because it wasn't a lifestyle she wanted to duplicate. It represented the past, and for that reason alone, she was happy to close out that chapter in her life forever. Adrienne's sights were on tomorrow. She had a daughter now, and she fully intended to raise her in a totally different environment, a place where a new identity could emerge, leaving all her yesterdays far behind, where no one could ever resurrect them. So changing her last name from Wynne to her mother's maiden name, Watson, proved added security that her yesterdays remained where no one could resurrect them again. The cornerstone of her dream was to own a restaurant, maybe to start small like her mother's tea room and then, as it grew, expand it into a major dining establishment. But the timing was off, and Adrienne had the discernment to know it. Good ideas at the wrong time wind up in the graveyard of unfulfilled expectations. She knew she had to pay her dues, had to learn the ropes before she was able to fly solo under her own power. So she landed a job as a desk clerk at the Normandie on the Sea Hotel, situated right in the center of town. At the time, the hotel could boast of having a thousand rooms and a spectacular lobby that held its own when compared to New York hotels like The Plaza. Open year around, the Normandie attracted patrons from all over the country, and its proximity to Atlantic City, only ten miles away, enabled guests to have a raucous night out and still retreat safely to a relatively quiet Peck's Beach, where the three-mile-long boardwalk was figuratively rolled up at night, unlike the glitzy city to the north.

Over a relatively short period, Adrienne was offered and accepted an assistant manager position, due mostly to her quick mind and her ability to handle the public. The promotion was a good one because it helped her develop excellent managerial skills while, at the same time, cultivating a network of personal and business connections throughout the town. Many prominent people from the big cities of Philadelphia and New York stayed at the Normandie for the summer. Adrienne accumulated a treasured black book diary filled with the names of the wealthiest patrons as well as of society's finest.

Having rented a small apartment when they first settled on the island, it was time to move up, so Adrienne and Ella were always on the lookout to buy rather than rent. There was a very small cottage for sale only four blocks from the hotel, and Adrienne thought it perfectly suited their needs. The price was cheap because it needed tons of work, but it seemed tailor made for her little family, containing two bedrooms and a bath, with a living room barely big enough to sling a cat around as they'd say. But the space worked, and so Ella and Adrienne, with baby Vivian in tow, rehabbed this one-story, pathetically tiny cottage into a home.

Ella was the linchpin that made the home tick like a well-oiled machine, with a precision that made possible the coordination of housekeeping, work scheduling, and childcare. Ella's "I can handle it" attitude enabled Adrienne to spend the very demanding hours that were required at the Normandie, again proving Ella to be a phenomenal blessing...not that there had been any doubt of that.

Addi, a name of endearment Ella had bestowed upon her long ago, proved a clever businesswoman, knowing innately how to promote the hotel to increase occupancy and service. Philadelphia society was where she aimed to drop anchor. The "pure bloods" listed in the Blue Book were prime candidates to reel in for weddings, graduations, engagements, sweet sixteen parties worthy of celebrating at the Normandie on the Sea. Addi worked hard to build a clientele base developed almost exclusively from the pampered and spoiled guests she met along the way, their wealth putting on display all their successes in life while Addi played it up for all it was worth. Even for a woman in the decade of the 1920s, she slowly positioned herself to become indispensable. Adrienne advanced rapidly from assistant to manager, though her promotions were not without battles. She maneuvered through the landmines with aplomb, and before the male opposition knew what hit them, Adrienne achieved her personal goals, and her enemies were forced to fade into the background, at least for the moment.

At the Normandie, Adrienne was enveloped in her work and became secure, finally feeling in control of her own life, something she desperately needed. She had lost not only her family but the father of her child—she was passionate about never risking the loss of someone she loved ever again. Life threw Addi many curves, especially at her early age. Yet with every assault came her determination to stay in control. In her mind, she planned to win every battle she faced. Her daughter and career were her life. Addi never let anyone get too close, so she constructed walls, living in a fortress built to her own specifications, yet she was always engulfed by old fears of losing those closest to her. Memories of Greg didn't ever fade; in fact, just the opposite was true.

On a Saturday evening in October of '27, Addi left Vivian with a playmate, Sandra Pettit, for a sleepover at the Pettit's suite on the top floor of the Normandie Hotel. Both girls were the same age, ten, and had been great friends since meeting at the hotel four years before. Samuel Pettit stayed at the Normandie exclusively every time he was in town on business, and he often brought his wife and daughter along. As a major stockholder in Normandie Hotel, Inc., Addi made sure he was well taken care of upon his arrival and straight through to the minute he departed.

Though the Pettits were out for the evening, Gammy, their maid of many years, would oversee the girls, assuring Addi that she need not worry. With Gammy at the helm, Addi had full confidence the evening's activities would be in good hands.

Addi went to Atlantic City with her good friend Jennifer. They went from work in the early afternoon to see a play at the Traymore Hotel, one of three or four five-star hotels along the boardwalk. Atlantic City was enjoying its Golden Age in the twenties, due in large part to prohibition. Drinking was prohibited nationally from 1919 to 1933 but was basically ignored in the city. Much liquor was consumed in the back rooms of speakeasies, nightclubs, and restaurants as racketeer and political boss Enoch "Nucky" Johnson quickly rose to power. Banning booze in Atlantic City was largely unenforceable. Local officials were "on the take," making illegal liquor flow like water in eating establishments throughout the town. The city's popularity grew steadily and soon became known as "The World's Playground."

Addi and Jennifer wanted no part of the darker underbelly of the city. They went for the lighter side, so after the play wrapped up, they walked the boards, taking in the sights of people parading like peacocks in their finest Saturday night attire. The sounds of the sea played background music to the masquerading masses. The evening was cloudy, cool, and very windy, but no rain was falling. Addi loved stormy nights. She unexpectedly broke stride and ran over to the railing of "The Walk," taking in the wild surf that had been whipping up. The waves were big, thundering toward the beach like a herd of wild horses, the incoming sea foaming at its edge.

Addi gazed southward, toward Peck's Beach, a distance of ten nautical miles, and all she could see was a massive glow of amber light bouncing off a low ceiling of clouds. By now, other people had noticed the unusual light, and then Addi heard someone say Peck's Beach's boardwalk had been burning for two hours and was threatening the entire city.

Addi was well aware of the proximity of the Normandie Hotel to the boardwalk, being separated by only two short blocks. Panicked, she turned to her friend and yelled, "Let's go! I've got to try to get onto the island even if I have to swim to get there!" Fortunately, Addi had driven her Model T Ford touring car to Atlantic City rather than taking the train, a decision that proved to be a wise one. Had it not been for the car, they would have been stranded, because the train came to a sudden halt once it got to Somers Point. The fire was consuming everything in its path, so all train service was cut off at the 8th Street boardwalk station.

They rushed to their car and drove like hell through the small towns that string the coastal beaches between Atlantic City and Peck's Beach, but the traffic was heavy, forcing them to stop, so they rode up the shoulder of the road, trying desperately to keep moving. Every minute counted, and the bridge was just ahead. The main access road was cut off to make way for all the fire engines from the mainland. Hundreds of volunteers walked or ran as they poured over the bridge to assist in the disaster. Addi and Jennifer managed to get halfway over the causeway when forward movement came to a screeching halt. Addi jumped out of the car, ran to the barricade right before the drawbridge, and pleaded with the policeman to allow her to get to the Normandie Hotel, screaming that her daughter was staying there and might be in imminent danger. Her breathing was labored, and the look in her eyes expressed a fear so deep that the policeman was caught off guard for a second, wanting to stop her in her tracks yet hesitating in a brief moment of compassion. In that split second, Addi broke away from his attempt to halfheartedly stop her. She ran like she was being chased by a tiger, over the bridge and down Ninth Street, toward the ocean.

Nearing the Normandie, the smoke was so dense she couldn't make out the condition of the hotel, but Addi was able to see flames lapping like tongues of fire from the bottom floors, and she became frozen in place. There was a sudden disconnect, a confusion as to what to do, where to go, her mind in neutral, short circuiting. Over and over, she heard herself cry, "I will not lose her, I will not lose her!" Internally she was screaming, but outwardly she knew she had to come to her senses or there would be no chance of saving her little girl. I must do something, run, yell for help… but move! And move she did, thanks to survival mode and adrenalin.

Addi knew every inch of the hotel and also knew she had to think clearly…no time for more panic. There was a private entrance to the building on the north side of the building that led to the upper floors. She was on the west side, and with no way to access the entrance from where she stood, she was forced to go around to the far side to get to the door off 8th Street. It was a longshot, but Addi knew Vivian was on the top floor, and the entire Pettit family may have been overcome by smoke.

With Addi a half-block away and the fire engines plus the police blocking anyone from closer access, she ran around the block in a full sprint to position herself so she could get to the side door. Through her tears and all the smoke, she was barely able to make out the outline of an old man standing protectively on the small portico of a Victorian house, with two small children, one under each arm. At first, what she saw didn't register. Running closer brought her into clearer focus, but her mind didn't seem to interpret what her eyes saw. The house brought the first flicker of awareness amid total chaos. This was the house Addi had seen the first day she'd arrived on the island. She had been on her way to the Asteria with Ella and fallen immediately in love with the house on the corner. She'd made a silent promise to herself that someday she would buy that house and open her very own tea room.

As Addi rushed closer to the corner, she couldn't believe what she was seeing. It was a miracle. She was afraid to believe it at first. Screaming through her unbelief, the word "Vivian" pierced the smoke-filled air. Vivian responded to the faint sounds of her mother's voice, pulling herself out from under the arms of the old man and running wildly into the safety of Addi's embrace. The reunion brought tears, kisses, and hugs so tight you'd think the two intended to break each other in half.

Neither Addi nor Vivian realized that the rain falling was not from their tears of joy. The heavens had opened up, pouring large drops of salvation on a city at the brink of extinction, a city where block after block had been blackened to the ground from the sea to the bay. The drenching that followed saved the town from even greater destruction than it had already endured, but the Normandie by the Sea had not been able to escape; its wooden-framed, one-thousand-room structure had gone down to the ground in flames.

In an almost hysterical voice, Vivian spilled out, "Mommy, Mommy, Sandra and I sneaked out of the hotel to spy on people walking along the boardwalk. We knew we'd get in trouble for doing it."

"Just take a breath, honey, and try to tell me what happened. It's OK. You're safe now. Everything will be fine."

"We went down the back stairway, you know, where the servants go, and we didn't make a sound. Everyone was asleep. We waited until it was late."

"Weren't you afraid you'd get in trouble?"

"Yes."

"But go on. Then what happened ?" Addi didn't want to affect the story in any way, but she needed to know the details as they unfolded.

So Vivian revealed a story that Addi absorbed with careful consideration. It was being told by a ten-year-old, so she was either making it up or she really knew the facts she was relating. Vivian told her mother how she and Sandra had gone under the boardwalk to see if they could hear what people were saying, pretending they were spies. The adventure was thrilling with every second that passed. They loved it. It was so dark neither girl could see very well, but they could make out who was talking, and it wasn't those strolling the boardwalk, but three boys smoking cigarettes.

One of them said, "I hate this town. Let's trash it!"

"Are you crazy!" another yelled.

And then, in a flash, a cigarette butt flew into the air, disappearing into a trash can.

Instantly there was an explosion that lit everything up like someone had just taken a photograph with a flashbulb. Then a kid screamed out some name Vivian couldn't remember and said, "Look what you did! Jesus, let's get out of here!" They ran like they were on fire themselves until they were out of sight. The girls were so scared they couldn't move.

"But the flames made us move, Mommy, and we ran as fast as we could onto the street. The fire followed us so quickly I thought we would burn up."

Later Adrienne found out the girls had ventured under the boardwalk further than they realized, so when they emerged onto the Avenue, they were at Eleventh Street, two blocks from the Normandie Hotel. They knew they had to get to the hotel before anyone discovered their absence. But the sky was black with smoke, and the sirens were wailing, crying out for help in a desperate attempt to rally every fireman from as far away as the sound could travel. The girls kept trying to run toward the hotel, but the sight of it became obscured by smoke. Both Vivian and Sandra were disoriented. Sandra stumbled on uneven pavement, fell to the ground, and burst into tears. Vivian, always the strong one, reached down and pulled her up. "Don't cry now, Sandra! There's no time for that! We've got to get back, and you're slowing us down!"

The girls were on Ocean Avenue – a street that ran north and south on the island – and they knew the hotel was almost in reach. A structure commanding half a city block; yet right then, it was wrapped in a blanket of black smoke, not visible from where the girls were positioned. Their trek home stopped short of two blocks from the Normandie, and they found themselves standing on the corner with tears running down their faces while the smoke choked off oxygen, making them cough, tear, and cry at the same time.

Jeremiah Fogg, a stately gentleman of some eighty-plus years, related to Addi how he had been standing on the porch of his Victorian home when he saw the two girls on the corner crying their eyes out. Without hesitation, he held out his arms to assure them it was safe to come onto his porch. He camouflaged his concern with a slight smile of warmth, even though the fire was two blocks away. But underneath that smile, he was very worried for the safety of his own home. However, sometimes miracles do happen. It's usually when your back is against the wall with no obvious escape , trapped with no way out, and no way to change or control it. It's then that you turn, begging for deliverance, to whomever you think will answer and pray you will be heard. Rain began to fall like the spigots of heaven had suddenly been opened, and the fire yielded to every blessed drop. When it was all over, the Victorian house on the corner of Ocean and Ninth Street, the home of Jeremiah Fogg and the first place Adrienne had coveted ownership on her arrival to Peck's Beach, stood proud and untouched by a disaster that had devoured nearly half the city. And when the smoke had cleared and the rain abated, amid the ruins, the Normandie by the Sea was no more.

Jeremiah took them all into his home and made them feel safe through the night. The fire was gradually brought under control thanks to the rain, a wind shift, and hundreds of firemen and volunteers. Besides, Addi, Vivian, and Sandra were homeless at this point and grateful to be able to wait things out until morning. Jeremiah lived alone, rattling around in this old seven-bedroom Victorian mansion, and he was delighted to fill the house with young people for a change.

Addi couldn't sleep, dreading that something terrible had happened to Ella. She felt trapped not being able to search for her lifelong companion. With too much confusion in the streets, people were crazy with fear, not knowing where their loved ones were, crying and screaming, shouting names in a futile attempt to locate a father, a mother, friends. So many lives were intertwined; so many souls were lost amid the smoke of a smoldering city!

When morning broke, the sun's rays edged over the horizon as though afraid to expose the blackened earth that covered what was once the thriving resort town of Peck's Beach. No building within a three-block radius of the Normandie escaped heavy damage or total devastation, with the miraculous exception of Jeremiah's home.

"Ella, Ella, where are you?" Addi awakened with a start. The room was strange. Where was she? Then memories flooded back, and she was out of bed and out the front door before she thought it through. Home, home, I've got to get home, but she couldn't get down Ocean Avenue; everything was roped off. Fire trucks were still on the job, putting out stubborn spots of burning embers, so she ran west for two blocks and then headed toward what she saw as the remains of her little cottage. Nothing but a shell was left; it had been gutted completely. Gone were the memories of a life only she and Ella knew existed. Pictures and furniture now lay in heaps of ashes that could never again reveal another place and time.

Some of Addi's neighbors were more fortunate than she; having been just north of the fire line, their homes had been spared. When they saw Addi on her knees, sobbing and crying out, "Ella, Ella," several of the women ran to her side to console her. Just then, Addi looked up through a waterfall of tears, barely discerning the most beautiful sight on this saddest of days, her dearest friend, Ella, running toward her with arms stretched wide, yelling, "Miss Addi, Miss Addi, you sure is a sight for these po' eyes of mine…! Child, child…don't cry, don't cry no more!"

As Ella helped Addi off the ground, they hugged each other with a bonding that reflected their many years of friendship.

"Vivian, child, where is Vivian?"

Addi unfolded the events of the past twelve hours while she walked Ella back to Jeremiah's home. They had lost everything, and there was literally no place, no one, to turn to except Jeremiah Fogg. When they entered the house, he was already up and fast at work in the kitchen. Introductions were made, and the three of them sat together on the enclosed porch. Addi was able to tell Jeremiah how Ella had come to be her dearest friend. By design, details of Addi's background were left out. All Jeremiah needed to know was how Addi had been left an orphan as a result of the swine flu, or, as it became known later, the Spanish flu, and widowed by the war. Jeremiah Fogg was deeply affected learning about Addi's past, which moved him to offer his house to all of them until they could find a suitable place to live. His home had never been touched by the fire directly, though the smell of smoke lingered for weeks. They were very grateful for the offer and accepted with alacrity.

The days and weeks that followed the fire were filled with anguish and then despair, but they were always mixed with a good helping of hope. Addi and Ella worked night and day to assist the townsfolk in a variety of situations. Jeremiah's house became a hospital, refuge, restaurant, and small hotel for the weak and weary, some parading aimlessly, not knowing where to turn.

CHAPTER 11

Slowly and with untold energy, the town began to recover. Peck's Beach took on a look of normalcy, though only on the surface. But the positive attitudes on display all helped to encourage people to look to the future and let go of something they had no control over: the past.

The police, however, were not so quick to bury the past as were the citizens. The city officials were determined to get to the bottom of the cause of the fire. Preliminary investigation revealed the flames most likely had begun under the boardwalk around Ninth Street where the Hippodrome Theater extended over the beach. Addi had heard rumblings among the citizenry that the police were questioning anyone who might have seen or heard something that night that could lead to evidence connecting the fire to a suspect.

Out of guilt, Addi went to the police, who agreed to ask Vivian and Sandra about their adventure the night of the fire.

The constable and several other authority figures questioned the girls as gently and with as little intimidation as possible, not an easy task since Vivian and Sandra sat there as if they were about to be hanged. Addi placed her chair between them both, arms embracing each girl like a mother hen protecting her chicks from the Big Bad Wolf. Both girls were able to recall, in great detail, what took place that evening, and Addi was transfixed, moving not a muscle the entire time.

The constable tried his best to jog the girl's memories to recall the names of the boys, without success.

"I just can't remember, sir. It was so dark, and we were hiding 'cause we didn't want them to know we were there. We were so scared. It was some kind of nickname, but I never heard it before, and I didn't know what it meant." Vivian looked sad and lost, and as she started to cry, Addi pulled her closer.

Addi terminated the interrogation by simply standing up and saying, "We are done here; the girls have told you all they know, and I don't want them to be subjected to any more questioning." With that terse statement, Addi gathered her little chicks and headed for the front door of the precinct's building. In a flash, the four of them were out of there and off to Jeremiah's house, their safe place. For Vivian, though, there was no escaping the idle gossip and innuendos from people in town, as unspoken suspicions lingered. The point was driven home when Vivian was doing an errand for her mother at the corner grocery store. She overheard two ladies talking about the fire in the isle next to her. One said to the other, "I personally know the constable that interviewed Addi's daughter and he was not entirely convinced she didn't have something to do with starting the fire. That said, he could not be positive, no evidence to the contrary, just a gut feeling she may be guilty." The passage of time dulled the effect, but Vivian subconsciously suffered from her inability to recall the boy's nickname, remaining incapable of vindicating herself. The shadow boy under the boardwalk had a name, a name that totally eluded her.

The assumption was that Sandra's parents never had a chance, most likely dying of smoke inhalation. Gammy had inexplicably awakened in a room engulfed with black, dense smoke, the kind that kills. In a panic, she'd run to the hallway and then collapsed, but a heroic rescue from a hotel guest brought her safely outside the building.

The loss was devastating for both. It was very fortunate Addi, Vivian, and Ella were there as a support system, because the grief, coupled with despair, was almost beyond bearing.

Life after the fire was a transition period for everyone, both in the Fogg home and in the town. The Normandie was gone and, with it, Addi's close friends and owners, James and Rebecca Rodgers. Their charred bodies were found on the third floor; they'd never had a chance to escape. Addi was on her own now, and once the emotional shock of the disaster began to fade a bit, she decided now was the time to bring to fruition the dream she had always sheltered...a tea room of her own, just like her mother's. There was a small building on Ninth Street for sale, and as it so happened, there was a three-bedroom apartment above the store. Addi scraped together all her savings, plus her small investments, and privately negotiated a real estate offer with the owner. The result was the purchase of a prime store location right in the center of town. Shortly thereafter, she proudly opened her very own tea room, Addi's by the Sea.

There was a flurry of excitement on opening day. People came because they knew Addi from the Normandie and wanted to support her efforts. Besides, the food was excellent, and the service impeccable. Ownership by a woman was a bold move to make in the decade of the twenties, and doubly so for a widow.

By now, Jerimiah had become a treasured friend, so Addi and Vivian were regular visitors. There wasn't a time Addi entered his gracious home that memories of her first arrival on the island didn't come flooding back and how she had made a vow hoping someday to own this most beautiful Victorian home.

When the Depression followed the stock market crash of October '29, people were not only broke financially but suddenly unemployed. Credit was almost impossible to get with disposable cash being nonexistent. They couldn't possibly find money to take a vacation, let alone have the time to do so. Their main concern was how to find employment to provide for their next meal.

Jeremiah lost everything in the crash except his home and a pile of cash under the mattress. In what seemed like overnight, the entire island was crushed at its financial core. Tourism trailed off to a slow drizzle, along with all the associated businesses that benefited directly from the tourist trade. Real estate fell victim as well: new construction came to a screeching halt, and existing homes for sale went unsold for months.

Fortunately, the tearooms early success allowed Adrienne to save money, so she was in relatively good shape financially to weather the storm of the encroaching hard times. Her tea room was taking a hit, daily meals served were down . Not a surprise considering the average patron was unemployed and trying to make ends meet just to put food on their own table. Having high tea was suddenly not high on the priority list.

Addi cut the staff to one person besides herself and Ella, allowing her to squeak by financially, being also very cautious about food buying. Addi had an uncanny ability to figure out what customer consumption would be long before the person sat down to eat. A plan began to take shape as Addi desperately tried to keep their heads above water: she decided to buy several small houses that had gone into foreclosure, renting them out to people in need of shelter who had lost their homes in the crash. She had the seed money, and slowly, one at a time, Addi built up a very viable little enterprise.

It took some time, but her persistence and patience paid off. Over a four-year period Addi was able to sock away a fair amount of cash, enabling her to make her move. The opportunity presented itself in a very natural way. Jeremiah called Addi at the tea room and asked if she, Ella, and Vivian would like to come to dinner. Mondays were the only weekday Addi was free to plan anything social. The restaurant was always closed then, so she was more than happy to accept the invitation.

Jeremiah cooked up a fine meal and set a beautiful table for the occasion. He had learned the art of food preparation and garnishing from his wife before her passing, having realized the need to be able to cook or otherwise be forced to eat out every night. Nellie, his wife of fifty years, had been a wonderful cook, spoiling him with her culinary delights.

The four sat down to eat in an elegant dining room replete with sterling silver flatware, fine lace tablecloth, and a gorgeous crystal chandelier designed by Tiffany's. Addi still found it breathtaking every time she had an occasion to enter the room.

It wasn't until they were almost through dinner that Jeremiah confided, "I have an offer to make to all three of you that I hope you'll seriously consider."

Addi shot a puzzled look at Ella, who did likewise to Vivian. What Jeremiah was about to suggest really caught them by total surprise.

"I'm an old man, and one who is fading in strength with every day that passes. I know I look like all is well, but it isn't. I have buried my entire family, and I don't want to spend the few years I have remaining to me fighting with my loneliness. The Depression has left me nearly penniless and feeling very insecure. It's taking a toll on my life, both physically and emotionally. I don't have much to offer, but if you would be willing to come and live with me, I would be most grateful. I know this is a lot to ask all three of you. I say all three because it affects each of your lives. I can sweeten the offer by saying you will inherit my house when I die, as well as whatever is left of my money. It's not much, but it's all I have to offer."

In stunned silence at the table, the women just stared at nothing discernible, speechless, with thoughts running wild. Addi had come to dinner looking for the right moment to broach the subject of buying the house from Jeremiah, and in return, caring for him. Now Jeremiah had completely turned the tables on them. It was as though he was handing them his home on one of his silver platters, and in fact, he was doing just that.

Addi broke the silence. "Jeremiah, I have never, nor will I ever forget the debt of gratitude I owe you for protecting my daughter and her friend the night of the Great Fire. Nothing I could do for you would ever be enough to repay you for what you did that night. It would give me the greatest pleasure to be able to repay the indebtedness I feel toward you, so yes, we are most blessed to be willing, and able, to love and protect you for the waning years of your life."

Tears rolled down Jeremiah's wrinkly, leathered face as Ella and Vivian, in unison, shouted a joyous "Amen!"

CHAPTER 12

On the last day of May 1934, Jeremiah, while peacefully sleeping in his bed on the second floor of his beloved home, graduated to heaven, forty years to the day after he first bought the house and four years after Addi and her little family made it their home as well. He lived just long enough to see the opening of Watson's Restaurant on a beautiful Sunday afternoon in May.

Two major life events came back to back...a joyous and very successful "Grand Opening" and a heartbreaking "Grand Departure." Two deeply held loves of Addi's. If there were to be any consolation, it was her remembrance of the look of total joy and contentment on Jeremiah's face as he watched people come and go from Watson's on opening day. Invited guests seemed so pleased to be part of the birth of what they all knew would become a huge success. It gave Addi great comfort to know Jeremiah had lived long enough to see his home be "the pot of gold at the end of the rainbow" for Addi, a final curtain for him, as though he knew the end was near, and so his bonds were loosed, freeing him into eternity.

Addi buried Jeremiah next to his beloved wife at the Memorial Cemetery on the mainland. The private graveside service was attended by only close friends. As his casket was slowly lowered into darkness, Addi reached in her pocket to retrieve a key. She lovingly kissed it and then gently place it on the casket like it was a beautiful, delicate rose. In a way, it was a rose to Jeremiah. It was the key to his most treasured possession, his Model T, the first car ever to be driven on the island and an object of much adoration from all who had enjoyed seeing Jeremiah Fogg sputtering down the road on a sun-drenched Sunday afternoon. Sadly, along with everything else, he'd lost the car in the Depression, but he'd told Addi he kept the key in a picture frame as a daily reminder of how you can lose everything you love in the wink of an eye when your eyes are on the wrong thing.

With Ella and Vivian flanked on either side and holding tightly onto Addi, she quietly said, "We love you, Jeremiah." Then came the tears.

Adrienne called the restaurant Watson's, the name she was known by after she came to town. It was a reminder of her mother and the tea room they both had worked so hard to make successful. Her childhood home in New Hope had commanded three hundred acres of the most bucolic landscape in all of Bucks County, PA. Her family had leased some of the farmland to tenant workers, providing an income and the chance to do what she and her mother really loved, creating and operating their own little restaurant, right there in the farm house. Adrienne may well have stayed right where she was, at the farm, comfortably enmeshed in a world she never wanted to see disappear, if it hadn't been for external forces beyond her control.

The establishment of Watson's was a lifetime achievement for Addi and a great sense of pride for Jeremiah. What better place to have your adopted family come to the realization of a passion deeply held, the fulfillment of a dream come true. Opening day was a big happening in the town. It was well known, even common knowledge for those who thought they were in the inner circle, that Addi someday would open a major eating establishment in town. So people weren't caught off guard when the gossip around town was that Addi would soon be serving dinners in an undisclosed property. They just didn't expect the new location to be Jeremiah's house.

The turnout exceeded all expectations. Seating capacity was one hundred, and dining hours were set for 4:00 to 9:00 PM, except Sundays. The Lord's Day hours were noon to 8:00 pm; that way, customers could enjoy a Sunday supper or brunch right after church. Dining later in the day worked well for patrons who desired to take a Sunday stroll on the boardwalk before eating.

Addi managed for the entire day to oversee almost every aspect of the restaurant, making sure the sum of its parts were pleasing to its patrons. She had been taught well at the Normandie Hotel by the Sea about service, and she knew how a satisfied customer would come back time and again when treated like royalty. Applying the same code of conduct at her own establishment was an easy transition, and she instilled her philosophy on all who ventured to work under her very exacting style.

Addi had become very involved in the town since the Great Fire. She was well connected and highly respected after fourteen years as a resident, a very classy lady with a personal style that captivated and charmed the most obstinate of characters. Men pursued her, and women imitated her.

To the ladies of Peck's Beach, Addi represented the best a woman could be...a person of substance, confident in who she was and where she was going. As a widow, Adrienne was not tied to a husband and all that represented in the thirties...a lady in the parlor, a cook in the kitchen, and a hussy in bed. Women envied her openness, knowing full well that Adrienne enjoyed a freedom quite contrary to their own roles in life.

She worked hard to make sure to keep a ring of security around herself and Vivian. Control of her life was paramount, and no matter what it took, she was going to make sure no person or thing would ever dictate her future again. She put her personal stamp on everything she tended; whether opening a restaurant or helping the poor find housing, her ultimate goal was to solidify her social status in the community, keeping her in a position of power and control, all with effortless dignity and grace.

CHAPTER 13

Ella continued with her story of Watson's. She found it easier to confide in me as she got to know me better. Over time, we chatted about many aspects of life while we ate together on the Porch, and slowly Ella was able to trust me with some of her very private feelings. She opened up due to loneliness, having no one to talk to anymore. Addi was gone, and Vivian had made friends with her bottle and prescription drugs.

I looked forward with great anticipation to every time I knew Ella and I would share dinner. This time was no exception, and when she began to talk, it was as though I were being transported to a time long before I was born...the year 1937.

By then, Vivian was twenty, soon to be twenty-one, and while waiting on tables at Watson's, she noticed a young man taking his seat at her station on the Terrace. It was 8:30 on a Thursday night, and business was slow. He looked like he'd just stepped off the front cover of Esquire magazine...tall, with pitch-black hair, a chiseled nose that didn't overtake his face, light blue eyes drawing you in like magnets, and a smile genuine enough to get Vivian to smile in return...involuntarily.

Vivian seized the opportunity and poured on her feminine charm in a style reminiscent of Scarlet O'Hara. She had no plans to let him escape, and he had plans to score with whomever he could...never missing a chance when it presented itself, confident this night would be no exception. A very self-assured Vivian approached his table. With an order pad in one hand and a pen in the other, leaning slightly forward at the hips to show she was listening, she looked into that handsome face and said in a somewhat flirtatious voice, "Anything that catches your eye...on the menu, sailor?"

Stephen was caught off guard with her opening salvo and let out a hearty laugh. "Lots...but it's not on this menu."

And with that line, it was all Vi needed; the rest of the evening was magic for both, and they flirted nonstop until Stephen paid his dinner bill some hour and a half later. He left a tip under the placemat with a note: "This table is reserved for tomorrow night." But tomorrow came and went without a sign of a customer named Stephen.

Vivian was crushed and wondered if she been too flip with him. They had joked around all evening, but he couldn't have taken her seriously, could he? It wasn't until Saturday night, right in the middle of the rush hour for patrons, that Vivian caught a glimpse of Stephen waiting outside in line for dinner with a young lady on his arm.

Vivian was sure he didn't see her peering through the Terrace front window, so she quickly tracked down Alice, one of the hostesses. Pulling her over to the curtains that partially draped the window, Vivian stood aside just enough to avoid being observed.

"See that so-called gentleman right there? Whatever you do, do not put that couple at any of my tables, do you understand?"

"Yes, Miss Vivian. I'll make sure nothing like that takes place."

Alice looked somewhat puzzled, a look that went unnoticed because Vivian was intent on her scrutiny of the lady on Stephen's arm. A lady of the night, no doubt, a tramp! The thought was fleeting, and just as quickly, Vivian ran off to the kitchen to pick up another dinner order. Simultaneously Alice was called to the center hall to assist a waitress who had just dropped a dessert on the floor after bumping into a patron.

Fortunately, Addi had been able to utilize the L-shaped design of the house so the different dining areas enhanced the traffic flow between the waitresses and patrons. It helped create less chance of waitresses running into one another, but bodily contact could not always be avoided, and collisions were, unfortunately, bound to happen. There were five dining rooms, the Terrace paralleling Ocean Avenue, the Porch overlooking Ninth Street, the interior Garden Room, with its many flower boxes filled with floral arrangements, the Boardwalk Room, where wall paintings had been done by a local artist depicting scenery filled with children and adults strolling along the boards, and then the Beach Room, right behind the Terrace, adorned with a wall tapestry weaving the sun, sand, and surf into a trio of solace. Three of the five dining rooms were accessed from the center hall as well as the kitchen.

Stephen and his lady had advanced to the front of the line, and another hostess, Ruth, had taken over seating patrons. She was not aware of the edict laid down by Vivian several moments before, so she proceeded to seat the party of two in the Beach Room, at a table just opposite the entrance to the kitchen.

As it happened, the deuce was one of the tables assigned to Vivian. It was not a happy evening, when Vivian swung the kitchen door wide open with a swift kick of her foot only to come face to face with Stephen and his guest. Vivian became the consummate actress in a scene she knew couldn't end. She wasn't about to tip her hand, to cave in. If she could have, she would have spit in his food and then served him with a huge smile on her face.

"Good evening, my name is Vivian, and I'll be serving you tonight. Is this your first time dining with us?" And so the scene unfolded, dripping with sarcasm and complete with verbal tennis, the ball being flung from one side to the other, all while the "other woman" had no clue what was being volleyed over her head.

When Stephen's "date" excused herself to go to the ladies room, he had a chance to write a note and leave it, once again, under the placemat while Vivian retreated to the kitchen to pick up dinners for another table of two. By the time she returned through the swinging doors with entrees on her arm, Stephen and his lady had departed. Vivian felt like crying when she saw the empty table, and she came very close to losing her carefully balanced plates when she came to an abrupt halt... What a good thing no waitress was tailgating her. Vivian's tip was partially hidden under the placemat, so when she began to clear the table, she picked up the mat and saw Stephen's note: "Lady is close friend/sets no sails for this sailor/please meet me at the Asteria... 9:30pm."

Nine couldn't come fast enough. The restaurant closed, and Vivian slid out the rear kitchen door before anyone knew she was gone. She wasn't about to do side work, not this time. What a perfect night to rendezvous, as her mother just so happened to be in Atlantic City with Ella for the evening.

Huck, a faithful servant of Addi's since earlier days at the Normandie Hotel, was reluctantly in charge of overseeing Vivian. Addi knew her daughter well, being fully aware of the trouble she could get herself into if not managed closely. Vivian told Huck she was going to walk over to a girlfriend's house several blocks away and would return in an hour. In fact, Vivian did return in an hour, but those sixty minutes began a passionate romance that took off like a bat out of hell. No one was aware of what was taking place, everything was done under the cover of dark, and if Addi found out what was happening, Vivian would be sent to a nunnery.

The summer months marched on, and through a close friend who worked at the Asteria, Addi learned not only of the romance Vivian was hiding, but who the suitor was...Stephen DeVries, the hotel owner's son! Addi's reaction was predictable and swift; it could have been scripted for a soap opera, one with a very predictable ending. Vivian dug in her heels, saying that nothing would stand in the way of their love for each other. Addi had a flashback to a different time and place, but although quietly sympathetic, she didn't give an inch. Vivian was underage and way too young for a man who could be her father!

"I hate you, hate you! You're a controlling bitch who can't remember what it's like to really love someone."

"Don't you ever disrespect me again with such gutter language, do you hear me?" Addi's words fell on deaf ears. "Oh yes, my sweet daughter," she said very cuttingly, "I do know about love. This I know for sure: you will never see Stephen again, Vivian. If the DeVries' ever find out about their son's little adventure into the arms of a young lady who is only twenty, they would be mortified, not to mention the scandal it would cause. You are scheduled to leave by ship for Europe for a year's study in Paris in one week, and I intend to be standing on the dock waving goodbye as you sail away."

Addi panicked at the thought of anyone finding out that Stephen was the twin brother of Greg, Vivian's father, and therefore her uncle. Vivian had been told her father had died in the WWI, and his last name was Watson. What a disaster! How could this have happened? Addi would die first before this truth was known. Just the thought of it made her sick and many nights were spent pacing the bedroom floor with sleep very slow to take her out of reality. The truth had to be buried, but how? Her daughter's romance had to be terminated. And as a result the seeds of deception were sown.

After mother and daughter's major altercation, Vivian was kept under "house arrest." She never saw Stephen again during the week she was preparing to leave for Europe, and Addi made sure Vivian was not out of her sight until physically boarding the Queen Elizabeth in New York in early September. A sense of calm flooded over Addi when she and Ella took the train back to Philadelphia from Grand Central Station. Knowing Vivian was safely out of the country gave her a little breathing room to work on a plan to deal with Stephen.

Stephen came to Watson's a few days after the QE set sail, looking for Vivian. He was totally unaware of her departure, and he very tactfully asked the hostess if he could be seated at Vivian's station, adding that she was a friend. The hostess informed him Vivian was not on duty, having left for Europe to study. Stephen looked dumbfounded, tightly holding back any response, when Addi approached him from the center hall. It was near closing on a Monday night. The bulk of the patrons were long gone, and a light drizzle dampened the night air, foretelling that fall was not far away.

"Mr. DeVries, please excuse my intrusion into your evening, but may I have a word with you?"

"Certainly, Mrs. Watson. Won't you join me at my table? I mean, as soon as I'm seated, that is?"

"I'll see to it that you are indeed seated right away. I do have some influence at this establishment, you know." A big smile from Stephen confirmed the understatement of the evening, and with that warm ice breaker, Addi directed the hostess to secure a desirable window table on the Terrace.

When they were seated, Addi decided to come right to the point about what she had to say to this obvious man of the world. It wasn't as easy as she'd first thought, though, because, as she sat directly across from Stephen, she felt like she was looking into the eyes of Greg. Even though the brothers were paternal twins, the resemblance was unnerving, and Addi had a rough time concentrating on keeping the conversation going in the direction she planned.

"Mr. Devries…"

"Please, call me Stephen. It's so less formal…"

"Stephen, I am very aware of your relationship with my daughter, and to be very blunt, it can't continue. Vivian is only twenty, and you are much older, I believe."

"I'm thirty-eight," he said very sheepishly, with eyes cast downward.

"Well, you don't look like you're out of your twenties yet. In any case, the age difference between the two of you is totally unacceptable, not now, not ever... regardless of the changing world we live in."

"Mrs. Watson, I had no idea Vivian was so young! She said she'd been out of college for several years, so I thought she was about twenty-four, maybe twenty-five. I don't know what to say!"

"Stephen, Vivian is going on twenty-five in looks and maturity, that part I can understand. She has always been perceived as much older, and it's caused her trouble on a number of occasions. You're not the first male friend that's been fooled. She is on her way to Europe at this very moment and will remain there for the entire school year. Vivian is not ready to get serious with any man right now, and when the time is right, it won't be with someone almost seventeen years her senior. She has much to learn and experience about life, and as her mother, I'm very aware of how strong-headed she can be. If Vivian doesn't have someone to keep her reined in, such as me, she'll make a mess of her life if left to her own devices."

His response was very open. "I lost a fiancée several years ago in Atlanta, and I have not rebounded from the hurt and despair that has caused. I'm acutely aware of my personal struggle to move beyond my loss, and at this point, I'm not looking for a long-term relationship. As you say, Vivian is a strong person. I was actually looking for a way to take a step back and keep our dating on a less serious level. I'm really dumbfounded by all you're telling me. Now that you have been so open and honest regarding your daughter, it seems only right to agree that I will cut off any further relationship with Vivian."

"Stephen, I hardly know you, but I am certain you would be doing yourself and my daughter a huge favor if you would follow through with the agreement you just attested to. Mothers usually know their daughters fairly well, and this has disaster written all over it."

With that, Addi dismissed herself by rising from her chair, Stephen following suit. She had no intention of dining with him, realizing her sudden attraction was taking over, and she wasn't about to go down that path.

To him, she said, "Good evening, and may we meet again under better circumstances. Please don't stop dining at Watson's due to any awkwardness you might feel. I would be most troubled if you carried any resentment toward me because of what we've discussed."

"Not at all, Madame Watson, quite the contrary, I assure you."

"And on a minor point, my name is Adrienne. Friends call me Addi."

"Well, I hope we can be friends, and until we meet again, Addi, I'm grateful for your counsel."

With that, she was gone, seeming to vanish as quickly as she had appeared.

Over the next month or two, Stephen dined often at the restaurant, inviting Addi to join him at his table one warm early August night. The scene was repeated many times in the weeks ahead as both were able to share their life's journeys, though neither realized the subtle attraction that was developing. How quickly the tables can turn.

Stephen was a carbon copy of Greg. Even with the passing of years, Stephen's face was what Addi had projected Greg would look like now. She had never been able to separate from Greg's memory, and on some level, she had immortalized him. When Addi looked into Stephen's eyes, she saw beyond the present and into a reality of her own creation, a reality that only held room for Greg. By inviting Stephen into her fantasy world, she was projecting his brother.

Stephen was attracted first by Addi's poise and charm, and then by her sexual elegance. He was drawn into this romance by forces that were indefinable. But he couldn't help what he was feeling, acting on impulse, moving forward in the relationship they had so carefully and somewhat innocently nourished. On balance, the risks were worth it. No staying safely in the harbor for this man.

The romance deepened well into the fall, after the restaurant had closed for the winter. Vivian was settled in school in France, and living with a French family as an au-pair. This was Addi's attempt to teach her daughter some life values extending beyond her own self serving world.

Her mother's parting words, " You're their problem now. Please don't ruin it."

Vivian was totally unaware of what was taking place between her mother and Stephen. Letters were sent in which Stephen tried to let Vivian down in stages, not wanting to hurt her but knowing full well this was not going to end on a good note. His last letter to her expressed his true feelings about not wanting to make any kind of heavy commitment at this time in his life. Vivian's response was raw, telling Stephen what a liar he was, how deceptive he had been, and that she had been planning to break up with him anyway, since she was in a heavy relationship with a gentleman she'd met in class. "You know these Frenchmen really are lovers." Was it true? Anybody's guess.

Stephen never expected such a cold and vicious response, to which Addi just shook her head as if to say, "Par for the course."

In the spring of '38, Adrienne and Stephen decided to marry…a decision not made lightly. The relationship was revealed to Vivian in small, well-thought-out steps over time that were designed to expose the true feelings each had for the other. But repeated overseas phone calls eventually ended in disaster, especially when all the small steps finally added up to the truth…her mother's marriage.

Vivian hated her mother for stealing Stephen away from her. It was inconceivable that her mother would take advantage of her absence to highjack the love she and Stephen had felt for one another, destroying any chance for their young love to reach maturity.

Once the truth was fully in the open, Vivian hit bottom emotionally, threatening to kill herself.

Addi knew her daughter, the drama queen, only too well. During one of the rare phone calls where Vivian was able to listen and not hang up in anger, Adrienne was able to convey to her, as difficult as that was, that Stephen was telling the truth when he said he was not in love with Vivian. She told Vivian he had really opened up to her about his past relationships, about his ability to play the "poser game," as he called it, until it was discovered that he was not who he wanted others to think he was. He wasn't proud of himself; the emotional wreckage left behind was heartbreakingly destructive for all the players involved.

He said, "Just look at me; I'm living proof. I come home at night to emptiness when I open the door and loneliness when I close it behind me. My father has basically disowned me ever since the war days."

The lessons learned proved to be a turning point in Stephen's life.

"And yes, Vivian, I believe him," Addi said with a heavy dose of conviction.

Back to reality. I always felt a twinge of disappointment when Ella decided she had said enough. Slowly rising, she gave me one of her warm, sweet smiles and said, "I'm gone upstairs, child. It's late, and I just know I talked your ears off. We'll dine again darlin." And with that, she was gone, along with her the past until she brought it to life once again at a table for two on the Porch.

The year of '65 slipped quietly into '66...no huge celebrations for the new year, just a lot of expectations. I graduated from college in late May with the rest of our gang facing another year before they had to confront the real world. Teaching elementary education in Lower Merion School District would be ahead of me in September, but for now, the entire summer lay in our immediate future, and we all badly needed the break and were anxious to pick up where we'd ended last fall. Summer flew by as usual and I missed seeing Laura.

CHAPTER 14

August '66... Thunderstorms built along the Intercontinental Convergence Zone...that place deep in the Atlantic where the trade winds blow along the Equator, near the Cape Verdi Islands, just off the west coast of Africa. It was mid-August, and the tankers were cutting through the shipping lanes, headed for the Eastern Seaboard ports from Charleston to New York. Reports began to arrive indicating a storm brewing, but early development was not impressive. Then suddenly radio signals sent messages that a major hurricane had exploded overnight. Seas were running fifteen to twenty feet high, winds clocked at eighty mph, and the storm was moving west at eighteen mph. The news of the hurricane trickled into the public's morning papers as an item of lowest priority.

The Jersey Shore was lost in its usual drug of choice...hedonism! Life is good, live it up because Labor Day is coming quickly and every minute of fun counts. Barely anyone was aware of what loomed ahead, far out in the Atlantic. Satellites and computer-driven technology were in their infancy in '66. The only way hurricanes or severe storms were forecast was through the ships at sea communicating with the National Weather Service. Buoys were strategically placed to capture readings for wind speed and wave action.

So, the fun times were relentless on Peck's Beach in the summer of '66, and 150,000 people were totally oblivious to the danger looming far out at sea.

Within a few days, the hurricane named Carmella would be two hundred miles off the Virginia coast of the Eastern Shore of the US. With its 145 mph winds and waves running over forty-five- feet, forecasters predicted a continual northeast curve out to sea, away from any land areas. The Friday before Labor Day, the public knew the hurricane was off the coast, but concern ran low since the storm was tracking as predicted, northeast, away from land.

Through forces not totally understood, the upper-level steering winds known as the jet stream dramatically shifted northward, blocking the forward movement of Carmella, rendering her stationary. The entire system became controlled by a high pressure system that slipped southeastward from New England, anchoring itself five hundred miles due east of the hurricane. Acting like a blocking wall, it forced the storm to move westward. This was not what the forecasters wanted to see, a disastrous scenario at best. If the course continued, the New Jersey and New England coastline would be under ten feet of water. The storm surge in Jersey was estimated to be fifteen feet measured at low tide. A full moon worsened the forecast, and should the tide be at its height when the hurricane landed, it could bring a catastrophe of major proportions.

With a forward movement of twenty-five miles an hour, Carmella would hit the Jersey coast within eight hours, given the fact that the eye was located just two hundred miles east of the Chesapeake Bay. Evacuation warnings were issued that all persons were to leave the island immediately or seek shelter in well-constructed buildings such as the high school, churches, and City Hall. People left Peck's Beach in droves, jamming the streets with traffic gridlock so bad it didn't make sense to leave...better to stay and ride the storm out than get stuck trying to make it to the mainland. There were only two major roads to enter or exit Peck's Beach, the Ninth Street or Thirty-fourth Street causeways and neither was able to handle thousands of cars leaving the island at the same time. The Long Port Bridge at the north end of the island was not an option. It arched its way over Great Egg Harbor, ending at a very low point in the wetlands that were flooding rapidly.

People were desperate to find shelter anywhere they could, so the crew and I didn't hesitate to open Watson's for their refuge. The building had stood the test of time for good reason, as it was constructed more like a castle than a Victorian home. Jeremiah Fogg had made certain no storm or flood would wipe him off his foundation. He liked to remind all who would listen that one was never to build their home on sand, but on solid rock, and he'd tell you outright that it was Jesus sweeping the houses away, as sand castles on the edge of the sea melted with the first incoming wave.

The hurricane came onshore at midnight on Sunday. The restaurant had closed early, around three in the afternoon, when it looked like a direct hit was inevitable, so almost all the staff had gone home. Laura took shelter upstairs in her living quarters, alone. Vivian was in Atlantic City for the evening, and JD was away in New York on business. Both were unable to get home because of the storm.

Dennis, the devoted head chef and being very capable, took charge in JD's absence. He dismissed everyone and left the restaurant as soon as he gave me the word that the kitchen was closed. I relayed the message to the staff. The hurricane was coming in fast, and Dennis needed to get back to his place on Simpson Avenue. He and his family rented the same small cottage when they came north from South Carolina every spring.

I let the staff know I'd be staying put. Our third floor walk-up on 1st Street would have been too vulnerable to hurricane force winds plus being close to the beach. A high ocean water storm surge was considered almost a certainty. I wasn't going anywhere because Laura was upstairs, so that clinched it for me. What no one saw coming was the influx of people heading straight for Watson's. It looked just like the usual Saturday evening line, everyone waiting to come inside. Only this time, it wasn't for dinner; it was for shelter. So I unlocked the door, and in they came. During this out of control time, Laura and I were on the verge of making our first real connection. Oddly, chaos brought clarity, and I no longer saw a teenager but a young woman, mature beyond her years. Traveling abroad and being educated in the best private schools had their effect on Laura, helping her to develop an air of confidence and refinement that certainly hadn't been apparent several years before.

The hurricane raged on for hours, the wind so deafening that it began to seriously unnerve people. There was no way you could block out the roar. If it wasn't the wind screaming, it was the roof being torn off in large chunks or glass shattering from third-floor windows that notched up the sound to almost intolerable decibels. And the casualties kept coming. How some people made it through the hell that was unfolding outside was a miracle.

I was grateful for the chaos, in a way. It gave me something I felt in my control. I took command, directing those few crew workers who remained in the kitchen to clear out the Beach Room, the main dining area at the back of the restaurant, in order to make space for anything that would serve as a bed or a place to rest for older folks. Windows were boarded up in as many places as possible in hope of safety from flying objects while the crew gathered flashlights, batteries, candles, and blankets, in an effort to keep people warm, dry, and able to navigate tight quarters in limited areas, as night was fast approaching. Laura jumped right in, not missing a beat, and we worked in tandem, anticipating what the other was about to do or what the other needed.

Watson's was a stronghold in the mist of havoc right outside its walls. The tide hit at its apex just as an invisible full moon was rising over the raging sea. The island flooded like never before, but the restaurant had been built six feet above the ground for just that reason. The water poured into the basement, right up to the boards beneath the main floor of the house. The dungeon, bakery, and changing rooms were ruined. The roof was partially torn off, allowing the rain to enter only on the northeast side of the house. All the third-floor windows were gone, and the office, where the financial nerve center of the restaurant was located, was destroyed. But the building stayed steady through an ordeal no one had ever experienced, and through it all, not one soul was harmed.

The two rest rooms were located underneath the spiral staircase with a small broom closet nestled to the right as you went back to use the Gulls or Buoyes rooms. Laura and I literally bumped into one another, crossing through the hall checking on the different dining rooms.

The lights had gone out long ago. I was worried about flying glass or other objects. Fortunately I remembered the broom closet.

Literally shouting over the roaring sounds of a massive hurricane, "Laura, take my hand and follow me." She did with no resistance. I took her into my hiding place and shut the door.

We couldn't see a thing in front of us, not even our own hands. Talking was impossible; there was no way we could compete with Carmella's rage taking place on the other side of the restaurant walls, walls that we prayed would hold up against the mighty force of the winds pounding the building relentlessly. We had to cover our ears to block out the sound. I held on to Laura, and she gripped me as though we might be ripped out of each other's arms, swept away like Dorothy in The Wizard of Oz.

With her beautiful face against my chest in the dark, I gently touched her trembling lips before I did what I had wanted to do for a very, very long time…kiss her. At that moment, a silence and calm like I'd never known before claimed the little broom closet and the entire universe around us. We were centered in the eye of Hurricane Carmella, but I felt centered in the eye of heaven. It was a kiss not even a hurricane could blow away, the beginning of a romance neither of us could ever have imagined.

The eye passed as quickly as it had begun, and the hurricane moved inland toward its next victims. The aftermath of destruction had not been witnessed since the March '62 nor'easter. Flooding was almost total throughout the island, with beach and bay front homes taking the biggest hits. The only saving grace in all this was that the hurricane landed at the end of the tourist season. The island had months to rebuild and, thankfully, the damage to Watson's was not that severe considering what other homeowners and businesses faced. The dungeon could be repaired and the bakery restored over the winter, as well as any visible damage to the outside of the building. A betting man would have the odds in his favor that Peck's Beach would be up and running by spring.

Once again, the summer came to an end, only this time a bit prematurely, thanks to Carmella. Laura and I were more desperate than ever to keep September from happening. We knew something of what we were up against if we were to keep our relationship alive, but how to work it out presented a challenge. I was 26. With Laura turning 21 in September, I would be in big trouble if our dating became known. We decided to see each other during the school year after Laura returned to Wellesley. It would be easier to visit while she was away, meeting her at prearranged locations off campus to deflect detection. I was starting my first year of teaching on the Main Line of Philly. No one would be tracking where I spent my weekends anyway.

CHAPTER 15

L ooking back on it, 1967 was a pivotal year. With my first year of teaching behind me, as well as the craziness of adjusting to an academic lifestyle, Laura and I managed to maintain an intimate relationship. Our letters and phone calls were the thread through which we were able to share all kinds of things, learning about each other on a number of levels. In our letters, we had time to convey and absorb the other's thoughts.

What do the poets say? "Absence makes the heart grow fonder." Well, I was about to burst open from all that "fonder." Absence worked its magic, and I couldn't wait to see Laura.

I was well aware of the risk I was running just to be able to see her, not to mention to be alone with her. Her parents were totally oblivious of our clandestine relationship, and we both knew it had to stay that way. Somehow we'd make it all work, but it was going to take a lot of clever maneuvering to keep our relationship from being exposed…not an easy job, especially with Laura's mother Vivian..

I was making a living now in the real world, while the rest of the gang were still laboring in the Halls of Higher Learning. For all of us, summer break was like being let out of prison. Kicking off the summer social season, I organized a beach party shortly after everyone returned to the "big W," as I liked to call the restaurant. Joining forces with our comrades who worked at the amusement pavilion and theater complex on the boardwalk, we met after closing hour in the parking lot of Watson's. It was about 9:30 PM when we caravanned out, bumper to bumper, with twelve cars hightailing it to the 22nd Street boat ramp, each vehicle heavily laden with all kinds of food from the restaurant. The cooks and kitchen crew had gathered an array of delectable steaks, lobster tails, fried shrimp made with Watson's special cornflake batter, hamburgers, its famous French fries, ribs, and all kinds of goodies from the bakery…truly a feast that all but guaranteed a beach party for the ages.

I had arranged for an armada of rowboats of dubious floating ability to be "borrowed" from Bob's Boat Rental Marina, supplying the necessary water taxis we needed to sail happily off to Shooters Island. It looked like a scene out of Robinson Crusoe, when, in fact, the island I'd chosen was a glorified sandbar, one filled with tall bay grasses, home for herons and a plethora of assorted sea life. And to think, all this was just a quarter mile from the dock of the bay!

As fun things tend to be, gatherings of this type were illegal, so the big adventure was a well-guarded secret, especially from the locals and, more importantly, from JD and company. The party had been planned to be at Shooters Island for one purpose only, to find a secluded place where everyone under the age of twenty-one could drink and not get arrested. Fifty people made the short voyage unscathed; beer and food flowed like an incoming tide. We kept the music low, making sure the noise was kept to a minimum, since sound travels loud and clear over night water. Even a whisper can be heard from afar if the wind is calm. The water was still, no wind and no moonlight. It was a perfect evening, with a million stars draped over a bay that was as quiet as a seagull asleep on a piling.

Laura and I, with four of my buddies, launched the last boat from the ramp. I wanted to make sure all our guests, the majority of whom were underage, had already loaded up and launched for the island. Laura was breaking all the rules, under aged and out with a man five years older, a risk of monumental proportions if events went south. I had asked her to come with us, and the timing turned out perfectly. Her father was away on business, and her mother was in Newport, RI, having been invited to the Great Gatsby Ball to raise money for the historical society, an event close to Vi's heart. That left Ella in charge, and Laura got her permission to spend the evening with one of her friends who lived on Pleasure Avenue over by the bay.

Knowing the risk she was taking, I made sure to stay close to Laura in case problems of the police type surfaced. Laura was calm, but her eyes reflected the brightness of feeling fully alive.

We made sure no one suspected there was any spark between us. I played the big brother role, carefully looking after his kid sister. When all the rowboats had landed on the far side of the island, we disembarked and moved toward the middle of the sea grass-covered sandbar, placing food and beer kegs on blankets. Everyone spread out in different small groups, keeping a comfortable distance from each other yet forming a wide circle around the food and libations.

Laura visited with some of her girlfriends, many of whom were waitresses she got to know well, while I checked around to make sure the party was going as planned. What a blast. We laughed, we drank, and we ate as though there were no tomorrow. For a few hours, all was well with our world, the winter fading from mind with all the expectations of the summer ahead, just within our reach.

And so were the police!

I was on the east side of Shooter's Island, facing the docks from which we had launched. I heard them before I saw them...two Coast Guard cutters aiming straight for us. They were running silent, and though their engines were cut to an almost undetectable hum, I knew an invasion was coming. I figured if the cops did find out about our little island excursion, the Coast Guard would be the guys to handle the situation, but from what I could see from their fast approach, the entire boys in blue from Peck's Beach had hitched a ride on the cutters!

With barely enough time to react, I reached into my bathing-suit pocket, pulled out a cigarette lighter, and lit a fuse, setting off eighteen Roman candles that I had carefully planted, all aimed in the direction of the invading forces. It was an awesome scene, and for a split second, I knelt in place without moving, mesmerized by the craziness of what I saw. Multicolored balls of fire rocketed high in the sky in wide arches, raining down on the incoming boats, and cops ducked for cover to avoid being hit by the hot cannonball-like spheres. For a few seconds, I was in a trance; then I bolted like a rabbit. I knew exactly where Laura was, and after I yelled her name, she came running towards me.

"Don't leave me , French Fries, no matter what happens.

Just hold on, follow me and don't look back! Trust me, OK?"

"Do I have a choice? I am all yours,'" she said with a laugh and a smile, moving right along with me as I grabbed her hand, and together, we slipped silently into the water.

I was so glad I'd had the presence of mind to bring two life jackets in case of an emergency. Others had done the same, but some of the guys were too macho to think they couldn't swim a quarter-mile back to the docks in the dark. Within seconds, the entire party was in the water or in rowboats, making their escape.

I figured we'd have a fighting chance to avoid being caught if we swam to shore and then hid somewhere. But there we were, in the bay at 1 AM, swimming our way to what we hoped was a safe place, and I began second-guessing myself, not exactly good timing to do that!

Laura held onto the life jacket for dear life, using it as a raft as I did the same.

"You OK?" I asked, my words muffled by a mouth partially filled with bay water.

"Yeah, I'm good as long as I can hold on to you, so please don't let go!"

"No chance of that… I can barely make out the docks. I think the cops have landed by now, and I get the feeling they're pretty pissed off. You couldn't see it but I did. It was a funny scene. The shocked look on their faces in the blaring light of a hundred fireballs falling on them was hilarious!"

We both started to laugh, and the more we did, the funnier it got, resulting in our inhaling bay water, laughing, and sputtering and spurting like two whales playing hide and seek in the sea.

"If we swim just north of where we launched, we can climb onto someone's floating dock and make it to my car; hold on, Laura!"

"I'm really getting cold, Sax."

"Hang on, we're almost there," I said, thanking God the water was not sixty degrees. Fortunately, a very warm spring produced early warm bay water, and the temperature was in the low seventies. Despite that, the night air was cool, and the tension of trying to escape the claws of the law didn't help warm our bodies, that's for sure.

Glancing back, I could see action on the island and hear voices barking orders to those who hadn't made an escape. I wondered who'd made it and who hadn't. We managed to find a dock and pull ourselves out of the water, and we quickly made a beeline for my car. Laura shivered so badly her teeth were chattering. I pulled her close to me, trying to warm her up by rubbing my hands over her shoulders, her back. I kept pressed against her to transfer some of my body heat and there was plenty of heat to transfer. When we got in the car, I threw a beach towel over her, put on the heater, and took off down the street with my lights off and windows up. I could see up ahead of us a roadblock at the intersection.

"Laura, quick, get out of the car and walk home from here. We're trapped. The police have us blocked in, and you'll be in deep shit if they haul you in. You can't be arrested."

Laura shot back, "But what about you?"

"Please don't worry about me. I'm over twenty-one, and I'll face the music if I have too. You're a different story. Please, go and don't look back. Take the alleys home. That way, you'll stay undetected."

"Ok, be safe. Thanks for everything." One fast kiss on my cheek, and she disappeared.

I slowly inched the car to the blockade. The police made me get out of my car and hauled me into a police van that was nearly filled with party rebels and drove us to City Hall, along with, as I found out, thirty others who'd been capture in the Great Amphibious Raid.

I knew I'd be asked by my buddies how Laura and I had wound up together in our escape, so I made sure I didn't blow our cover. My story was well rehearsed.

"When the alarm sounded on the island, I took off toward the water and heard Laura right behind me, yelling, 'Slow down a little! I'm following you!' I yelled back, 'Stay down low and close to me. It's not that far a swim." I very quietly asked my buddies to keep it quiet that Laura was with us, saying that she'd be grounded for months if her parents ever found out.

Police headquarters were jammed with more young people than they knew what to do with. In fact, there were so many staff members from Watson's, Seaside Fun Spot Amusements, and Harry Blake's Boardwalk Kettle Fudge that none of the businesses would have been able to open the next day, not if we all remained in jail. So Harry posted bail at fifty bucks per head. After being released, we all slinked home, wet and very weary.

The next day, we dragged our sorry asses to work with employee productivity at an all-time low. JD had no clue about what had gone on the night before—not until some idiot from the kitchen who was not a team player spilled the beans. From then on, it was downhill in the kitchen. JD knew something was up but couldn't quite figure out why everyone was dragging their butts. When the truth came out, he was more than happy to play the drill sergeant, making the kitchen crew step into high gear. It was an evening in late June, a very hot Saturday night, when everyone on the island must have decided to eat out rather than heat up their kitchens. So, they trundled over to Watson's, eating everything that wasn't nailed down or dead. The restaurant was swamped, serving 1200 people and setting a record for so early in the season.

Laura told me, as soon as she could, that she had been able to sneak into her house, making it to her room without being discovered, or at least, that was what she thought. Turned out Ella's antennas were up. She told Laura she'd heard her come in at 2 AM, said she'd say nothing, and didn't ask where she had been, that she trusted her and left it at that.

The headline in the Philadelphia Inquirer read: "Peck's Beach Police Launch Amphibious Raid." A court hearing ensued the next day, with Harry retaining a lawyer for all thirty employees. A case was made that the police raid had occurred outside the jurisdiction of Peck's Beach. Shooter's Island was beyond the protective limits of the city, so the police had no legal authority to make the arrests. In addition, Harold Cabot, an outstanding citizen of the community and proprietor of Cabot's Department Store on the Avenue, was the owner of Shooters Island and didn't want to press charges.

The judge ruled in favor of the defendants and agreed, reluctantly, to dismiss the case after delivering a dressing down from the bench. I sneaked a look at my buddies in the row adjacent to where I was standing, catching no eyes looking back in my direction. Their faces were without expression, no smiles, and their heads were hung low.

When the ruling came down, there was an audible sigh of relief. No one could believe it, especially the underage drinkers. I had a feeling Harry Blake had worked his magic with the judge. Harry had connections all over town, and way beyond for that matter. I never did find out, and I didn't care to know. All I cared about was Laura and the fact that she hadn't gotten caught by the police and her parents. That was paramount in my mind. Everything else took second place. By the grace of God, Laura had slipped under the radar by the skin of her teeth.

JD refused to attend the court hearing because he was so pissed off. Vivian, according to Laura, didn't know about it. She was nursing a bad hangover from too much partying in Newport the night the raid had taken place. Harry was the hero of the day, of course. He collected his bail money from everyone involved and picked up the tab for the lawyer. All in all, it was a pretty nice ending to what could have been a disaster. Most of the gang were working their way through college, and an arrest with a record written in indelible ink on a rap sheet would have really screwed things up big time. It would have had far-reaching implications, and when we all rendezvoused the night after the court hearing at Gail's house, individual escape stories were relived and somewhat embellished in great detail. We laughed so hard I thought I'd double over. It was our way of letting the tension dissipate, but when the roar of the crowd faded and we were left alone with our private thoughts, I felt we knew just how fortunate we were... We'd gotten away with our fun and frolic this time and not without help from a loyal ally, one Harry Blake. Any lessons learned? I doubt it.

Ever since the hurricane the previous year, Laura and I had been inseparable, convincingly acting out our charade on Shooter's island and then in public, managing to keep everyone off guard about our relationship.

We were adults at this point. Laura turning twenty-one and me turning twenty-six. It's crazy how that space between our ages was not that big a deal. The first time I laid eyes on Laura, she was sixteen, and I was twenty-two. She was a junior in high school when I was a senior in college. The age difference was huge then, but as time moved on, it didn't seem so important.

The coming summer could not come fast enough for me. This was the first time Laura would not be away at camp or in Europe or somewhere else her mother would find to hide her or, at least, remove her so she wouldn't have the burden of overseeing her during the summer. Laura was actually going to do some small jobs for JD in the kitchen and in "Take Out," the place where customers picked up dinner orders, avoiding the crowds and saving money while enjoying the same outstanding food. This way, we'd see each other at work on a somewhat daily basis. Our hooking up after work was calculated on a minute-by-minute basis. Vi was always coming and going, dividing her time between living upstairs at Watson's or her home on the Platinum Coast, one of the most upscale beach front sections on the island. Fortunately, her social life consumed much of her time, allowing us to continually scheme about where to meet after hours, if only for a few stolen minutes.

As things turned out, even our stolen minutes were snatched away by Vi. She must have had some sixth sense about us. She set a trap that we fell right into. It was a weekday evening, and the restaurant had been slow that night, so I said I'd hang in and close up the place. The last customers had left, and I was checking to see if the waitresses side work was completed. Laura surprised me when she came into the dining room as I was turning out the lights. I took her arm and pulled her into the little broom closet, where we had our first kiss and where we often went to duplicate as many kisses as possible.

Laura had said her mother was out for the evening, but in fact, Vi had no intention of going out. Instead, she positioned herself at the first landing of the center hall stairs and listened while totally out of sight. She heard me whisper, "Laura, come here, honey," as I whisked her daughter into the closet.

When we emerged a few minutes later, quiet as church mice, who should be looking down on us from the lower landing but…Attila the Hun, Vi, live and in person. Actually, Vi was a beautiful woman if you didn't know her. People used words like stunning, captivating, sensual…all true if viewed as a package. Interesting how her beauty seemed to fade once her mouth opened.

"What the hell are you two doing?"

"Mother, we've been dating, and we—"

"Don't bother with an explanation! Get your ass up these stairs, daughter! And you, Mr. Sax, I'll deal with you later!"

I stood there, stunned, watching Laura slip away from me and into the clutches of her domineering mother.

Laura gave me a scared look of concern and then ran up the steps as ordered, feeling diminished under the thumb of her mother, even at the age of twenty-one. I couldn't relate. When I was twenty-one, my mother had been the total opposite of Vi.

I heard the upstairs door to the family compound slam shut. I didn't make a move, unsure how to handle the situation from this point on. What I really wanted to do was climb the stairs, beat the door down, grab Vi by her broom handle, toss her to the floor, and yell, "I'm in love with your daughter! Age makes no difference, and we have every intention of continuing dating with or without your consent!"

But I didn't… I wimped out, head hung low. I turned and walked into the kitchen, only to be confronted by JD staring down at me from a six-foot ladder he had climbed to fix an exhaust fan. "I heard part of that."

I answered, deflated. "How could you miss ? Vi has a way of screaming without screaming, if you know what I mean."

"Sure do."

JD was always at the wrong spot at just the right time. For him, of course.

"Got advice, boss?"

"I sure do. Keep your cool and let me see what I can do. Then, looking at me squarely, he asked, "Sax, do you think I didn't know about you and Laura? I'm her father. A father knows when his daughter is in love. I could see it in her eyes whenever she looked at you; it didn't take a rocket scientist to see that. It reminded me of a love I had... Brings back memories. I'll go to bat for you because of two things and two things only...I trust my daughter, and I trust you."

I was speechless. These were words coming from a man who guarded very closely the limited words he chose to use. It was like a message from Moses on the mountain top. JD, up on the highest rung of the ladder, looking down on me from the grease-stained ceiling, proclaiming words of both wisdom and encouragement. Amazing, just amazing and I could not have been encouraged more.

I stood there, looking up, not sure how to answer. "Your trust means everything to me, JD! I won't let you down. We love each other very much, and I have no intention of breaking Laura's heart or hurting her in any way."

JD nodded with a look of approval as he slowly descended the ladder. No more was said. He went downstairs to the dungeon, and I walked out the rear door into the pouring rain. JD did confront Vi about our situation; however, Vi was ready for battle, and for JD, the battle was lost before it began. She let loose with one of her drug-induced tirades with alcohol for an appetizer. Relentless about seeing things her way only, she was very clear that we were not to see each other except at work. JD lacked the balls to fight her head on. From what Laura told me, he decided on a more passive-aggressive move… "I've got your backs covered; steady as she goes." Trouble was, Vi was anything but steady. She dealt with her demons by coating them with pain killers so she didn't have to feel anything…and they were all too happy to oblige.

I didn't see Laura after that for several days. Vi took her to New York on a shopping spree, probably trying to ease the tension and pacify her daughter….who knows what conniving thoughts lurked within that woman's crazy, convoluted mind.

I was bereft, and spent the days turning over options in my mind. How could Laura and I have a future together unless we ran away and got married? The timing was off. I was just settling into my career, and Laura really needed to finish her education. It was a dilemma without an apparent solution.

After Vi and Laura took off for the Big Apple, Ella surprised me by coming down for dinner. We sat down at her favorite table on the Porch. She had a way about her that soothed the savage soul, and boy, did I need soothing. I decided to confide in her about Laura and me, so I painted a word picture, one good enough for a novel, about how we'd fallen in love. I left nothing out.

When I finally got quiet, Ella looked right into me, not saying a word. Her sweet face and soft brown eyes betrayed her feelings. A slight smile turned her lips up just a bit at the corners, as though she were taking in the sweet lingering smells of a warm South Carolina morning and it pleased her soul.

"Child, you ain't about to surprise this old lady. I saw it comin' as sure as the tide rolls in. You think you two can pull the wool over these tired eyes? Ain't no way."

"Were we that obvious, Ella?"

"Sure was to me. You see, child, I know Laura better than you know yourself. I helped raise her from the time she laid eyes on the world. I was there at her birth, when she poked her little face out, lookin' like a head of cabbage. She's like my own. Wish I'd been blessed to have a child, but the Lord knew it wasn't the best for me. It breaks my heart to see how Miss Vi treats her. It ain't right, and it makes me angry, but I don't say nothin'.... Keeps my mouth shut, that's what I does."

"Yea, seems that's what we all do when it comes to Vi. We just keep our mouths shut and let her get away with all the crap she dishes out. Ella, Vi's half in the bag most of the time when I'm talking to her. She'll call down to the front desk on the house phone and rag on JD like he was the worst person God ever created. I don't get it. She's got everything a person could want in life, a good husband, beautiful daughter, and a famous restaurant in one of the best resort towns on the East Coast. What more could you want? But she sure is one unhappy lady. What are we going to do?"

"Take it slow, slow as molasses in January. Breathe easy, child, and let time work its magic. Good things come to those who waits. The Lord knows all about your love, honey. Trust Him for guidance."

It's what I loved about this true servant of God...a better friend you could never have, devoted beyond all expectations, and trust? It wasn't even up for consideration. It was a given. One look in those eyes, and you knew the word "disloyal" could never have found a home in her spirit.

"I do, Ella, I really do. I prayed I would find a girl like Laura long before I knew she existed. I know our love is as real as it gets, and I'm not willing to let anyone, particularly Vi, drive a wedge between us, no matter what I have to do."

CHAPTER 16

"Sax, honey, let me try as best I can to unravel some of the past, and maybe, just maybe, it will shed some light on why Miss Vi is the way she is… I ain't makin' up excuses now… We is the way we is. Us poor souls on this here earth carry a bag full of hurts and pains, and Vi is no exception…only she don't know it. That's why we all need Jesus, child, to forgive us, wipe our sins away, and make us new again."

I marveled at Ella, a remarkable woman of considerable substance. Baptist preacher's daughter number five in a line of seven, she fought hard for her independence, leaving South Carolina to find her way in the world somewhere "up north." Her travels took her to New Hope, PA, where she was able to find employment at a tea house right on Main Street. She didn't have experience when it came to the finer things in life, but she sure knew how to cook. And cook she did.

Adrienne's mother instantly recognized the gifts Ella possessed that went far beyond cooking. It was the gentle spirit Ella exuded, and as a result, she embraced Ella as though she were a part of the family, encouraging her to be a friend to Addi. That way, she would be a companion and look after her while Addi's mom was overseeing the restaurant.

Leaning over the table, as though hard of hearing, I homed in on Ella's compassionate face, not willing to miss a single sterling word. It had been a while since she'd opened up to me, and these rare encounters were like lost treasure found in the depth of the sea, treasure brought to the surface in time to garner the gold. One snap of the winch, and the treasure might sink back into the deep, possibly vanishing forever. She had my full attention.

"Now, I can't rightly remember where I was going with all this," she said. Her momentary lapse of memory was but a heartbeat in length. Ella quickly regained her thoughts and segued to another time and place.

The year was 1938.

In 1938, the wedding of Adrienne and Stephen was a private affair held at Watson's with only a few close friends in attendance. Absent were Stephen's parents, for several reasons. From the start, they'd been highly critical of the relationship; a widow with a daughter in her late teens didn't fit their image. And they were suspicious as to why Stephen had moved back in town after his absence for so long. They felt he was being blindsided by the idea of marrying a woman with money and social status, which was odd because Stephen came from both money and class. But also his parents never let go of the fact that he'd dodged military duty when he was young.

As for Vi, she was livid with rage when she arrived home from Europe in May. To say she was devastated to learn of her mother's marriage to Stephen was to vastly understate her emotional state of mind. Addi knew she had to travel to New York and meet the HMS Queen Elizabeth when it arrived. It was the only way she could solicit an explanation and try to control the situation as best she could.

The arrival section of the moored steamer was overcrowded, packed tight with family and friends anxiously waiting for the passengers to disembark, jockeying for position to get a first glance of their loved one, be it family, friend, or guest. Somehow, through the mass of humanity between them, Addi managed to catch a glimpse of Vi descending the gangplank to the pier. Running to greet her and with arms extended for a hug, the look on Vi's face stopped Addi cold. Vi's frigid stare pierced her mother like a dagger, and her expression was devoid of life or love. Addi's hug died in midair; no such move from Vi was forthcoming. Huck, who had been at Addi's side, reached down and retrieved the luggage as Vi made sure he received a hug. The gesture didn't go unnoticed by her mother.

The ride back to Peck's Beach was mostly silent and definitely tense. The few words spoken between mother and daughter put together would not form a compound sentence. The future was not looking very promising, leaving Addi very depressed and at a loss to figure out how to bring healing into their relationship. As was often the case, Addi would turn to Ella when events got out of control.

That evening in her apartment, Addi called Ella to join her and said, " I need to share some things weighing heavily on me right now. I treasure your discernment."

"Thanks Addi, I'm listening."

Addi opened up about seeing Vivian again at the ship, the deadly ride home and the depression she feels settling in again.

From social clubs to historic committees, the town ladies were in high gear. Gossip ran its usual course, traveling down the same path of reasoning as that held by Stephen's parents. But it fell on deaf ears with Addi, who had faced harsher critics than the whispers and innuendos of the town magpies. Addi was always able to compartmentalize her thinking, so she put all frivolous gossip behind her and moved on.

Teaching Stephen the restaurant business from front door to back, and everything in between, was challenging enough. There was no room for anything unproductive. As time went by, Addi and Stephen developed into an unbeatable team, building the business to even higher levels of success. Stephen became totally immersed in entrepreneurship, and his love for Addi was only as deep as he was capable of giving. He had a gift for "carpe diem," seizing the day, which he accomplished with aplomb, and the benefits paid off.

He was well aware going into this relationship that there were more important things in life than love. Addi was, in large part, a key to Stephen's emerging success and respect throughout the town. He was basically disinherited from his father's wealth, and the gossips knew it. Addi brought a lifestyle and prestige that would have taken him years to build on his own, if at all. Of course, he had his parent's pedigree, a yoke he was banned from carrying. Stephen had a very poor relationship with his father. Gregory was the favored child, the firstborn by two minutes, who could do no wrong, and Stephen detested his father for viewing his brother as perfect, the favored child. Stephen came to resent Gregory to the point that he turned in a totally opposite direction.

He came to resent Gregory and since perfection was unattainable, he decided to lower the bar to meet his father's expectations. He became what his father saw him to be, a person not indebted but entitled. And it was to that end, entitlement, that Stephen seized the opportunity to embrace the Watson package for all it was worth.

Through this period in her life, Vi was bitter and unforgiving toward her mother for stealing Stephen from her. She vowed to have nothing to do with her mother, let alone Stephen. It was a toxic relationship, to say the least.

In the summer of 1940, Adrienne invited Andrew Todd III to dinner at Watson's. He was the 27-year-old son of Andrew and Margaret Todd Jr. of Villanova, PA. Andrew Sr. was the founder of Todd Industries, producer of some of the world's finest military weaponry, a major company located just outside Philadelphia's city limits, which was chosen by Vought-Sikorsky Aircraft Division to manufacture helicopters. The Todd family had been close friends of Addi's ever since the Normandie Hotel days. Andrew III stopped in to visit Addi when he was in town for an overnight. It was a quick trip, but he loved the shore, and Peck's Beach brought back childhood memories that were recaptured every time he put his feet on sand or took a stroll along the boards. He had business at the Air Force base in Absecon, just northwest of Atlantic City, and he expected to finish his work by the end of the week, allowing him the rare pleasure of slipping into town without anyone trailing him.

Once seated at Addi's favorite table for two on the Porch, Andrew caught her up on all the latest family news, and she did the same. Vivian's name never came up, a fact that didn't go unnoticed.

"Aunt Addi?" he asked, using a title he bestowed upon very few close friends. "You haven't mentioned Vivian; how is she, and what's she up to these days? She was like my little sister growing up."

Taken a bit off guard, but not surprised by the question, Addi said, "Andrew, I didn't want to get into all the details with you about Vivian, but let's just say we've had a falling out, and it's a major one. Vivian has not forgiven me for marrying Stephen, and the result has been a lot of bitterness and hurt on Vivian's part. I love my daughter very much, and I long for reconciliation, but we're far from that right now. Forgiveness is a process, but I don't think Vivian wants to even entertain such a thought."

"But why wouldn't Vivian want you to be happy.? It doesn't make sense. Something's not right," he responded.

"Andrew, the root problem here is deception. Vivian believes I intentionally took Stephen away from her while she was in Europe. It's not that simple, nothing ever is, but she doesn't see it that way."

"Aunt Addi, if it's not being too presumptuous, what way was it?"

So, Addi told Andrew a condensed version of how events unfolded that led to her and Stephen falling in love after Stephen realized he did not reciprocate the same depth of commitment that Vivian felt for him. She opened up to Andrew because she trusted him explicitly. He was no stranger to her, and she had been in his life periodically for more than twenty-seven years. He had matured into a fine young man, and maybe she confided in him with multiple motives. Who knew the reasons, but here they were, sharing confidences, with age being no barrier.

"Vivian!"

Vivian appeared, interrupting the conversation.

Andrew quickly went to his feet and gave her a big hug. She, in turn, embraced him warmly. Then she turned to face her mother.

A blind person could have mustered up more expression. "I'm only here to get some of my clothes upstairs; I still have a key, unless you've changed the locks, so I hope you aren't inconvenienced by my sudden appearance. I can see you're busy trying to steal somebody else's man again." And with that cutting remark, she took off for the center hall.

She hadn't gotten ten steps away when Andrew, whose mouth had fallen open in disbelief at her crassness, followed her into the hall. The fallout from Vivian's bombshell lingered over the table like an incoming fog. Addi sat frozen in her seat as one small tear slowly traveled down her flushed cheek, the only evidence of anything melting.

Andrew caught up with Vivian just as she was ascending the staircase. "Vivian, wait," he said.

She turned and looked down from the first landing, "Don't get involved, Drew. You have no idea what that woman has done to me."

"Ok, point taken, but I do know this, she's still your mother. She loves you no matter what, and someday you two are going to have to make your peace. That's it; I'm done except to say, do you have any plans for tomorrow night?

She coyly answered, "Thought you'd never ask, especially from this vantage point looking down on you…my favorite position." She relished having the advantage over anyone in any situation.

Andrew's hands gently clutched the newel post, looking up at Vi like Rhett Butler had looked up at Scarlett O'Hara in Gone with the Wind. He shot back, "Oh, it surprised me too" then he continued, "I'd pick you up at seven if I knew where you lived."

"Twelfth and West, Northeast corner" came the answer while Vi ascended the stairs.

Andrew turned to go back to the table, but he glanced up to see Vivian retreat to the second floor. He couldn't help but think what a stunning woman she had become… glossy, coal-black hair, deep blue eyes, and with a figure like Grace Kelly. Possessed of her mother's sophistication, but she was wild and untamed. Andrew was a happy man just thinking about the next evening. But right now, he had to console Addi, which he was not looking forward to. But ever the lady, Addi had composed herself, and when Andrew took his seat again, she apologized for her daughter's rudeness.

"No need to soften the blow, Addi. Vivian was totally out of line, which I tried to tell her when I abruptly left and went after her. She said to stay out of it. I got nowhere except a backhanded "yes" to my asking her out."

Addi didn't respond, so he filled the silent gap in conversation by looking straight into Addi's eyes and said, "I really want to try to understand her more, now that I know your side of the story. Since I'm somewhat detached from the emotional aspects of all this, I figured I'd take your daughter to dinner and see where the evening goes."

Addi warned, "Good luck. Be prepared, the evening could go down the drain fast. She's not the same young girl you grew up with, Andrew, and I'd hate to see you get hurt. There's a Praying Mantis underneath all that beauty, and you know what they do to their mates." She shot him a look that said it all and then slowly moved her right forefinger across her throat. "I know what she's capable of doing. Despite what you may think, I love my daughter, but there are times I really don't like her, and this is one of those times."

Andrew's date the next night with Vivian progressed in a way he never would have guessed.

They hit it off as if they had been together for years. Not a word was said about Addi. Andrew felt he had said enough, so the subject was taboo, far from forgotten but just not discussed. They settled into enjoying each other's company, reminiscing about the years gone by and how the families were such good friends. Vivian told him how she'd had a childhood crush on him, that she'd often dreamed of him "riding in on a black stallion, like in the movies" and carrying her off to some place far, far away.

Later that evening, at the Bala Inn along the bay in Somers Point, tongues were gradually loosened by wine. The Inn was a very popular dinner and dance establishment with food, live music daily performed by local groups at the edge of the bay. The music worked its magic, drawing them closer together. Andrew reached over the table, took hold of Vi's hand and led her to the dance floor while the band slowed it down with "I'll Never Smile Again" and whispered in her ear, "Maybe I really am that rider on a black stallion after all!"

The daughter Addi had described and the woman he took to bed that night could not possibly have been the same person.

Love is like a diamond. It has many facets, and sometimes one of those facets reflects a beam so intensely that all the others are absorbed into its light.

Blinded as they were, both Vivian and Stephen believed marriage was in their future, and in the interim year, Vi and her mother worked on reconciliation one step at a time. Loving Andrew made it possible because Vi slowly began to realize how immature her obsession with Stephen had been. Her renewed relationship and budding love for Drew defused her rage and bitterness over Stephen until it faded away, and her emotions pulled her in a totally new direction.

On October 7th, 1941, Andrew and Vi were married, and the wedding was first class all the way. The guest list was a "who's who" of both Peck's Beach and Villanova. As it turned out, half the social registry of Philadelphia's Main Line was in attendance. The reception was held at the Atlantic City Country Club, followed by a brunch the next day at Watson's. Then it was off to Barbados for their honeymoon. It was a happy time for everyone.

But like everything else in Vi's life, her timing for happiness could not have been worse.

Two months later, Pearl Harbor was bombed, and WWII began. In an instant, Vi's future and security were lost, along with a nation ill prepared for war.

Andrew was drafted immediately into the Naval Air Force, leaving Vi alone in a town where she hadn't had time to open her mail, let alone meet new friends. She decided to lease their small apartment in Bryn Mawr and return to Peck's Beach, making absolutely sure she found her own place to live. The idea of living with her mother and Stephen was never a consideration. Just the thought made her sick, reconciliation had its limits, after all. As a war bride, Vi had to make it on her own emotionally. Financially, she was golden, because the Todds were exceptionally wealthy and made sure Vi was well cared for. Very few people really knew Vi, which is exactly how she wanted it. She was complicated, and she drew strength from the misery she created around herself. Vi was a mixture of loveliness and grace one minute, pure selfishness and venom the next. It caught people off guard, as well as dissolved friendships. No one wanted to be on the receiving end of Vi's fury. Once experienced, there was no desire for more.

Vivian found work as a volunteer in the war effort. The Todds were very pleased at Vi's successful efforts to support herself despite their available monetary offers. They still remembered the early years when they'd been penniless, though it was a memory they wanted to forget. Being poor was such a yoke to bear; it was best left in the vault of things you cared not to remember again. The move back to Peck's Beach made Vi feel somewhat secure, while knowing full well there was no such thing as security, when you're a war bride. At least the surroundings were familiar and under the circumstances, that feeling of comfort was enough.

Vivian had a childhood friend, Alice, from the yacht club, with whom she had remained friends and who also shared her tough situation as a war bride. Alice owned a boarding house on Central Avenue at the south end of the island and was looking to find someone to help her run the business. She had converted her three-story, ten-bedroom, Edwardian-style home into an inn. Alice had some creative ideas when it came to interior decorating, as well as with building a customer base, but she bit off more than she could chew. She needed help, and Vi became the perfect addition to the team. So, during the summer months of the war years, Alice and Vi managed the Mallard Hotel. A ton of work but lots of fun too. The women were an ideal match. Alice was very kind and interested in people; Vi was more businesslike, managing every penny that crossed her desk, showing no patience when it came to people owing them money. She was tough, known on the streets by some as "Hatchet Lady."

For the most part, it was a cash business. But cash flow dwindled when maintenance and employee payroll outstripped the income. As the war years lengthened, they had their effect on occupancy, with the tourist business slowly tapering off. To keep her from worrying, or so she convinced herself, she always painted a rosy picture whenever Alice would ask. It became somewhat apparent that tourism was down, but, being an optimistic person, Alice always looked on the bright side of things; she could never entertain the thought of losing the inn.

What Alice didn't know was that Vi could see they'd be in a non-reversible financial position by the fall of '44, a fact she kept to herself. So she cut a deal with a wealthy friend of her mother's, the Howards. It was simple, as she put it: "Stay in the background and be ready to make your move as soon as I let you know when the collapse of the Mallard's about to become a reality. After the bank has foreclosed, you show up and buy the inn at a rock-bottom price. The value of the property is in the land, which will appreciate literally overnight the day after the war ends. With all our troops returning from foreign lands, housing will be at a premium. We split the profits."

The deal was struck.

In October of '44, the bank foreclosed on the inn after Vi did what she could to save it from happening, a lost cause from the start. At the proceedings, a well-heeled gentleman known only by one person in the courtroom stepped forward and bought the property for an amount equal to the taxes owed and all the arrears in payments. Alice was devastated by the reality of it all, and she was sincerely considering leaving Peck's Beach to return to her roots in Philadelphia. Leaving the courtroom, Vi tried her best to comfort Alice, who, at that point, was quietly crying. Making their exit, Vi caught the mystery gentleman's eye as he stood by the door. In a fleeting second, to the unobservant, the smallest of smiles on Vi's lips could have been easily overlooked.

On some level in Vi's mind, what she had done was not deception; it was strictly a business deal. She rationalized it from every angle possible, always coming out innocent. Her way of thinking? It would have happened anyway. The fact that she walked away with a bunch of cash from her clandestine deal bothered her not at all.

To insulate herself from projected rejection and possible loss of her G.I. husband, Vi reached out to various male friends to fill the void. She was haunted by visions of naval officers knocking at her door to deliver a message of death that made her legs turn to jelly, the sheer weight of the news causing her to collapse to the floor.

No problem—she learned to take care of the pain; it couldn't hurt her anymore if she didn't allow herself to feel. Should the "angel of death" show up, she was numb already.

Vivian lived her life like tomorrow would never come, and she made no excuses for it. She partied till dawn but never cheated on her husband. Contrary to her perceived reputation, Vivian remained faithful to Andrew. On some level, she couldn't cross that line... Infidelity trumped a marriage, whether good or bad every time, so she wasn't about to travel down that road.

On June 6 of '45, the morning paper landed on Vi's front sidewalk along with Andrew, both announcing the end of the war. Against all odds, he'd made it home in one physical piece, but Vivian could tell he was not the same man who had left.

For the next two years, from 1945 to '46, Andrew and Vi tried to make a marriage out of a love that had little chance to mature. They were different people, and neither liked what they saw in each other. They had become strangers. Andrew suffered badly from night terrors, reliving the carnage of his comrades on the ship he'd lost, followed by the screams of the sailors who'd jumped overboard after a torpedo hit only to be eaten alive by frenzied sharks. Vivian no longer knew the man who'd gone to battle. She couldn't possibly connect with what he was going through, and she didn't try. She was too self-absorbed to even try. It was always all about her. It didn't take long before they found themselves slipping into a life of separate living, both emotionally and physically, the result a type of informal separation. Vi spent most of her time on Peck's Beach, while Andrew worked every waking hour flying between Todd Industries' local office in suburban Philadelphia and the Flight Development Center in San Diego, CA.

There was a lot of company pressure on Andrew to be at the forefront of research and development of the newly designed helicopters for the government. The world political scene was heating up again, and Todd Industries once gain became a major player in the war game. At this point, Vi was a wife in name only. Andrew still held onto the hope they would somehow work things out, though the hope was thinly disguised. He was caught between loving Vi and hating what she had become: a woman detached to the degree that her emotions never seemed to surface beyond her skin.

John David Chandler, or JD, a relative to Conrad Chandler, the hotel magnate bearing his name, arrived in Peck's Beach with a definite agenda on his mind. He stayed at the Asteria Hotel for a fortnight because he was engaged in scouting new locations for the Chandler Hotel chain. JD was thirty-five, a bachelor, and employed by the Chandler Real Estate Development Division out of Newport, RI, where he resided.

He'd graduated from Cornell University, the school of hospitality, spending more than several years paying his dues by successfully managing several prominent hotels. When Chandler Corporate headquarters offered him a chance at a lucrative career change, John grabbed it. With both parents gone in a private plane crash when he was twenty-five and a sister who chose to be anonymous, he had the freedom to travel wherever he was required to go and was without any ties to the domestic life so many of his friends were tethered to.

CHAPTER 17

While on the island, JD made an appointment to interview with Adrienne Watson in hopes to learn about the success of Watson's and its influence on the commercial environment of Peck's Beach. The restaurant was a major player, and an in-depth knowledge of its origins would help the Chandler Corporation to make an informed decision regarding the development of a new concept in the hospitality industry…a version of their flagship hotels that they would call "cottages," clusters of small units marketed to the "upper end" clientele.

JD and Adrienne met as planned, a dinner for two on the Porch, and the meeting was moving along nicely until Vi entered the room.

"Hello, Mother. I figured you'd be on the Porch having dinner. You're such a creature of habit."

"Well, my dear, this 'creature,' as you put it, is having a business meeting. Seems as though you also have a few habits of your own, like suddenly appearing at inopportune times."

John Chandler was on his feet at this point, mesmerized by the beauty standing before him.

"Mother dear, where are your manners? Who, might I ask, is this handsome man?"

"Oh, forgive me. John, this is my daughter, Vivian… Vi, meet John Chandler." Lightning could not have produced a stronger charge!

JD stumbled over his own words, trying to speak coherently while at the same time practically speechless at this lovely vision whose hand he was now shaking, not wanting to let go.

Vi never took her eyes off him. "It's OK. You can let go now. I think we're done meeting."

JD was really embarrassed. " I am so sorry. I was so fixed upon your beauty I completely disconnected from everything else around me."

"Well, that's about the nicest compliment I've had come my way for quite a spell now. And I'll accept it on one condition."

"Name it."

"That I return the compliment. You're just about the handsomest man I've had the pleasure of meeting since my husband left me."

Addi sat there listening to them both verbally sparring, but when she heard Vi say her husband had left her, she nearly fell out of her chair. She shot her daughter a look that could kill, but Vi knew her mother and she also knew full well that silence from Addi's lips would validate her lie. There were way too many worms in that can to open it now.

JD faked a concerned look on his face, but immediately his mind zeroed in on what she didn't say. He took the bait like a shark to chum, and Vi knew it the moment he looked so concerned.

"Vi, any chance that after your mother and I have concluded our pleasurable meeting, we could have a drink somewhere? This evening has been like dessert, but a yes from you would be icing on the cake."

"Well, aren't you the silver-tongued one. But you'll die of thirst before any drink is found on this tee-totaling island. God bless those founding fathers, they made sure to hide their sins. Not a drop of alcohol in our town can be found in public, but plenty lies behind closed doors."

"Maybe all that will change someday, but before it does, let's go over to the Bala Inn. It's in Somers Point and the perfect place for that elusive drink. I understand the founding fathers were known to escape to that whaling town watering hole themselves on occasion."

"How right you are, and I've been known to pay a visit myself to the old inn from time to time. Sounds like a fine idea."

"Wonderful! Let me finish here," he said, motioning to her mother, "and when we're done, I'll meet you in the center hall. I'm quite sure Addi will be glad to find you wherever you may be."

"I'll be upstairs, powdering my nose. Just give a whistle." And with that, she took her leave.

JD sat back down and stared into space, trying to collect his thoughts and make some sense out of what had just happened.

"You've now met my daughter. She has that effect on men," Addi said.

"You mean it's that obvious?"

"Quite so, I'm afraid."

Addi had seen that look before, a dazed expression as though one had just been shot with a pistol loaded with lust.

"Your daughter is lovely, and I want the chance to get to know her."

Addi didn't respond to JD's last remark. Instead, she got up from the table, at which point John rushed over to pull her chair out, saying, "Thank you very much, Adrienne, for a delightful dinner and, even more so, for the conversation. I really appreciate your willingness to share your thoughts about the business and your perspective on the future of Peck's Beach. Hopefully, we'll have a chance to meet again."

"I share your thoughts, John, and I thank you for a most enjoyable evening as well. I'm quite sure we shall meet again," Addi replied with a slightly devilish look in her eye as if she knew what the rest of his evening was going to be like.

"Now, enough of these serious matters of building empires, as it were. Follow me to my suite, and you can begin another adventure, one with much more mystery and risk than any hotel chain could ever imagine."

Following Addi up the stairs, JD couldn't resist saying, "No risk, no reward."

And what an adventure it was. Neither of them could ever have imagined what roads their lives would travel, what twists and turns lay ahead. From the moment they met, they never looked back. The lust, the love, the laughter and tears were all right there for the taking. They knew they were running a risk that could prove fatal, yet both were determined to face the consequences come hell or high water.

Their love affair went on for six months, and they cared nothing about who knew. Just add adultery to the long chain of whispers uttered since the great fire of 1927.

Addi avoided even asking the hard questions. It wasn't worth the fight.

Vi received a short note from Andrew asking her to come to their apartment in Bryn Mawr. He would be in town for a short stay and had something important to discuss. Curiosity more than anything moved her to reluctantly make the trip, and when she arrived at their place, Andrew was comfortably ensconced in his favorite chair with drink in one hand and a cigarette in the other.

"Please, don't get up. Wouldn't want you to spill your drink."

"Same sarcastic tongue, I see, nothing ever changes, does it, Vi?"

"In our case, not really. We seem to have an appetite for degrading each other."

"Can't we, just for tonight, try to meet halfway, try to get along without filleting each other?"

Vi made herself a drink and took a seat opposite Andrew, next to the fireplace.

"I'm listening."

He said, "I've been handed a major promotion at Todd Industries, one I would not want to turn down, but it involves moving to San Diego."

The idea of moving to California with a man she did not love was absolutely not going to happen, no chance in hell. The edge of Vi's glass barely touched her lips when the "good news" of a move came floating through the air and landed like a ton of bricks in her lap. In slow motion, she lowered her glass.

"Andrew, let me say this as calmly and with as little sarcasm as I can. Moving for me is out of the question. Go if you must, but I'll stay in Peck's Beach. Why would you want me to go with you when you know full well our marriage is one in name only? We haven't slept in the same bed for months. I don't love you, Andrew, not the way you want me to, and as hard as that is to comprehend, I don't think you love me either."

Andrew got up and came over to Vi as she stood up to face him.

"Vi, the trouble is, I've always loved you, but you've just never been able to allow yourself to feel it."

"Andrew, that has not always been true, and you know it."

He reached gently to embrace her, and for some reason, Vi let him do it, and then he kissed her. During their entire screwed-up marriage, the one thing they were always able to agree on was making love... Who knows, maybe it was the only time Vi could connect with anything worth feeling. But on that night, Vi had unrestricted sex with her estranged husband, and she had no clue why.

Lying in bed, Andrew looked over at Vi. "Wow, what happened there?"

"I don't know, but it isn't ever going to repeat itself. Make a note of that."

"Why, 'cause you couldn't feel that either?"

"So perceptive of you." Vi got out of bed, put her clothes back on, and went into the kitchen to fix a drink.

The phone rang by the bed; having not moved, Andrew fumbled for the receiver.

"Hello… Yes, this is Skitters, old buddy… This must be Matt… No one's called me that in years." After this instant recognition of his childhood friend's voice, the conversation continued.

What Andrew missed was the look of absolute terror on Vi's ashen face. Her body was frozen, and her mind was trying desperately to put together the fragmented pieces of an event that had taken place a lifetime ago…and then the pieces fit into a full image, resurrecting the picture of a frightened little girl with her dearest friend in all the world…the town, Peck's Beach…the place, under the boardwalk with Sandy… year, 1927.

"Oh my God, it was you!" with that, Vi rushed into the bedroom with a knife in her hand and blindly lunged toward Andrew, who dropped the phone and made a quick move to get out of bed. Her cry of utter anguish became the audible sound of all the years of silent agony. Andrew's image danced in her head, forming an image of a ghostlike little boy…one second appearing, vanishing the next. Suddenly it all materialized, a boy long ago with matches in his hands.

Andrew understood nothing of what was happening. There was a look of total shock on his face as he successfully blocked Vi's attempt to put a knife through his chest. Vi swung wildly, trying in vain to desperately grab hold of those elusive matchsticks, yelling incoherently about flames and fear and death.

And then it hit him…she couldn't know…no one knew…no one except Matt, and he would never talk.

"Vivian, what's happening? What's wrong?"

Andrew tightened his grip on her shoulders and looked directly into her eyes, which revealed a horror that told him she knew. There was no longer a dark place to hide.

His deeply guarded secret moved irreversibly into the light.

"You know, don't you?"

With tears streaming down her face, fighting to loosen Andrew's grasp on both of her arms, she screamed, "You son of a bitch! All these years, I've lived under a cloud of suspicion, and all the time, it was you, Skitters, the name I would have sold my soul to remember, but couldn't! I hate you, I hate you, you vile murderer, killer of young and old. Coward, coward, coward."

Andrew hit her in the face with a force that sent her slamming into the bedroom wall, knocking her out cold. He threw his clothes in a duffel bag, grabbed his briefcase, and headed for the door. Glancing back, he saw Vi struggling to sit up, looking dazed and confused, blood running down her face from a mangled lip. With total detachment, he slammed the door shut, shattering forever the life they had shared so intimately long ago.

Badly shaken, Vi literally crawled to the bathroom on all fours. Pulling her body up by holding onto the sink, she got a glimpse of her image in the mirror, and then the tears came.

Her hatred was beyond rage. "That bastard will burn in hell, so help me God!."

Struck with the reality of it all, Vi had to make a plan, one that explained the fact that she'd come to Bryn Mawr without anyone knowing it. She'd tell people she tripped and fell outside her apartment while coming down the stairs. No big deal, happens to people all the time. Fortunately, when Andrew had thrown the punch, it hadn't landed high enough to give her a black eye. The other bruises were in places no one could see.

The drive back to Peck's Beach gave her plenty of time to figure out her next move.

CHAPTER 18

Andrew was going to suffer, just like she had suffered all these years. For an hour, her mind was filled with diabolical plots to grind Andrew Todd into the ground like one would stomp on a roach crawling along the floor. Revenge is a meal best served cold, and she was going to relish serving him dinner.

Andrew caught the red eye back to San Diego, his life in shambles. He didn't know how he was going to pull it together again. He knew Vi didn't love him, but now her indifference had been replaced by hate and terror. He'd seen it in her eyes, eyes revealing her tortured soul.

It was a rainy, raw Monday on Peck's Beach, with winds out of the northeast, almost as though nature herself sensed an inevitable change. When the phone rang, Vi picked it up to hear her mother-in-law say, "Vi, our son is dead."

She stood motionless, the receiver still held to her ear for what seemed like forever. She was able to respond with only one word, "How?" Then, in halting sentences accompanied by sobbing, the details were relayed.

Andrew had been killed flying a test helicopter. Circumstances were mysterious at best. Todd Industries was launching an investigation, and the official statement showed pilot error. Vi didn't buy that for a minute. Andrew was the best pilot there was at experimental flight. No way was it pilot error.

His body was brought home to Villanova. The funeral was attended by a myriad of Main Line blue bloods and industry personnel from both coasts.

Vi went through the paces in a state of numbness that was interpreted as grief when, in fact, it had nothing to do with grief. It was all about the emotional wreck she had become. She was in limbo… She couldn't vindicate herself from her past, from people's suspicions in particular, and she lived with unresolved anger over Drew's death…anger rising from her lost chance to serve him that cold meal of revenge. She knew forgiveness was the hallmark of the Christian, but for her it was for the weak and weary…no such word existed in her playbook.

Vi knew only one person in her world in whom she could confide, and that was Ella. Ella had always understood her, though she'd been far from approving many of the choices Vi had made, especially her rejecting God at every turn. Ella shared her faith, and better yet, she lived it, but it fell on a rock-hard heart that hurt Ella more than anyone could ever imagine. Vi unloaded the events that had taken place at their apartment, and Ella just held her in her arms. They cried together, and then Ella prayed for peace for her special little girl. Prayer was definitely not in Vi's vocabulary, but a hug from Ella spoke volumes.

Telling her mother about Andrew's involvement in the fire was a conversation that was never going to happen. The outcome was so predictable it bordered on the absurd.

Vi knew that underneath it all, her mother had always held onto some bit of doubt regarding whether she actually had started the fire under the boardwalk. Telling her now that she suddenly remembered the one word that had eluded her for years would be ridiculous. Andrew's involvement would seem unbelievable to anyone at this point after so many years had elapsed. What were the chances that Andrew, of all people, was linked to such a tragic event. Her mother would find it too coincidental to accept. She would say, "How convenient with Andrew now dead, you suddenly unearth the fact that he set the fire." It would look once again like Vi was trying to vindicate herself through the confessions of a dead man's revelations.

No, Vi had to take comfort in knowing that at least one person close to her believed her story.

The thought that Vi was now free to marry JD enabled her to get through the ordeal of Andrews's wake. The "poor, grieving widow" was consoled by her late husband's life insurance policy. Couple that with Todd Industries financial contributions, and Vi never had to worry about making ends meet. The funeral was attended by those at the top as well as those at the bottom of the social ladder. Andrew had many close friends from high school as well as college. Include the Todd family and their friends, and it didn't take long to fill the Presbyterian Church in Bryn Mawr to overflowing. Vi went numbly through the motions, as expected, but with an underlying sense of relief. Even if her hidden pain formed a tear made of glass that fell to the ground, it would make only a hollow sound. Emptiness encircled her, yet the moments of real depression were brought on by her anger at having been the complacent wife in a marriage that had so little chance of survival.

At the end of the wake, as everyone was getting ready to leave, Addi embraced Vi warmly and whispered, "You are my daughter. I love you, and, despite all our differences, I need you now more than ever to be my friend as well."

"Let's work on that together, Mom." The hug lasted a little longer than expected, and it didn't go unnoticed that Vi had used the word "Mom."

For obvious reasons, Vi's sudden marriage to JD would be kept quiet. They caught an early plane out of Philadelphia International Airport for Sandy Lane Estates in Barbados, West Indies, and were married exactly a week after she'd put her dead husband in the ground. There was no display of black wreaths on the doors or mourning clothes for this widow. She was on a mission to change her life, and it was about to begin on a faraway island.

On returning from their honeymoon, still heady from self-indulgence and hedonism, JD and Vi leased a small apartment in the town of Newport, RI, where he had an office with the Chandler Hotel Corporation. They needed to be flexible, not tied to a mortgage just yet, wanting to be sure Newport was where they envisioned themselves settling down.

Seven weeks into their marriage, Vi told JD there would soon be three, covering her tracks by adding two months to her due date. JD was thrilled, although also a little taken aback by the news. For him, it was the exclamation point to a love affair ending in almost fairy-tale style; for her, it was a question mark, one filled with all kinds of emotions.

John failed to do the math when their baby, Laura, was born early, but there was no reason in the world he would ever suspect Vi had a one night stand with her late husband.

Vi supported John's need to stay flexible in their living arrangements. Newport had many interesting sections in which to buy a home, as did Providence. No matter where they wound up settling, Vi was not content to stay at home and play the devoted mother to their newborn daughter. She was way too self-centered to play that card.

Vi figured that since JD traveled a great deal for the Chandler Corporation, leaving her alone, she was free to immerse herself in the town's society. This, of course, was at her daughter's expense. Vi loved Laura, at least as deeply as she was capable of loving anyone. But Laura was a constant reminder of Andrew, and not a day went by that Vi didn't look into that beautiful face of her daughter and feel pain, not from losing him, but from living with all the hurt and deception that continually haunted her. She couldn't just let it go; it ate at her. She knew it was not Laura's fault. Laura happened to be a casualty in the play called "Andrew Todd," which featured deeply flawed main characters.

By hiring a nanny to assist her in parenting, Vi found a way to tamp down any pangs of guilt that might surface periodically. Laura was tended, fed, clothed, and given plenty of attention, just not from her mother. Evie, short for Evelyn, was a loving, dedicated nanny, and Laura seemed content in her nurturing arms.

Vi spent hours working with the prominent women of Newport to further the goals, aspirations, and funding for the Historical Society. In an ongoing effort to maintain the "cottages" of Newport, Vi was never content, no matter where or what she was doing. She couldn't just live in the moment; she was restless, always striving for the next thing to accomplish. Then there was the "male factor." Vi was and continued to be a woman that men automatically wanted to make a variety of sexual advances on. And there were plenty of chances to be accommodating, but she had no interest in crossing that line. She loved JD very much, so she made a concerted effort to resist men's blatant desires. Vi enjoyed being hunted but never caught; she was a flirt and a tease, and men fell for her beauty and sensuality knowing full well they stood no chance in hell of scoring with this crafty vixen.

CHAPTER 19

In 1955, Adrienne and Stephen were invited to Grace Kelly's wedding in Monaco. Adrienne was a friend of John and Margaret Kelly, originally as an acquaintance at the restaurant in the early years and then on a closer level at Peck's Beach Yacht Club. Adrienne and the Kelly's loved sailing, and they easily developed a lasting friendship. Besides, from the very start, Margaret had always admired Addi's independence in raising an only child and her steadfastness in giving her daughter the best advantages in education and social upbringing. The Kellys had a summer home along the Platinum Coast, the most ideal real estate on Peck's Beach if you were a beach lover. If not, property along the bay was the next favorite location, as sailing and fishing were ideal in the backwater bay and offered an alternate lifestyle that beachfront properties could not.

The entire Kelly clan became the focus of both the national and international media. Grace's career skyrocketed her from girl- next- door to movie star in a few short years, and her engagement to Prince Rainier was an event of global fascination. Through it all, Grace's family never lost touch with old friends, even though dinners for the Kellys at Watson's became very infrequent.

So, it was not unexpected that Addi and Stephen would be invited to the wedding of the decade. Addi desperately wanted Stephen to attend with her, but the timing could not have been worse. The restaurant was due to open the weekend of Mother's Day, and there was simply no way Stephen could be absent at such a crucial time. Not wanting to make the trip alone, Addi invited Vi to attend as her guest, and though Vi didn't outwardly show it, she was very pleased her mother had reached out to her. It would not only be an extraordinary adventure, it was a rare opportunity to spend some time together, even if it would be sparse. And the timing was perfect for Vi, as JD was traveling to the orient on business and would not have been able to attend the wedding even if invited.

Even though it was just a long weekend in Monaco, each day was more impressive or memorable than the last. The little kingdom was nestled along France's southern coast, surrounded by mountains and breathtaking scenery. Every day was precious, especially the moments that brought some genuine healing between mother and daughter.

The night they decided to gamble at Monte Carlo, a suggestion coming from Addi that was so beyond the borders of sensibility for a person as conservative as she, it left Vi speechless. Of course Vi loved the idea and couldn't wait to have an evening out in the play yard of the rich and restless. What fun they had, especially at the roulette wheel; everything clicked, the money piled up, one of those rare nights when you could not lose. The camaraderie continued into the next day when they took a carriage ride through the mountain terrain of Monaco. Being side by side for hours of shared adventures, laughter and conversation created a new warmth between them.

Small steps toward healing started before the marriage, then were built upon in Monaco. It was a slow process at first, but at least, movement was in the right direction.

The wedding was as close to a fairy tale as one could get, right down to the four white horses drawing the carriage that whisked the bride and groom away to their never-never land. It truly met every expectation any little girl could ever have dreamed of living.

Addi and Vi were on top of the world when they returned home. Stepping off the plane in Philadelphia, Addi spotted Huck getting out of her car to put their luggage in the trunk.

"Hi, Huck, thanks for meeting us, but I thought Stephen was coming."

"He was, Miss Addi, but last night, when I was leaving the restaurant, he told me he was feeling poorly and asked if I would please pick you up... Gave me proper directions too."

"Well then, I can't wait to get home and play nurse to Stephen."

"I'm sure, Miss Addi, he will like that very much, 'cause I know he must have missed you."

Vi had continued on to a connecting flight to Newport, so the ride home was quiet and gave Addi a chance to reflect. What a wonderful time she and Vi had enjoyed, and, from her vantage point, Addi never wanted to wipe away the happiness and joy she was reliving. She wanted the contentment and peace she was clinging to on the ride home, to last at least until she'd had the chance to share it with Stephen.

When Huck pulled the car up in front of Watson's, Addi couldn't wait to tell Stephen all about her trip. So she rushed inside, leaving Huck to gather the luggage and take it to their apartment.

A quick check in the bedroom showed the bed was made, but the room was empty and felt sterile.

In response to "Stephen, where are you?" there was only silence as Addi moved into the office. There was a note with her name on her desk, written in handwriting she knew very well.. She was shaking when she opened it and once read,, she slumped weakly into a chair, dropping the letter and staring at the wall.

When you read this, June and I will be well on our way to California. You remember June Davis, don't you? The pretty blonde, my "Girl Friday" and backup bookkeeper...? The one who's 20 years my junior, but then again, who's counting? You've always said, age is just a number. Totally by accident, I found a letter in your desk buried in a file marked, "archives," addressed to you from my brother, dated May 1920.

What a fool I've been. All this time I never figured out why I couldn't measure up. Now I know. It all makes perfect sense now that the truth has come out. I never stood a chance, did I? How could I ever replace the love of your life, the very person who proved impossible to replicate...my brother. Once again, even from the grave, he has bested me again..

Goodbye, Addi, enjoy the rest of your days fantasizing about the life you missed with Gregory... Hope it keeps you warm at night.

My condolences,

Signed, "Carbon Copy"

Addi hit the depth of depression over this, realizing she lost the two men in her life who meant the most to her. She never saw this coming, much to her discredit, never recognized her role in it, how she had transferred Greg onto Stephen with little effort. Addi really never saw Stephen for the person he was. As a result, when he got to know June by working closely with her, he found it easy to talk with her. He wore his feelings right on the surface, and she came to love him for the man he was, not for some fantasy unfulfilled. Stephen could never quite put his finger on just what it was about their marriage that seemed distorted, but he often confronted Addi about her ability to cause him to feel as though it wasn't him she was connecting to. She always criticized Stephen's "schoolboy emotions," never able to consciously recognize what she was projecting onto him.

Her depression was both severe and lengthy. Adrienne had only Ella to hold onto now. Vi was gone to a new life, and Addi had no intention of telling her daughter what had just happened, at least not now. Addi needed time to think, but she couldn't even remember her own name let alone try to figure out her future. She swore Ella to secrecy and then never spoke of it again. The winter seemed endless.

The winter was long and cold for Vi too. She was alone quite a bit due to JD's continued business travel, but fortunately, Vi was kept busy with a heavy social schedule and, oh yes, a part-time attempt at motherhood.

JD had grown to hate corporate life and all the politics that came with it. He had been seriously considering a major career move, but he didn't quite know whether to remain in his field or try to reinvent himself. He answered the phone one evening, and it was Ella on the other end asking to speak to Vi, saying that it was important.

Vi, taking the phone, said, "Hi, Ella, hope everything is going well with you and Mother."

"Not so good, Miss Vi. Your mom has had a nervous breakdown and is at the U of P in the psychiatric wing."

"Oh, Ella, this can't be. Tell me it's not true. Mother was just getting to a good place in her life, and even we were working things out. What happened to cause it, do you know?"

"Yes, Miss Vi, but I was told to keep quiet."

"Ella, that won't do now, and you know it! If Mother is in the serious mental state you say, keeping information private helps no one, especially her."

"Well, Miss Vi, when Addi came home from France, she found a note on her desk from Stephen telling her things that broke her heart."

"Can you get it and read it to me?"

"Yes, I've got it right here." As Ella proceeded to read the note to Vi, the tragedy of it all made Vi sick to her stomach. For a second, she couldn't think, and then she began to cry. The tears were shared on both ends of the phone, and soft sobbing was the only communication for several minutes.

"John and I will be at The Institute of Pennsylvania tomorrow, Ella. Then we'll talk to you after consulting with the doctors."

When they arrived at the institute, they were escorted to Addi 's room, and what they saw shocked them both. It was hard to realize the person sitting motionless by the window was the same person weighed down with such emotional pain. She seemed crushed by something unseen, a force so heavy that it almost smothered her.

Vi and John were silent as they slowly inched their way over to the window, coming from behind Addi. They were aware that the clicking of their heels on the tile floor should have alerted her that they had entered her room, but the sound fell on deaf ears. When Vi reached out to gently touch her mother's shoulder, Addi was unresponsive, mute, slumped over and still, making no eye contact. Vi and John left the room in a state of shock and confusion. They consulted with Addi's doctors and were told she was catatonic and that it might take months of therapy, including electroshock treatments to bring her out of her clinical depression, with no clearly projected time frame or prognosis. Life changes quickly. After a long and in-depth conversation, Vi and JD realized it made sense for them to take over control of Watson's. Who else knew the restaurant as well as they did or had a more vested interest in the welfare of the business?

Vi and John were hit hard by the gravity of the situation, and the reality of their decision to leave Newport weighed more heavily on them than they expected. The change in their lifestyle and future plans had been altered to the point that they suspected they could never go back to life as they knew it.

The move to Peck's Beach was swift. Vi took charge, reconfiguring the second floor of her mother's apartment to suit their taste, making it comfortable for them to live until Addi's return, when they would find a house on the island. Their home in Newport sold within a month's time, although finding a house on the Platinum Coast of Peck's Beach traditionally took much longer. The demand was greater than the supply in this heavily desirable section of the island, but they knew it would be worth the wait.

Vi and John made a united front during this time in their lives. John completely handled the kitchen responsibilities and staff, while Vi took command of running the dining room, maintaining the personnel and quality control needed to continue the restaurant's excellent reputation. Vi did an outstanding job, having been well trained by her mother.

She and John found the perfect house, right on the beach, exactly where they wanted to live. The timing could not have been better.. Four months had passed since Addi had been institutionalized, and now she was nervously making a huge transition, coming home to Peck's Beach to slowly integrate into her old life again. Vi made sure Addi was well cared for, and Ella assisted in settling Addi comfortably in her apartment. It was an ideal setup having Ella living on the third floor. She was able to provide much-needed physical comfort and emotional support for Addi. For Addi, having her closest friend by her side meant a great deal.

Although Addi remained in control both legally and as majority owner, she was ineffective much of the time. JD took the helm in running the restaurant, with Vi assisting. Addi and JD came up against each other on more than one occasion...her sticking to her tried and true formulas for success...him insisting on innovation and flexibility, acknowledging the times, an ever-progressing landscape.

Peck's Beach began to redefine itself in the late 50s and early 60s. People's lifestyles and dining habits were shifting...life was much more informal. In years past, one had to be dressed in their Sunday best to walk the boards or dine at a fancy establishment. It was a reflection of the period, but the winds were blowing in a new direction, though slowly at first. The blue laws were still in effect, prohibiting Sunday sales. All retail stores, drug stores, and the like were closed on the Sabbath, without exception. No alcohol was served anywhere on the island, in public at least, a rule set down in concrete by the founding fathers. It would have taken an act of God Himself to bring the devil's spirits to the lips of the good citizens of this Methodist enclave. But the old mores were changing, and political pressure was mounting in hopes of removing those antiquated laws.

Slowly, JD was free to wield more control of Watson's, due in large part to Addi's chronic depressive state of mind. She needed electroshock treatments twice during this five-year period, and JD, with Vivian's somewhat reluctant help, was able to bring the restaurant into more contemporary times. JD was a man of the world...

tough and strong, well able to handle the busy world of the restaurant industry. He had no awareness of a need for God, but started to attend church, mostly out of sympathy for Addi. He saw she really needed the support. After one of the services, JD asked the minister many questions about God and faith, none of which were satisfying answers. Then over time he became a believer in Christ on his own after devouring the CS Lewis book, Mere Christianity. With the wisdom found in the book, he reasoned out the existence of God and took a giant leap of faith. Unfortunately, Vi was driven up the wall over the spiritual split it caused between them.

During the dark days of her despair, Addi cried out desperately to God. She had always known, deep in her soul, where her true strength lay. But falling into the abyss of human madness allowed her to see for the first time the meaning of her faith and to know without question that God loved her beyond all understanding. And it all began at a church meeting.

She knew she had failed miserably to make a success of her personal life, and she was weighed down with a heavy sense of guilt. At a small church service, she heard the preacher's words, "God's Grace is an undeserved gift, freely given to those who confess the name of Jesus and believe that God has raised Him from the grave." It was a gift Addi boldly embraced that evening with outstretched arms and palms turned toward heaven.

Healing is not an event, it's a process, and it didn't happen overnight. It took time and counseling from both professionals and preacher alike, but slowly Addi's life began to move in a new direction. She was emerging from a long, dark tunnel of despair, and the light she experienced was as though she had been given her sight back again. She gradually integrated into the restaurant, doing tasks she could handle without heavy pressure. Being cashier was a great place to start and a place where she could connect with customers, chat about their lives, and stay connected to her loving public. The waitresses didn't handle the money. Diners passed to the front of the restaurant to pay at the register. It was also the perfect place for Addi to keep a critical eye on the waitresses, making sure they provided the best service with the highest standards possible.

Step by step, Addi became a functional part of Watson's again, finding herself taking on the familiar rhythm of nightly orchestrated chaos.

While eating with Ella one night on the Porch, Addi saw an old friend, Harry Blake, enter the center hall and wait to be seated. Late though it was, Addi excused herself to greet him.

"Harry, I haven't seen you in quite some time."

"Addi, what a nice surprise. How are you feeling? I'd heard you were a bit under the weather, " he responded.

"Oh...they do like to say that, you may be sure. I'm doing just fine, Harry. I've had a rough year emotionally, and I'm recovering well. Nice of you to ask."

"So glad to hear that. You look wonderful, and business seems to be booming from what I can see."

"Yes, we're very fortunate... Many blessings have come our way over the years, and we're grateful. Are you a party of one tonight?"

"Yes, I am. Just had to come over for a good meal and escape the boardwalk madness."

"Well, please join me for dinner, if you would. I just sat down with Ella, and we'd love to make it a party of three."

They had a wonderful dinner, and the conversation flowed freely. It was jovial and felt comfortable despite the year that had transpired. Ella genuinely enjoyed Harry's company, though she had a slight check in her spirit about him, one that she dismissed very readily.

When dinner was finished and Ella excused herself to go upstairs, Harry asked Addi if they could have another "dinner date" so they could continue where they had just left off.

"Of course we can, anytime. I speak for myself, but I think we've enjoyed catching up on our lives."

"I couldn't agree more, so it's a date. I'll check in with you later this week." With that, Harry turned in the direction of the cashier to pay for his meal at which point Addi put her hand over his before he could place a $20.00 bill on the counter.

"Don't even think about paying. For me, the conversation was worth the cost of the meal."

"Thanks, Addi, I owe you one."

"No, I think I'm the one who owes you. I needed tonight more than you know. It's been helpful to reconnect with an old friend, so I thank you."

Addi gave Harry a warm hug and then turned to go upstairs to her apartment. Harry watched her leave for a moment, grateful he had come to dinner and happy to see Addi looking so well. He left Watson's thinking how fortunate he was to live on this island called Peck's Beach, a place in which he had invested so much of his time and effort. Suddenly a flood of nostalgia swept over him as he walked to his boardwalk penthouse. The two-block distance between the restaurant and his home proved to be time enough to get lost in reflections.

CHAPTER 20

Harry had built his small empire by himself, and he was very proud of his accomplishments. Raised by a single mother who held down three jobs to survive, and having never known his father, he was on his own early in life. Tired of being poor and seeing his mother struggle to make ends meet, he dropped out of high school and came to Peck's Beach in his late teens to find work. Employment choices were pumping gas or slinging hash on the boardwalk... He opted for the hash.

In 1948, a devastating hurricane slammed into the Jersey coast, coming close to wiping out the boardwalk. Land value suddenly tanked; people wanted to get out of town, wanting nothing more to do with Peck's Beach. There was no one with enough chutzpa to get people fired up and ready to make the sacrifices necessary, stay in the town, and rebuild...no one except Harry. By now, he was a successful businessman. He had been able to buy a movie theater at first, then added three more to the chain, plus an amusement center he named Seaside Fun Spot and, of course, the Boardwalk Kettle Fudge shops...all because he'd taken advantage of knowledge gained as a real estate agent. Timing was critical, and the post-war years seemed to yield unbelievable opportunities for young entrepreneurs like himself.

Harry became a very popular figure on the island as a fun-loving guy, very generous with his money and time. For someone were in need or wanting help getting started in business, Harry was the first to lend a hand. The reasons for this were really two fold...he had an intense desire for acceptance and a business mind with vision that understood how important young entrepreneurs were to the future of Peck's Beach's growth and maturity as it moved into the next decade.

Harry worked hard at placing himself in critical positions to further his political career. He was well aware that if he needed to get anything done on such a very conservative island, he had to maneuver carefully through the political maze at City Hall, not an easy task, but it presenting a challenge Harry relished.

I'm ready for you, he thought. Let me have your best shot. Their best shot came close to his, but he beat them at almost every turn. Over time, the goals he sought for the town were realized, though some not quite as he would have planned. His concept for a major high-rise with retail stores and a convention center, rising ten stories high next to the boardwalk, were voted down by the city council despite Harry's all-out effort to gain grassroots support. Other projects, however, managed to see the light of success in their completion...the multilevel parking for the downtown shopping area, the grassy strip on Asbury Avenue from Sixth to Fifteenth Street, with free trolley service, along with the continued expansion of the Seaside Fun Spot amusement and water park to offer a broader variety of rides, miniature golf, and eating establishments.

The city council was well acquainted with Harry Blake, and they knew in advance that when his agendas appeared on the docket, things were about to heat up on the debate floor. Invariably, Harry was well prepared to state his case and even more prepared to stand his ground, resulting most often in his achieving success in getting what he came for. He'd adroitly endeared himself to many political stalwarts, so when it came time to present his agenda, whatever it was, he usually came away with a big smile on his face.

Harry's personal life didn't always follow the same path of success as his political one. Regardless, he gave new meaning to the phrase party animal. He drove a white Lincoln Continental and partied hearty at two famous night clubs over at "The Point" as people called it. Bayshores or Tony Mart's, pick your poison: Bayshores, easy for under age beer hounds to get past the front door bouncers. If the place got raided, a weekly occurrence, escape by jumping out the back window into the bay was available, always preferred over a night in jail and big fines, not to mention your parents finding out, as well as the school you attended. Tony Marts was home to some great bands, more difficult to slip by with your fake ID card and no readily available escape route. Owners and friends alike loved seeing Harry arrive at either establishment, knowing drinks would be "on the house" and the fun times would rocket up to a new high. Harry attracted attention wherever he appeared, unintentional but unavoidable. Though loved by many for various reasons, his lifestyle was right out front for all to see. He had enemies as well. Not all were captivated by his charisma. They weren't enamored by his charm, nor did they like the direction he envisioned for the future of Peck's Beach. His liberal ideas and costly zoning changes did not mesh with their plans to rein in taxes while limiting new home construction. Conservatives were bent on keeping the status quo, everything as it always had been; conversely, Harry was the poster boy for change.

By far the biggest change he proposed was lifting the city ban on alcohol.

The influx of tourists coming to Peck's Beach had been stagnant for some time. Harry was convinced that if drinking was allowed, major hotel and restaurant chains would eventually invest on the island, raising the quantity and caliber of the tourist market.

Harry often frequented Watson's as a dinner guest at the invitation of Addi. More often, than not, while dining on The Porch, Ella joined them from time to time. What began as a casual relationship and a good friendship developed into a deeper involvement, at least on Addi's part. She was following a well-traveled road, continuing to get emotionally involved with younger men. Youth served with a topping of maturity was the combination that really attracted her, and while she was barely aware of it, a man twenty years her junior made her feel just as young. For a man in his forties, Harry exhibited a level of sophistication and worldliness beyond his years, a combination to which Addi was helplessly attracted. The bigger question was whether Harry had similar feelings for her. The answer was that he was completely devoid of anything resembling romantic feelings toward her. In his mind, they were only friends and no more. Their renewed acquaintance was well timed for Harry, whose personal life was very private, isolating him from people he could trust and confide in. Addi offered what he viewed as a platonic relationship with no strings, no attachments, and no expectations that couldn't be met...a buffer zone that Harry really desired, promoting conversations at dinner that covered many subjects and encouraging the confidences that good friends share. These were rewarding times for both, and two or three times a week. It was Ella's observation that Harry could be found sitting with Addi at a deuce, always in excess of an hour, deep in conversation, while waitresses buzzed about, trying to wrap up their respective stations so they could close out for the evening.

Harry made Addi feel alive again, and the feeling, following her long depression, was extraordinary. She hadn't felt so connected to life in a long time, relishing her dinners with the Mayor of the Boardwalk, as Harry was known. Dinners at Watson's morphed into dining at other restaurants in town, as well as social events at Peck's Beach Yacht Club and the Asteria Hotel. This bubble of euphoria was something Addi enjoyed to the utmost, keeping her deeper feelings well concealed. While she showed warm affection for Harry on the surface, deep down, Addi was blocking her true emotions for him.

She just couldn't face another failed relationship, always falling into the same trap: a young man, with a striking presence who worshipped and adored her...at first.

But for now, Addi was infused with new life and renewed hope. She and Harry were together more than not in the summer of '62. They were confidants, advising each other on business matters, and Harry often talked about how he would like to become involved in town politics. Addi offered her views only when asked. Harry was anti-blue laws and pro- alcohol for the island, but he didn't get into that debate with Addi, because she was adamantly opposed to drinking. Her father had been an alcoholic, and the hell he'd caused was an inheritance of indelible traumatic memories.

When it came to the blue laws, she could be more flexible, but if pushed to vote, she'd opt for no change in the status quo. By early June of '63, Addi was on the verge of making her move and telling Harry how she really felt toward him, and of course, the risk would be huge. This could be a fool's journey, one that could ruin a wonderful friendship, and if her openness backfired, her already fragile mental state could be greatly compromised.

The restaurant was no longer under her control, as she'd abdicated her position of "one-woman ruler" to her son-in-law, one of the passages in her life she had not relished. The result was the return of an old unwelcome visitor, depression. Addi prayed for relief, asking God to keep her from the abyss of despair. She knew in her heart that God had taken all her self-accusations and buried them in the garden of forgiveness. But her mind told her it was all lies.

And then…

CHAPTER 21

After a long pause, Ella looked at me. "It sure is a sad tale, Master Sax, and it's heavy on my heart tellin' it." Her words snapped me back into the here and now.

"If ya'll don't mind, I'll be goin' upstairs now."

I got up from my chair, went over to her, and gave her a kiss on the cheek.

"Thanks, Ella, for sharing all this history with me; it helps me to understand where people's lives have led them and why they are what they are. We all have our demons."

What I came to learn later from Ella was Addi's decision to confide in her close friend, let her feelings out, go for the gold ring, risk everything, and hope she wasn't knocked off the horse in the process. She took a deep breath and dialed his number around 11 pm, on a rainy July evening. There was a lot of static on the line, and then it went silent. The thunderstorm in process seemed to echo the turmoil racing through her mind.

As fast as the storm came, it passed. The heavy downpour stopped, and the late evening night suddenly became deadly quiet, so Addi decided to walk over to Harry's penthouse, which was only two blocks away. She figured what she had to say was better said in person.

No one was aware Addi left the building and the pastry chef wouldn't arrive to work until about three in the morning.

The entrance to Harry's apartment was accessed from the parking lot behind his retail store on the boardwalk. It was familiar to Addi, since she often paid a visit after closing hours at Watson's. She could hear the ocean as she approached the stairs, a sound she much loved. Tonight the crashing of the waves seemed angry, riled up, even though the ocean was not visible in the dark, stormy sky.

There was a deck on the second-floor level, and when she climbed the stairs, she didn't notice the sliding door was ajar...her thoughts were in turmoil, and she was not totally confident she should be doing what she planned in the next few moments.

The lights were low as she entered the apartment, and except for the agitated ocean, all was quiet. Addi was seconds from announcing her presence, but the words got stuck, never crossing her lips as she stood there in the hallway. From where she was positioned, she heard a lot of commotion coming from the partially opened bedroom door, and then a distinctive male voice that wasn't Harry's was heard saying, "Good to know this is more than a one-night stand!"

Addi lost all sense of reality; spinning around, knocking over a small table lamp, she tore out of the apartment.

Hearing the breaking glass, both men cautiously moved into the hall but could see no one. The rear sliders were wide open, making it obvious that the intruder had entered from the deck. Slightly disoriented at first, Harry regained his bearings, making a sudden rush forward to get over to the railing.

To his shock, he was able to discern the figure of a woman running down the alley, a woman he knew very well.

Yelling Addi's name to stop was not an option...it was way too late for that.

Harry's friend, trailing close behind him, said, "Did you see anyone?" as he scanned the darkness for any movement.

"No. I can't imagine who that would have been!"

The earlier evening rain turned into drizzle, darkening Addi's already black thoughts. She felt genuinely victimized by her circumstances; life was once again crushing her as though she were some kind of giant vise. The pressure in her head was too great to bear. The walk back to Watson's seemed endless.

Addi rushed into the center hall, crying for Ella all the way to the top of the stairs.

Ella came to her with arms outstretched, giving Addi a long enduring hug, words unneeded. Through Addi's tears and shaking, Ella knew there was no gold ring. She guided Addi to the bedroom while her dear friend slowly unfolded what had just taken place.

Suddenly an inexplicable calm washed over her when Ella left the room. Addi sat down at her desk and addressed two envelopes, one to Harry and one to her daughter. With a steady hand, she penned two notes, signed each, folded them carefully, then was overcome by stillness, almost as though the stillness was waiting for permission to allow her next step to take place. A look of satisfaction tinged with a subtle touch of revenge floated across her face as she inserted the letters, each purposefully placed in the other's envelope.

Addi took the letters, and with quiet determination, walked downstairs and out the front door, heading across the street to the mailbox. Not a person or car was in sight. By now, it was after midnight. She hesitated, staring at the mailbox like it was going to swallow her up. Then she slowly slipped the letters through the opening. The quiet sound of the envelopes hitting the bottom of the empty box exploded in her mind like a bomb. She turned and walked robotically back across the street, oblivious to the screeching sound of brakes from a car trying to avoid hitting her. The driver yelled some profanity at her, but Addi heard nothing. She closed the doors of Watson's behind her, slowly climbed the stairs, and entered her apartment. All was eerily quiet...all but Addi's tormented mind. She lay down on her bed, calmly emptied a bottle of pills into her hand, consumed them all, and then closed her eyes while whispering, "I'm unshackled, unshackled from this world at last." As she fell asleep, a tear found its way down her cheek.

They say time heals all wounds, but what is not said is: How long is that time? For Vi, her mother's suicide evoked the gamut of emotions: anger, guilt, and selfishness to name just an identifiable few. Vi's way of dealing with all this was to rely again on an old friend...drugs, the prescription kind she was so adept at securing. She had every doctor on the island in her phone book. She convinced them of her need to get through the worst crisis in her life. She hadn't slept through the night since the funeral, so doctors were very willing to give her what she wanted; none of them, however, were willing to put the brakes on an endless supply of her little round "crutches" in a bottle.

She took a more active role at Watson's, showing up at unexpected times in the dining room, playing hostess without advising me in advance of her plans. The first time she did this, it threw me "in the weeds" even before the evening began. The line was already forming, it was a hot Saturday night in mid-June, and if the seating was not done correctly at the beginning of the night, chaos would reign for both waitresses and diners. Added to that was Vi showing up under the influence of what, at first, I thought was alcohol but later realized were those nasty little treats from the pharmacy.

I tried to have Vi seat parties of two, so she could easily move from the Terrace, on the Ocean Avenue side of the restaurant, to the Porch, which ran along Ninth Street. Many of the old-time patrons of Watson's were deuces, parties of two who had been coming for dinner forever. Somehow Vi was able to maneuver herself down the aisles, seating the parties without losing her balance. She was never far from a chair or side stand, so in case of an emergency, she could grab onto whatever piece of furniture was available.

The night was moving along nicely until Vi lost her balance and fell into the arms of a waitress who happened to have seven desserts fanned out on one arm and two in her other hand. Both hit the floor simultaneously, followed by the cascading of nine under liners, whose entire contents covered Vi's and the waitress's heads. It was all I could do not to laugh. Ice cream and assorted toppings dripped down their faces and clung to their clothes. The crash could be heard around the world…well, at least our world. Even the kitchen heard the noise over the crazy rush-hour sounds. Various people came to the rescue. Somehow Vi bounced to her feet like it was some kind of circus act. The waitress was not so fast…she felt sick and had to go down in the dungeon and clean up. I had a sudden flashback to the grand entrance I'd made on my first day at the Big W…gave me chills!

Vi looked disoriented, and she fled upstairs without a single word to anyone…typical. She knew if JD ever found out what had happened and why, she'd be looking for a place to hide. Vi could hold her own against the best of men, a virtual bulkhead. Little, if anything, got past her except when she was under the control of drugs. She secluded herself before anyone knew what was happening…without a word of compassion for the girl she'd caused to abruptly land on the Terrace floor.

The collision was big-time news for the kitchen crew, and it wasn't long before I caught a glimpse of JD's head peering out between the swinging doors, not an unusual occurrence for him. He liked to conduct periodic spot checks to survey the main dining rooms during the rush hours, believing it was good management. But this time, he never saw Vi, her exit was so swift. JD was unaware she'd caused the accident. He motioned to me to get someone to follow the girl down to the dungeon and make sure she was ok. He asked what had happened, and for some unknown reason, I covered for Vi. Maybe it was out of pure sympathy, I don't know, but I played it down, saying the waitress had slipped on the hardwood floors; must have been some water dropped on the floor... JD wasn't buying it.

By now, he had moved from the kitchen door into full view of the diners, dressed in his faded whites and dirty sneakers. Looking down at the mess as busboys scrambled to clean it up, JD bent over to pick up a familiar brooch, one his mother-in-law had worn on many nights when she'd tended the register. He just looked at me and said, "Interesting; where's Vi?"

"She went upstairs," I said, not willing to divulge any more information, at which point JD disappeared into the kitchen, back into his cave. I had a sinking feeling Vi would catch it in spades from her husband behind closed doors. Their fights were becoming legendary, exacting an emotional toll on Laura. Not long after the funeral, Laura began to come down from their apartment toward the latter part of the evenings, when dining generally calmed down, and she would ask to sit with me while I ate. The answer was always "yes," of course. I was thrilled she asked, so no objection from me. Considering our age difference, coupled with the fact she was the owners' daughter, it was a compliment just knowing she was feeling comfortable joining me for dinner.

I knew from our openly honest conversations that life behind the walls upstairs was anything but pleasant. Laura's mom was her usual tough cookie, while Laura was at a very rebellious age. I had to watch what I said, but in subtle ways, I conveyed to Laura that she must not jump off the deep end, that things would get better, and, from the sounds of it, her parents were going through some rough times right now.

Laura questioned me about her mother's use of prescription drugs, and I said that while I really didn't have a good understanding of the issues, she'd definitely been out of control that night and should never have come down on the floor to hostess.

Laura was going to try to talk to her dad about it, because the drugs were causing her mother to be combative, more so than usual, and trying to communicate with her when she was under the influence was beyond impossible…thus the nasty fights, both with Laura and JD.

It was from these frequent conversations on the Porch, at a table for two, that I really got to know this teenage kid named Laura. Not only was she beautiful, she was intelligent and could hold her own in a conversation about a whole assortment of subjects…conversations most teenagers would likely pass over.

CHAPTER 22

One evening, I told Laura she would make a great waitress, something she had thought of as well, but we both knew the idea would meet major resistance from her mother, although her dad had no objection. In fact, he had brought the idea up several times, but Vi had emphatically opposed, saying she didn't want her daughter working for the family. "It always causes trouble."

So I said, "What if I bring up the subject tomorrow evening when your mother comes down to hostess? She and I have been hitting it off in some strange way recently. It may have to do with us hosting together. I help her out when customer madness starts to get out of control on the floor, so let me have a swing at it."

Thankfully, when Vi made her entrance the next evening, somewhat late to the task at hand, she seemed fairly stable on her feet...always a good sign. I was able to broach the subject when it came up rather naturally. Close friends of Vi's had come to dine, with Vi striking up a warm conversation among the three of them. In an interesting turn of events, these friends owned a small restaurant on the Avenue, and they told Vi how well their daughter was doing as a waitress, even though she was only 16, she was learning responsibility, both with handling money and the public. I got pulled into the conversation because these patrons recognized that I had recently eaten at their place. As one thing led to another, I soon had the opportunity to tell Vi why I thought Laura would make a great waitress. I couldn't believe her reaction; it was a complete turnaround from what Laura had conveyed to me.

"Sax, the more I think about it, the more it makes perfect sense. Laura needs to learn that things in life aren't just handed to you on a silver platter with roses and champagne or, for that matter, trips to Paris. She's spoiled, period. Her father just can't see her unhappy and gives in on everything."

I didn't buy that for a second, but of course, I said nothing.

Vi continued, "She's got a lot to learn, and Watson's is the place to teach her. Working with a seasoned kitchen crew, under the thumb of her critical father, plus dealing with the public will show her what she's made of. Just because she's the owners' daughter, she's not going to be given a break; I want you to treat her like everyone else. No favors, do you understand?"

"Absolutely. No problem with that." I was dying inside. I couldn't believe the 360-degree about-face Vi had just made, and she didn't look like she was "under the influence" at all, at least not from what I could tell.

Laura was ecstatic about the news and soon got her mother's blessing to begin work. After considerable mentoring from me, trailing one of her waitress friends was the next step in learning the system, especially arm service. The ice cream sundae dessert she served me on the Porch for my dinner as part of her training didn't go unnoticed. It was larger than usual. My instructions were to go down the line of all the ice cream toppings and put it on top of a vanilla scoop. I was in heaven just looking at such a delight! Becoming a waitress was a major break for Laura, and I told her it would be a small, but invaluable step on her way to independence, one she'd always remember. I also said I'd show no partiality; otherwise, she'd be seen by other waitresses as getting preferential treatment as the owners' daughter, so I had no intention of cutting her any slack.

Laura fit right in with the work crew on both sides of those famous swinging doors. Whether serving patrons in the dining room or picking up entrées in the kitchen, she mastered the system with agility and grace. Laura was a quick study, nailing down all the "rules and regs," the do's and don'ts that went into creating the ideal "Watson Girl."

I, too, was well acquainted with the manual, especially what wasn't put down in writing. Our week days began at 3:30 pm every day, when the waitresses reported to work. I would have them line up in the center hall like they were about to do the Can-Can, only facing me. Standing at attention, each had to jump over six basic hurdles: hair properly styled so it did not fall on the shoulders; uniform clean and ironed; head cap properly pinned in place; nylon stocking seam in straight line; spotless side towel folded over forearm. And last, but not least, the perfect apron bow, tied on the girl ahead by the next in line.

Should any waitress fail the inspection, I would call her out and send her to The Dungeon to make the proper adjustments. How lucky was I? Off the radar, Laura and I laughed about this sudden turn of events. Now I got the daily job of inspecting the one waitress in the line I was falling hopelessly in love with. I treaded cautiously, managing to carry it off well.

THE MANUAL

GREETING

Let courtesy and happiness be uppermost in your greetings and let the customers know that they are welcome here at Watson's. Be sure each person has been given a glass of water containing ice cubes.

TAKING ORDERS

Stand a few steps back from the table and, when guests are ready to order, step forward. Greet them pleasantly with "Good afternoon" or "Good evening," as the case may be. "May I take your order?" Hold check book in hand. Never rest it on the table while writing. Start with one of the ladies of the party. Bend the body slightly at the hips, thereby assuming an attitude of attentive listening. Write clearly and briefly and firmly. If your handwriting is poor… PRINT. Once the order has been taken, read it back to the guests quickly. Be sure they know what they ordered.

If a baby is in the party, suggest a bib. Children under twelve may have the child's portion from the children's menu. Never argue over a child's age.

In serving your platters, "Ladies First" always, and do try to remember who gets what without asking. If you are in doubt, make a guess. If you are wrong, they may straighten you out on the whole order. Good service does not include "Who gets the flounder? Who gets the meatloaf?"

Once the order is taken, say, "Thank you," and return the menus to the menu boxes or give them to the hostess. Do not throw them on chairs or window sills or carry them to the kitchen.

While your guests are eating, if all your immediate duties are taken care of, stay alert at your station. Keep hands off face and out of your hair. Be watchful for if your guests need additional service.

There should be no critical discussion of any Watson's personnel within hearing of other employees or patrons. There should be no discussion on the methods of operation or problems of our organization within hearing distance of our guests. It should be assumed that they have problems of their own and are trying to forget them by dining out in a relaxed atmosphere.

And that was just the introduction!!!

Often, during closing time, Laura and I would relive the evening and laugh at the crazy things the public did, and the kitchen crew as well...laughing till our stomachs hurt.

Being new to the job, Laura said, "Sax, do you know about Charles, the steam table guy? He talks to the food all night. When it gets really crazy and the dinner slips are piling up, I hear him saying, 'Don't leave me, French fries,' and then, when he gets in the weeds, he says to whoever is up next, 'Take a walk on the boardwalk, take it slow an easy now, take a walk on the boardwalk.'"

"Oh yes, Laura, I'm very familiar with Charles. He's in another world when the orders come flyin' in. If Popcorn, the deep fryer, gets in the weeds, as Charles likes to mumble, then the system breaks down, because fries, as you know, are one of the most popular items on the menu. When supplies end, dinner orders back up big time. It's beyond me what magic Popcorn conjures up, but there must be something in that frying oil of his that makes those fries like none other. Take everything else off the menu and keep just the fries and the deep-fried jumbo shrimp, and people would still line up outside!"

"When I met Charles on my first day, I came up behind him to introduce myself. I stopped quickly because I thought he was talking to someone and I didn't want to interrupt. Then it hit me, he was talking to the food. Popcorn chimed in from behind Charles, saying, "Ignore him, he runs at the mouth like that all night."

"Like Ella loves to say, 'You know it too.' They are, for sure, the two most requested items on the menu. Unbelievable. 'Don't leave me French fries.' I think I'll be hearing that in my sleep," she said, and we laughed again.

In the weeks that followed, Vi seemed to have a breakthrough. She worked the floor maybe three or four times a week, and for the first time, I saw no signs of drugs or alcohol, no slurred speech, no balance problems. I don't know if she'd had an epiphany after the "collision heard around the world" fiasco, or a blowout with JD that had woken her up, but whatever it was, she was different, and even Laura commented on it.

On my end, I missed Laura and our evening hook-ups on the Porch. But I figured a way around that. I had her serve me dinner every night. I often sat down to eat after 8:30, when the line was finally in and everything was basically under control. Previously, I'd alternated waitresses so I could evaluate their quality of service. In other words, make sure the service lived up to the high standards of a "Watson's Girl." An added benefit was I could slip Laura notes, like the night I asked her to sneak out somehow and meet me at a friend's house on the bay for "Night in Venice," the creative theme boat parade held every summer in July. Starting at Peck's Beach Yacht Club, the boats navigated their way for two miles in and out of the lagoons. Home owners showed off their bayside palaces with Christmas decorations and lights. The event was a stroke of genius for public relation and tourism. It brought thousands of visitors to the island, many of whom stayed the weekend because they were too inebriated to drive home after having partying hearty into the wee hours.

Laura was able, with the help of Ella, to break free and meet me. Her mother was out for the evening to the same event, making it easier to escape. There were so many party crashers at the home I was in that no one noticed Laura's arrival. We were able to steal an hour together. The hell with the parade of wealth on water. We hid out in my car, held tight to one other and kissed non-stop. Well, it seemed like that. It was so rare to have those moments all to ourselves. Laura looked at the dashboard clock and said, "I better get home, I promised Ella I'd obey the rules she set...be home in two hours."

"Tell Ella I love her. Not quite as much as I love you though."

"She knows that already and when I tell her, she'll say, "You know it too?" And do you know it too that I love you?"

"Sure do" and with that we put parting on hold for longer than planned.

As Laura stepped out of the car to walk home, I leaned over toward her side and said," Don't leave me, French fries".

With her back toward me as she walked away, she turned her head ever so slightly to say,

"Never!" came shooting back, loud and clear; I loved it.

In this new situation, I had to be careful not to make it so obvious that Laura was the favored one to serve me. She was off two nights a week anyway, and I'd switch servers often enough that it didn't seem like I was playing favorites. Actually, waitresses hated serving me dinner because they knew they were being critiqued, a tried and true technique Adrienne had proved to be very effective years ago.

I could never be quite sure how any given evening was going to go; because of Vi's unpredictability, it was always a mystery. But something changed with her. She was cutting back appearing on the floor to hostess. Something was up that I couldn't quite put my finger on, at least not then.

CHAPTER 23

After countless conversations at a table for two with Ella, I came to know this: throughout all our sharing, nothing Ella said conveyed the depth of trust in me as what she displayed in revealing a personal and extremely delicate piece of correspondence.

"Sax, late on the day after Addi died, I received a letter from Addi. You can't imagine what an impact seeing her handwriting on the envelope had on me, I was terrified to open it. This is what it said."

Ella then reached into her pocket book and handed me a letter. I couldn't believe what was taking place. I took the letter, opened it and began to read with a great deal of trepidation.

"Ella, I never had the chance to say goodbye and I wanted you to know how much I love you.

When you read this, I'll be gone, but only from this life. Take comfort. I'll be with your greatest love and Rock, Jesus, whose life you beautifully mirrored by living out your faith in so many ways for all of us.

Two days from now, Harry will receive my letter, and Vivian as well, explaining some hurtful truths.

I love you so much. Ella. and we will meet again. That is our eternal hope.

The letter was signed "Addi" in very shaky handwriting. I sat across the table from Ella, not saying a word for what seemed like a long time, then thanked her for sharing such intimate information, assuring her it would remain confidential forever.

As I came to know much later, after many far reaching events had taken place, Addi's letters did arrive at their appointed destination.

Dear Vivian,

I am leaving you all the rights and ownership of Watson's, reverting to Laura upon your death someday. I beg your forgiveness for taking my own life; I can't stand the pain any longer and have pleaded for help from the Lord, but I've heard nothing in return but silence.

Tormented, but now no longer tethered,

Loving you always,

Mother

Harry was confused and called Vivian to ask if she had received a letter that should have gone to him. He explained the situation and sent his letter over to Watson's. Vivian denied any knowledge of having received a letter, taking great delight in the lie.

The note she had received began with "Dear Harry," and then it continued in vivid detail to describe what Addi had seen when she'd gone over to tell him how much she loved him, how she had witnessed his homosexuality up close and personal, and how totally devastated she was. The letter left no doubt as to the severe depth of depression Addi had been experiencing as she'd penned her last words.

Vi had been stunned as her hands released the hold she had on the letter, letting it drop to her desktop, smiling slightly as she did, but she revealed the contents to no one, nor did she tell anyone she possessed it. Harry was no fool; he knew Vivian was lying, and to say he was paranoid was an understatement.

Vivian couldn't believe her luck; being the sole owner of his letter was priceless, like finding a diamond on the beach. Now she had the weapon, better than any gift she could imagine. Harry was very prominent politically on Peck's Beach, pulling in all types of favors and working his connections to the hilt in an all-out attempt to grab the mayoral seat in the next election. He and Vi were at opposite ends of the political spectrum, about as opposite as two people could get. So, like a spider weaving its web, Vi thought out loud in a whisper, "Be patient. Timing is everything. I'm going to strike, all right, but not now. That's for another day." Vi needed to collect her thoughts. Move too fast, and she'd miss this golden opportunity to land a fatal blow. No second chances here, no reruns.

Among the many papers and files Vi combed through in Addi's safe deposit box were important documents having to do with the restaurant and deeds to the property. At the very bottom of the box, bound together by an old rubber band and in envelopes turned yellow with age, were letters postmarked 1919 with a return address marked US Army."

Vi carefully unwrapped the package and began to slowly savor each letter. She sat there for what seemed like hours, taking in the beauty of the love expressed in each note, and for the first time in her life, she recognized who her real father was. The discovery was life changing, and now everything Vi had wondered about or doubted concerning many serious family issues suddenly started to make sense. It was like finding a secret treasure you thought was always there but that you could never quite prove, never knew for sure where it was hidden, yet you believed one day the truth would surface.

That day had finally arrived, and with it came ammunition she never thought she'd have, an emotional gun she could aim, at will, toward whomever she pleased. Locked and loaded, she had several victims in mind.

CHAPTER 24

This new revelation that Samuel Devries was her grandfather took time to sink in and for her to embrace the reality it presented. When her mind calmed down a bit, she got slammed with this wake up thought: she had dated her uncle and had loved him, which goes to why her mother was so adamantly opposed to her dating him and by extension, why Addi fell in love with Stephen. Her stomach was in a knot. After a few seconds of total disconnect , she came back to life thinking, of course, there was Laura to consider. Vi knew she had to take things gently with Laura, letting her ease into accepting Samuel as her biological great-grandfather, but only after he had accepted the fact that Greg had fathered a child, a child he never knew existed, birthed by a woman he didn't realize he knew.

When Vi told Ella about finding the letters, she pleaded with Ella to tell her what she knew about her mother's romance. Ella was blindsided. She had no choice but to sit down with Vi and tell the tale of her mother's beautiful love, a tale she had sworn to take to her grave. Vi understood how important loyalty was to Ella—her word was her bond—so she didn't come back hard on her with the whys and what ifs questions she was dying to ask. Instead, Vi asked Ella if she would accompany her, for moral support more than anything else, when she set up a time to pay Samuel DeVries a personal visit.

"Child, I'm right there with you."

Samuel was a widower by now, old and frail, having no family left except Stephen. Samuel had been a lieutenant in the US Army and could never forgive Stephen for being a coward. In later years, Samuel bought the Normandie Hotel, only to see it burn to the ground in 1927. Determined not to be defeated, he purchased the Asteria Hotel in the early thirties, which turned out to be a financial bonanza, since the cost for the entire complex was obtained at a rock-bottom price, one of the few financial perks of the Great Depression, and, to his benefit, Samuel had the cash to pull it off at a time when very few did.

A phone call to the Asteria Hotel was put through to Samuel, who was kind enough to answer. Vi promised him it would be to his benefit to meet, as she had crucial personal information concerning Gregory, information essential for Samuel to know.

He replied, "Given our family history and that you're the one doing the calling, there's a chance it just might have an element of truth. Make arrangements through my secretary," and then he abruptly hung up.

When the private elevator doors opened, Vi and Ella stepped into Samuel's penthouse suite. He rose from his chair with the help of a cane, and they exchanged greetings. Then Samuel said, "It's been quite some time since I've seen you. Please accept my condolences for the passing of your mother. Years ago, when we worked together at the Normandie, she was an outstanding employee, one who brought innovation and integrity to her position. But let me say, right from the start, I never approved of your mother's marriage to my son, a fact I'm quite sure you were well aware of. Once again, Stephen proved his worthlessness, managing to show his true character by taking off with one of your mother's employees, never to be heard from again. My relationship with Adrienne might have been a good deal different had my son not manipulated his way into her life. My one consolation has always been Gregory, a man of substance, whose loss in the war is my greatest sorrow."

Taking a seat, as Samuel motioned to do so, Vi picked up the conversation where he'd left off, thinking, How much harder would that last comment contribute to making things even more difficult.

"Please let me say thank you for your willingness to meet. And to get right to it, the reason for the visit centers not on Stephen, but Gregory. I wish I could convey to you just how difficult this is for me, but I've come across some information I found in my mother's safe deposit box…letters dated 1917. I'll leave them here with you to read. They are letters written by my mother and Gregory to one other. I'll call you in a few days, as I know you'll want to meet again."

She opened her pocketbook, pulled out the bound letters, and placing them on the coffee table in front of her. As she did, she saw the look of skepticism on Samuel's face.

"The letters are real," she said. "What they express was almost too much for me to handle, so I can only imagine what the effect will be on you. As I said, we'll talk later."

Ella, silent up to this point, said, "Mr. Samuel, I just want you to know I was there from the beginning, God be my judge."

Samuel was basically at a loss for to what to say. "Since I'm in the dark about what you're hesitant to reveal, I'd best read the letters." Picking one out of the pack, he studied its postmark, he said, "When I have finished reading them all, you may be sure, Vivian, you will be hearing from me."

"Thank you, Mr DeVries, and please, it's not that I don't want to tell you of their contents, it's just that I couldn't do justice to how much love is expressed in their writings. You'll soon understand what I'm talking about."

Vi stood up, followed by Ella. They shook Samuel's hand, and he then brought up the elevator. They left the Asteria arm in arm, walking back to Watson's. Vi and Ella shared a bond, one many times tested, that went back a lifetime, a history written with the same pen.

Samuel, in his final days, found a place of redemption. In the days that followed, lonely and bitter as the man had been, much of it self-imposed, he was able to reconnect with Vi. The letters reshaped his life, softening the inner soul that belied his tough exterior. He built a new relationship with Vi and his great-granddaughter, Laura, that brought unspeakable joy beyond his wildest imaginations. When Samuel died in 1965, Vi and Laura experienced profound sadness. VI was angry that her mother had kept so many secrets from her, secrets that had a profound effect on everyone in her family. She had never been given the chance to really know her grandfather, although in the intervening years since Addi's death, Vi tried to do what she could to bring some modicum of happiness to Samuel. Though it was not always easy, Vi made an effort to include him in her life, dining together when possible, bringing him to family events, paying visits when she could and including Laura.

One evening when they had made a dinner engagement at his penthouse, Vi felt compelled to tell Samuel about the great fire. As she began her story, Samuel said how pleased he was that she felt comfortable enough with him to discuss such a sensitive subject. He knew the gossips in town had held onto their convictions like a seagull with a newly found sea clam, that Vi was the one who started the fire. A wave of release came over her while she unleashed the story about Andrew Todd And in an uncharacteristic show of emotion, she began to cry.

In one quick movement, Samuel jumped up from his dining chair, came over to Vi, putting his arms around her from behind. " It's Okay, let it out, I believe every word of it . What a heavy load for you to carry around all these years. Let it pour out now."

"Thank you, Samuel, you have no idea what your words mean to me. To have a person like you believe in me, is so freeing. I am so indebted."

A sincere, warm embrace followed with a new sense of bonding slowly beginning to take hold.

To say Vi was shocked to be informed through Samuel's attorney that she had inherited almost his entire estate, including the Asteria Hotel, would be an understatement. With the stroke of a pen, Samuel changed the lives of Vi and Stephen forever. For Vi, it validated her power play, her well-orchestrated plan to endear her way into the heart and mind of the old codger. For Stephen, the outcast son, it dealt a devastating blow. Adding insult to injury, Samuel's last will and testament mentioned leaving Stephen a stipend, $100 a month for the rest of his life. Samuel got the last word, and he might as well have shouted it from the grave: "You're just one hundred dollars above worthless!"

CHAPTER 25

With the acquisition of the hotel, Vi became even more of a player among the town's movers and shakers. It marked the beginning of a new empowerment, as Vi became someone with a mission in life, focused on who she wanted to be in the eyes of the town, no longer satisfied with dulling herself with drugs. There was a renewed sense of confidence and agility as she moved among the power brokers of Peck's Beach, always working the crowd to mold an image of herself unrelated to reality. That old cloud of suspicion from the Great Fire clung to Vi like black smoke, along with a mystical sense that the town had somehow passed on to the younger generation a verdict of guilt, never believing her innocence. A perfect bitch beneath the facade, Vi artfully covered her flaws with a combination of kindness, caring, and cunning.

Knowing full well the art of timing, Vi waited to strike, coiled like a snake with eyes and fangs locked on its prey. When Harry decided to run for mayor of Peck's Beach, she realized the opportunity to destroy him might never present itself again in such an ideal way. Patience was about to pay dividends.

Vivian had blamed Harry for Adrienne's death, and her secret vow for revenge had never diminished, despite the intervening years. In 1968, she summoned Harry to Watson's late one night.

"Hello, Harry...it's Vi."

"Yes, Vi," he replied somewhat sarcastically, "I know your voice. What can I do for you?"

"I'd like it if you'd come over tonight; I'm at Watson's."

"Isn't it a little late?

"It's never too late to talk politics, and besides, what I have to say could prove very advantageous if you ever hope to be mayor."

Harry was no fool; he knew better than anyone that without Vi's support in town, his election would be dead before it got off the ground. Her connections were invaluable, as she'd endeared herself to anyone with influence. She had toyed around with running for office herself, but that was only a "head game" she could never seriously follow through on. At the time, only drugs and alcohol were worth running for.

"I'll be over. Just give me a few minutes."

"Come in the front. The door is unlocked."

Vi hung up the phone and waited. Everyone had left the restaurant long ago. The last to leave was always JD, but she had checked before she'd made the phone call and had seen from her bedroom window overlooking the parking lot that his car was gone. They lived separate lives now. JD's life was Watson's, and Vi's life was the Asteria. She often stayed at the hotel in one of the suites, and JD went to their house on Wesley Avenue or crashed at the restaurant. Ella, they decided, would live with JD. The decision was mutually satisfactory, and Ella was happy about it. JD was much easier to live with than VI, and because Laura was a young adult needing supervision, it made sense to have someone always there to oversee family activities. JD's work schedule was crazy...twelve-hour days, seven days a week. Vi, reluctant at first to not have Laura on a daily basis, eventually accepted the decision, and Laura did her best to live out her life between both places.

All was quiet. The restaurant was, as Vi had planned, empty.

When she heard Harry's car pull into the parking lot, she waited at the top of the staircase. The front door opened, and Vi called down, "Come on up, Harry. We can talk where it's comfortable."

Harry slowly ascended the stairs, only to lock eyes on a face as cold as stone.

"Hello, Vi."

Not a word was returned; her body language screamed volumes as she turned abruptly, heading for the living room with Harry in tow. What he really wanted to do was run in the opposite direction. He'd known from the moment he'd heard her voice on the phone that this was not going to be pretty.

Entering the room, Harry didn't even get a chance to sit down; Vi wheeled around to face him, handing him the letter.

Puzzled, he said, "What's this?"

"Read it" came the cutting response.

He opened it, and as he read, it was as though Addi were standing right there in front of him. The letter disclosed what he had feared would surface, and as he felt his knees weaken, he slowly lowered a very shaken body into the armchair behind him to avoid falling over. Finishing the last sentence, he couldn't even look up. He curled into a sitting fetal position, his head wedged between the palms of his hands and his elbows resting on his knees. The realization that he had caused the death of a dear friend, a gracious companion, a fellow entrepreneur whom he respected and loved, was almost too much to bear.

Not one to let this triumphant moment linger in silence, Vi moved in for the kill.

"Harry, you are the scum of the earth, and I hope you rot in hell someday. Come to think of it, someday is already here. This is what you will do. You will withdraw as a candidate for mayor, sell all your island holdings, and leave Peck's Beach forever. You have a slim chance at best grabbing the throne of power on this island, not to mention the chances should this letter ever hit the press. And here's a thought: have your lover help you vacate. I'm quite sure you two will live happily ever after, but not on this island, not now, not ever. And by the way, the original letter is in my safe deposit box with instructions to publish its contents should I be harmed in any way. You have twenty-four hours to make your exit from this island. Now, leave before the stench in the room begins to overwhelm me."

"I'll fight you, Vi, with all I've got," he said as he stood up and walked toward the staircase. But his gut was tied in knots, and he knew she had him trapped. It was the sixties, no one was "out of the closet" yet, especially not on an island that was as conservative as a Methodist minister preaching abstinence on Sunday morning. The letter, if it hit the press, would convict him in the court of the public on two counts, the second being that he was an accessory to the death of a beloved town icon...Adrienne Watson DeVries.

Vi watched Harry disappear down the stairs, and she heard the front door slam behind him, which said it all. He was pissed. No, he was enraged. Now she knew she had him right where she wanted him. It was like a chess game, and her queen had just checkmated his king...no moves left. As she settled into her mother's favorite chair, she realized how sweet revenge could be...it truly was a dish best served cold.

A twenty-four-hour deadline was not much time to make life-altering decisions. Harry was so distraught at this point he couldn't even think straight. When he returned to the penthouse, his lover was asleep...lucky break because he needed time to think. What was his next move? He felt trapped, like an animal in a cage, no escape, only a feeling of doom. His dread was so heavy it was crushing him, with no route to take that would bring his life back to where it had been minutes before he'd answered the call from Vi.

The following night, Harry telephoned Vivian to say he needed to talk. It was the last thing she wanted to do, but she could never resist her curiosity. Vi agreed to meet him at Watson's later that evening. When he arrived, he once again went upstairs. Approaching the top landing, he was greeted with;

"Come on up here, queer."

"You of all people know what it's like to be under suspicion. Please don't do this, Vi."

"Go to hell."

Just as she stood and turned to face him, he unleashed a tirade of accusations, unloading hatred he had held onto for years. Vi never saw his fist coming, and Harry leveled a crushing blow across her jaw, knocking her out cold. Picking up her slight, five-foot-three-inch frame, he carried her to the adjacent kitchen, one used years ago as a bakery for Adrienne's fledgling restaurant, one that had been virtually unchanged since those early days.

Harry dragged Vi to a bentwood rocker, tied each wrist to the arm of the chair with nylon rope from his coat pocket, closed the kitchen door after stuffing all the openings with towels, blew out the pilot light on the old stove, and turned on all the gas burners. He sat down facing the unconscious Vi, delivered an incoherent soliloquy, and waited...waited for the inevitable while the small room filled with fumes to the point of lightheadedness... Then, he reached into his shirt pocket, and he took hold of his lighter just as Vi was coming back to consciousness. Then as though he was casually lighting a cigarette, one flick and two lives ended.

When Laura tried the rear door...the key opened the deadbolt, but the door was chained on the inside. No way was that going to work, so she stumbled around the building to the front door. After chasing the keyhole around in circles, she waited a second until the spinning settled down. Then she said quietly to no one in hearing range, "I swear I'll never drink again!"

 Finally, her key caught up with the lock, and the door magically opened. Slinking like a panther closing in on its prey, she entered the center hall. All was deadly quiet, almost too quiet. Standing in the dark alone, with all the smells of the past evening's dinners mingling with the aromas of pies and pastries still in the air, gave her a really strange feeling. It was spooky, as though the place were coming back to life. Only hours ago, Watson's had been filled with people milling about in all directions, hauling kids behind them or standing in the hall as they gathered other party members.

By now, Laura was starving, so she took a quick right into the kitchen, raiding the walk-in. She could always find something to munch on in there: rolls, butter, small paper cups of homemade blue cheese dressing you squeezed to pop their contents into your mouth. Ah, manna from heaven. And heaven was just the place her mind was taking her; could the ring on her finger be real? Could the night that just ended have actually happened? She felt like she was floating as she left the walk-in, quietly opened the swinging doors into the center hall, and then climbed the stairs.

Just as she got to the top landing, an explosion blew the roof off the upper-floor of the kitchen.

CHAPTER 26

I was suddenly released from a nightmare. My feet were no longer trapped in the sand; the adrenalin surged through me, not unlike what I had experienced once before when the ring on my finger had snagged the intake grate and trapped me under ten feet of water in the Asteria Hotel's pool.

The fog and daze I had felt through my body evaporated. All my senses were focused straight ahead...the flames, the roar of sirens, the flashing of lights just beyond the boardwalk buildings crushed in on me while my mind tried to process what was taking place three blocks away. I ran as never before in my life. In a dream, you run to escape the monster. I ran to face the monster, screaming Laura's name with every step I took.

Fire trucks, police cars, and ambulances were converging from all directions as I bolted through the parking lot, breaking past a hastily made police barricade, still screaming Laura's name. I was quickly blocked by two linebacker cops who stopped me dead on. I remember yelling incoherently to anyone who would listen that my fiancée was inside those flames.

"Hey, buddy, stop, stop! It's too late; no way are you getting close to that building!"

"My fiancée's in there; I've got to find her! Oh God, please, please, I know she's in there. I just dropped her off not even thirty minutes ago."

The cop's grip on my arm relaxed enough so I was able to rip myself free and make a run from the barricade straight for the front entrance. The cops went ballistic, forcing me face down on the sidewalk, snarling, "Make one move, and it'll be your last!"

I lay there crying...totally out of my mind with fear... Was Laura dead? How could such a wonderful night turn on us like this? It was too much to process, and suddenly I was overwhelmed with panic; all rational thought was gone while I froze, paralyzed with shock. The next thing I remember was hearing, "We found her. She's alive..." The medical team brought Laura out on a stretcher, and I couldn't even make out her face. They had her all wired up as three guys hovered over her body in a frantic attempt to stabilize her enough to transfer her to the hospital. I watched, then the thought hit me, I've got to make a break for it, get to my car, and beat the ambulance to the emergency room.

By now, what seemed like the entire police force was well immersed in controlling the crowd while the full force of Peck's Beach Fire Department fought with all they had to put out this major fire and save Watson's. As I was to learn later, the explosion had been confined to the second-floor kitchen and rear upper wing of the building. Fast action on the part of the firemen helped to prevent the fire from spreading and taking the entire building down.

I made a move so quick it surprised even me. I sprinted over to my car, jumped in, and drove unimpeded straight onto Ocean Avenue. No one saw me, since the police were all preoccupied at that point. The worst thing that could have happened to me was I'd be caught and arrested. Tough shit, it would have been worth it, and fortunately looking in my rear view mirror, there were no cop cars in hot pursuit. I drove like a maniac over the Ninth Street causeway, hooked a right at the circle in Somers Point, and managed to arrive at the hospital at the same time the ambulance pulled up to the emergency entrance.

There was no way of knowing Laura's condition, no way to know she'd even survived the ride over... I prayed, really prayed, for the first time in a long time, begging God to spare Laura's life, to bring her home to me. "I don't care what condition she's in, God. With your help, we'll get through this, and I'm here, I'm here for her. You know my heart, Lord."

When the ambulance rear door opened and Laura was brought out on a stretcher, I was right there to see her chest rising and falling with the assistance of a bag. She wasn't breathing on her own. The docs were all around her while the emergency room was set in high gear. She was immediately transferred to an adjacent room, where she'd be triaged and evaluated.

I was told by the nurses to move to the waiting room and that as soon as the doc had completed the immediate tests, they would update me with her condition, results, and prognosis. Try as I might, I lost the battle to stay by her side, and then the long, endless pain of waiting descended like a lead cloud over me.

JD was jolted awake from a deep sleep by the phone ringing on his nightstand; seldom does a 4 AM call carry good news. He was at Watson's in minutes, the depth of the unfolding tragedy having not even begun to set in. Pacing back and forth just beyond the barricade like a zombie out of a B-movie, JD tried to comprehend what had just taken place. The fire crew knew JD personally, and they asked him if he knew if anyone else was in the building. They told him a young girl had been taken out and rushed to Shore Memorial Hospital and that a young guy had been crying and yelling that Laura was in the building, that he'd broken through the barricade trying to get to her.

In a semi-dazed reaction, JD said his wife was in the building and that Laura was his daughter. The fire chief said they were unable to go into the back end of the second floor because the fire was still smoldering and access to the upstairs rear kitchen area was too unstable to attempt a search and rescue.

JD started to freak out at this point. He was beside himself. His wife was in the building, but where? Or maybe she wasn't; maybe she'd stayed overnight at a friend's or at the Asteria Hotel with a boyfriend. Who knew? Too many scenarios were possible, all with possibly deadly endings. The fire chief told JD he had searched the building, and so far, no one had been discovered, dead or alive. Realizing he was standing around waiting for bad news with "scared to death" written all over his face, JD told the chief he was no good to anyone in his state of mind and had to get to Laura, then he took off for the hospital.

Pacing back and forth at this early hour in an empty waiting room, my imagination started to run wild, and the road it took me down did not have "Happily Ever After" on a signpost anywhere. I sat down, put my head in my hands, bent over, and prayed, making desperate deals with God, and then I felt a touch on my right side. Raising my head, I saw JD standing over me with a look of such pain I snapped out of my self-absorption, stood up, and with tears slowly running down my face, I reached out for him as he did the same. With arms around one another, we both lost it. I stood to lose my fiancée, and JD, his wife and daughter. In the midst of what seemed like our valley of death, I will never forget the bonding that was created between two desperate people with huge unspoken fears. Whatever was to come, it was a pivotal moment.

It was killing me not to tell JD about our engagement, but I just couldn't bring myself to drop that bombshell in the middle of all he was facing. So far, he had not mentioned Vi, and I was too afraid to ask.

Waiting together for what seemed like hours enabled me to be there for JD, to be there and just listen. It turned out to be a good thing because he started to open up, saying he had talked to the fire chief, who had not been able to confirm or deny if Vi had been at Watson's at the time of the explosion. JD was still hopeful she had left the building and gone somewhere. Talk about being hit over the head with a sledgehammer... He didn't know; he thought Vi may not have been in the building. But I knew only too well she'd been there because Laura had told me so when she'd slipped out just after midnight. I had no choice at this point. My heart pounding, I took a deep breath and blurted out what had to be said before I lost my nerve.

"Laura sneaked out of Watson's just after midnight to meet me in the parking lot, and Vi was in her bedroom, asleep, or at least, that's what Laura thought. Your daughter was with me all night until I dropped her back at the restaurant around 3 AM. We went to the south end of the island, where I proposed, and gave Laura a ring." I can't remember breathing.

JD looked at me without a sign of emotion and asked, "Are you sure?"

"Yes, I'm sure. I am very sure we love each other."

"Are you positive my wife was at the restaurant?"

How insensitive and stupid could I have been. I had been so focused on my own personal agenda that I'd been completely obtuse regarding what JD had really been asking me.

I couldn't look at him. My eyes were cast down so I wouldn't see his face. "I am, and I'm very, very sorry, JD!"

My words hung in the air, cold, void of any comfort, but I was at a total loss, not knowing how to handle the situation. There I was, my future father-in-law standing before me, motionless, while I'd just handed him life-changing proof his wife was most likely dead. I suddenly felt like I was going to throw up.

At that critical moment, the doctor came in and delivered the good news that Laura was going to recover. Her injuries were serious but not life threatening. Two ribs, her left leg, and her left shoulder were all broken, and she would require a long period of healing, rest, and rehab, but her prognosis was good.

I introduced Laura's father to the doctor, and he was glad to make the connection because she was in need of surgery immediately, with permission essential. The doctor encouraged us to take a break, get some breakfast, and try to relax if possible, because the operation would be long, followed by an extended period in the recovery room.

After the doctor left, JD turned to me, trying hard to hold himself together, said, "God's taken my wife and saved my daughter, all in a matter of seconds. Why?" He turned, moving slowly toward the waiting room door, telling me to look after Laura, that he had to get back to Watson's to tell the fire chief what I had disclosed. With all the strife and turmoil in their marriage, all the hurt caused by brutal words spewed over time, JD was a defeated man leaving the room, a grief-stricken body bent low. Not a word of acknowledgment about our engagement was exchanged between us.

Alone again after the door shut, I was in a kind of non-alcoholic stupor, present but not really, just barely hanging on, when the nurse came to say Laura was coming out of recovery and I could go in to see her. I was so eager that I had no idea what the RN was in the middle of saying when I cut her off. Get to her, that was all I cared about. Which room? I literally ran down the corridor, checking each room as I went. The nurse's station was just ahead, so I stopped dead in my tracks. "Laura's room?" The answer came back, "Two rooms down the corridor on your right." I started to enter the room but was not prepared for what I saw. Laura lay there in traction, and it seemed as if every movable part of her body was in a cast or wired or strapped to something that made movement impossible. It was a shock, and I had a feeling the nurse had been about to give me a heads-up on what I could expect; too bad I hadn't listened.

I stood at the door, started to tear up, and then I knew I had to "man up" and get myself under control. Moving quietly to Laura's side, I leaned down and kiss her. The nurse said it would take a while for her to respond, as the anesthesia would cause her to be in and out of consciousness.

I whispered in Laura's ear, "I'm here, honey, right by your side, and I'm not ever leaving. Count on it." As I went to pick up her left hand, there was no ring on her finger. I freaked out, but tried hard not to completely lose it, I turned to the nurse and said intensely, "Her ring, it's gone. We just got engaged. It was right there!" I held her hand and pointed at her finger. In a calm voice, the nurse responded, "Mr. Saxon, I think it may have been put in the locker with her other possessions. Jewelry is always removed before surgery; I'll go check for you." The nurse returned smiling and holding a plastic bag with Laura's diamond, one remaining earring, and a necklace. I was so grateful I gave the nurse a brief hug. Then I turned around and went to Laura's bedside. I took her left hand, and as I slipped the ring on her finger, her eyes focused on mine for a second. I could swear I caught the faintest glimpse of a smile.

As I was to learn much later from Laura, she was almost at the top of the staircase at Watson's when the force of the explosion propelled her backwards and down three flights. Had she not stopped to raid the walk- in freezer, she would have made it all the way to the second floor, placing her much closer to the explosion. When the first responders found her, Laura was on the floor of the downstairs hall, unconscious and barely breathing, half-covered with debris.

I talked to JD later that morning when we connected by the nurse's station. He told me they had found Vi's badly burned body and he was going to have to identify her at Shore Memorial. I gave him an update on Laura, that she was awake, though groggy, and able to talk to me. He said he'd be there shortly and would come in after he was finished at the morgue. JD asked that I not tell Laura about her mother's death, that he felt he needed to be the one to handle it. I said Laura was starting to ask questions, foggy as she was in her state of mind. I suggested I'd wait for him outside the room so we could go in together.

We entered her private room as planned, and in a very heart-wrenching talk, JD told Laura her mother hadn't made it. Laura's reaction was very stoic, and her eyes fixed on some distant object. I could tell the death of her mother wasn't getting through, that her walls were up and that in order for her to survive, she had to stuff what she was just told...stuff it down deep.

My heart was breaking for Laura too, witnessing this personal and private interchange. I felt like I was intruding, so I turned to leave, but JD stopped me,

"No Sax, please don't leave. I want to talk to you both."

I moved toward the Stryker bed, and JD pulled up a chair to be closer to Laura as he told her, "Losing your mother but gaining a future son-in-law all within a few hours is more than overwhelming."

It was the first time JD had acknowledged our engagement, and I was caught off guard. I nervously waited for the next line. Laura started to quietly cry, motioning me to come closer and hold her hand.

"You're both aware of how difficult Vi has been over these last few years. It hasn't been easy on me or you, Laura. But to lose her like this..." he paused as though asking a question. "It's really knocked me down. I'm hurting in every fiber of my body right now, and if I had lost you too, I don't know where I would be right now... probably getting ready to jump off a bridge somewhere. It's a miracle you weren't killed, Laura, and I know in all of this hurt and pain, God's got a plan, but I sure as hell don't know what it is. I feel like I've been crushed to pieces, very much like you, and the only thing holding me together is you. If you hadn't sneaked out with Sax, you would have been asleep when the explosion hit." The relieved and grateful look he shot me conveyed a huge "thank you." A wave of relief washed over me.

"I'm numb at this point, and I'm having a difficult time trying to cope, but I am clear about one thing, and that's your engagement. Right now, it may be wrapped in tragedy, but in time, with healing, it will turn to joy. I believe you both love each other very much, and you have my blessing."

Laura started bawling. I was holding her hand and kissing her through our tears. JD stood up, motioning to form a team hug, and then he put one hand on her cheek and the other around me.

When the nurse came in to do her routine assessment, JD motioned for me to follow him into the hall.

"Sax, I didn't want to burden Laura with any more than she has already been through, but there was another body they found in the same room with Vi. It was too badly burned, so they're trying to identify the person through dental records, but it's believed to be a male. I don't know what to think, or if I can think at all. The police have questioned me. I have no clue who this person could be. Please don't mention any of this to Laura; it would just be too traumatic for her right now. Her need to know won't matter one bit; there's nothing Laura could do about it anyway except obsess, and what good is that? She has all she can handle just trying to heal physically and, at the same time, emotionally."

"And how are you handling all this?" I wasn't sure at all if JD would really answer me.

"I'm numb right now. Self-protection, I guess. Vi's gone, there was another body found with her, an explosion of a yet-to-be-determined cause, and a daughter I came way too close to losing. And oh yeah, add to that my restaurant that almost burned down. If I let all that really sink in, I'd lose it completely."

Making a move to leave, he continued, "I've got to get back to the island. Ella is a mess, as you can imagine. This has hit her hard, and I need to be with her. Take care of Laura, will you? I'll be back as soon as I can."

"I won't leave her side for a second; you can count on it." And with that, JD took his exit.

I went back into the room, and I could sense the guilt that seemed to hang in the air when I looked in Laura's eyes, a guilt we shared for different reasons. There was no love lost between Vi and me. Laura was well aware of that fact, but, at the same time, I found no satisfaction in a life lost, especially my fiancée's mother, in such a tragic way. It hit me more intensely that we were free now to live our lives without Vi's unbelievable control over Laura. I knew Laura would have similar emotions, but it was her mother we were dealing with, and yes, Laura was free now, but at a price. She had no mother, and that was really painful.

"Honey, I know you're hurting so much right now and things look bleak, but I really believe it will get better. I just know it. We've got to hold on to our trust and faith in God, hold on to His promises to be there for us no matter what. Our engagement and all the good things the future has for us, they're so worth the fight. It's a long road ahead for us both, but the payoff is going to be your total recovery and then our marriage. This is all good. We have your father's blessing too!"

"I can't handle all this, Sax. I feel like I'm broken in a million little pieces right now. Mother's dead; I might as well be too. Suppose I had stayed at home and not gone out. Maybe she'd be alive today."

"Laura, honey, don't give in to those mind games, please. What-ifs have no winners. Second guessing only causes more guilt, and believe me, I have plenty to go around for both of us. If I hadn't planned the whole evening, maybe circumstances would have played out differently and your mother would have survived somehow. But I didn't; I followed my heart and wound up giving it completely to you. I have no regrets, but this I know to be true: we captured the beautiful memory of a magical night. No one has the right to take that away from us."

I rarely left her side after Laura's transfer to the rehab center in Peck's Beach, and I slept overnight whenever I could. I was her "go-to strength" during the healing process in those early days. What became very apparent over time was that the real challenge in healing was not only the physical part; the emotional recovery facing Laura would take much more than a month or two of rehab to overcome, if ever.

I told Laura, "Let's put marriage on hold for a while. When you know you're ready, we'll plan the wedding we've dreamed about. That way, we'll do it right, the way it should be for both of us." I was not surprised when my suggestion of a "hold button" was met with a nod and smile that suggested she was grateful I hadn't pushed the "fast forward" button.

I had no doubt Laura's care, lovingly delivered by Ella, would be excellent when she returned home. Ella was the person you'd most want to have at your side when you were in serious trouble, physically, emotionally, or spiritually for that matter; she should have been an RN with a Doctorate in Divinity!

JD came to visit Laura quite often, and during one of those visits, he brought up a topic he dreaded. The police report stated that the physical evidence proved it had been Harry Blake's body at the apartment, that his body had not been bound like Vi's, that the explosion had been caused by a gas build-up. The investigation had led to a search of his penthouse and Vi's apartment. Among her his possessions, they found a letter written to Harry from her mother that had somehow wound up in Vi's hands. The letter revealed his sexual preference and what had happened when Addi had caught him in the act.

Laura's response was clipped. "Is there no end to all this?" Then she pulled the bed covers over her head, trying desperately to become invisible, which might have worked except for a faint, barely controlled sobbing.

In frequent conversations with JD, I told him that Laura and I wanted to get married but we knew we had better slow things a bit until she was fully back on her feet. JD agree with our decision to wait, since I was a poorly paid teacher and in night school at Villanova's MBA program with no means of finding a major paying job until schooling was finished. Knowing the question would surface, I told him my mother had finally met and married a great guy, Brian McGuire, and that she would be moving permanently to Peck's Beach, where my new stepfather was owner/broker of a real estate office at the south end of the island. That would leave her apartment in Haverford empty, so Laura and I could live there until I graduated in June, and then, hopefully would find a job. My mother liked the plan because she could come visit once in a while, see old Main Line friends, and feel welcome to stay overnight if she wanted.

JD said if we needed some breathing time, we could stay at the family house on the Gold Coast until we could afford to have our own place. I thanked him for his offer and said Laura and I would talk it over, which we did, deciding to split the difference. We'd stay at my mother's apartment until I graduated and then with JD until I found a job. It seemed like a good plan until we were blindsided again...big time.

CHAPTER 27

A few weeks after the explosion, while confined to her bed at the rehab center, Laura asked me to go to the bank and retrieve papers from her mother's safe deposit box. She told me where she had very carefully stashed the key in her home dresser, but I told her there was no way the bank would allow me to have access to the box. I suggested to Laura that I contact their family lawyer to get the necessary legal papers stating Laura had power of attorney. She could then write a personal note, along with the doctor's validation of her physical condition, requesting the bank allow me access to her mother's safe deposit box, and we would have it notarized at her bedside.

Vi had told Laura as recently as the last month that she was going to make her executrix to her will and that she was revising it to include some changes. Laura said she'd be glad to accept the designation, but why now? Was she planning on dying, and why not choose Dad for the job? Vi had just stared at her with that "Are you nuts? Have your father be executor? Not a chance" look, which was followed with "Just do what I ask. No questions, please!"

As expected, with letter and the legal documents in hand, the bank manager had no trouble escorting me downstairs to the vault. He guided me to the correct box, one of what must have been two hundred others securely sunk within a very long wall.

I turned the key, pulled out the metal box, and sat quietly alone at a large conference table. The manager disappeared, but not quite out of sight. I rifled through the documents, barely looking, as the contents were not my concern, but then I stopped. My eyes fell on an envelope with Laura's name on it marked, "To Laura, Personal."

I pulled it out from the other papers and stuffed it in my coat pocket, walked up a short flight of steps, went to the front desk, and then signed out and left. I went over to Laura's family lawyer, Jim Hughes, and gave him the papers, letting him know Laura was in no condition to rifle through all the documents. I kept the letter with her name on it. Since it was personal, I figured Jim didn't need to read it; Laura did. I asked him if he would please use me as the go-to person while Laura was trying to put herself back together again. Not a problem, he said, telling me to give Laura his best and that he'd take care of any legal details that needed addressing.

I told Laura my mission was accomplished; the lawyer had the papers and would consult with her should anything of a legal nature come up. Laura was relieved at the thought of not having to deal with any family matters when she was having a difficult time just performing the physical therapy required at the rehab center.

"Laura, when I was at the bank, I found a personal letter to you in the box, mixed in among other papers, so I pulled it out to be read privately. Jim doesn't know about it; I didn't mention it when I was in his office because I thought it didn't concern him. I hope I did the right thing," I said as I handed her the letter.

Laura didn't say anything. There was a long pause. The envelope was old, and her name was addressed on stationery her grandmother would have used. She glanced over at me with a strange expression of sadness and excitement all mixed into one bewildered look... Her hand was trembling, and her eyes began to well up. I could tell from the way her expression tightened up she was afraid to open the envelope and read it. Inside were two letters, one from her grandmother to Harry, which cleared up a lot of questions about Addi's suicide that Laura had wondered about— though, in retrospect, it raised a bunch more questions than it answered. Like, how did a letter addressed to Harry wind up in Vi's conniving hands rather than his? The other was an official medical record from Regional General Hospital of Cape May, dated September 27, 1946. It was Laura's birth certificate and listed the name of her father as Andrew Todd.

There seemed no end to Vi's venom; even from the grave, she managed to reach out to drive a knife right into the soul of her own daughter. Laura was absolutely destroyed over this unearthed secret. Why hadn't she known who her real father was all these years? Why hadn't JD, her "stepfather," told her? How could they have let this family skeleton stay in the closet? Laura's head spun with questions that only her mother could have answered. But now that Vi wasn't here anymore, she didn't have to deal with the trauma of it all… Just pull up the trash truck after you're gone and dump all the dirt on me, Laura must have thought. Why not, mother? You're dead, so why would you give a shit?

At JD's next visit to the rehab center to see Laura, she had her guns locked and loaded. She heatedly confronted him for his unforgivable deceit, which he, of course, tried to explain, but Laura couldn't hear a word. She felt blindsided; no amount of justification on his part was ever going to be forgivable, not now, not ever, as far as Laura was concerned

JD had her full attention when he said as sincerely as he could, "Hear me out on this Laura, if nothing else."

"Vi had wanted Laura to know, eventually, who her real father was. Also, Vi had wanted to make sure that if the opportunity ever arose, Laura had proof of who her biological father was, which might then factor into the Todd family fortune. It was a way to punish Andrew posthumously to have both a daughter and granddaughter the family never knew existed. JD told Laura he had never known until ten years ago, after a huge fight with VI. At which point, one drink over the edge, she'd proceeded to drop the bomb, and this is how it had gone down."

"You're not Laura's real father," said with a certain amount of satisfaction

JD just laughed in her face. "Boy, there's no depth to which you will not sink, is there?"

He didn't believe a word she'd uttered, so she walked over to her desk, pulled out a small vertical drawer, behind which was a hidden compartment, took out a folded piece of paper hidden there, and handing it to him. It was Laura's birth certificate. Startled, JD read it and then slumped down in the nearest chair in shock.

"Why didn't you tell me this before!" he finally said. "How could you deceive me and Laura all this time, you unbelievable bitch?"

"Let the 'bitch' speak, John," she replied. He did, and she continued. "I went up to our apartment to end my marriage with Andrew. My husband was furious and raped me. When I got pregnant, I knew it was Andrew's… I just couldn't tell you, not at that point in our relationship, when you and I were actually in love. Remember those days?"

"You were probably high as a kite, just like you are now. Are you sure you didn't rape him? And I'm expected to believe all this? This is me you're talking to, Vi, and I know you like a book! You've got to win, to always have the upper hand. Laura's hidden birth certificate is a perfect example. It plays right into your sick, pathetic mind… Stash it away until some crisis makes you dig it out so you've got the perfect weapon to destroy whatever or whomever you think is trying to destroy you."

After telling his story to Laura, JD stood there at the bottom of the hospital bed, willingly taking the verbal abuse. The right words didn't come. There was no way he could comfort his daughter because he knew his explanation just didn't cut it. He hadn't known the truth about her birth father at first, but he could have stepped up to the plate after he'd found out. Because he hadn't, he had lived in his own private hell for what seemed like forever.

Laura told JD she would never step foot in Watson's ever again.

"The place is toxic. It has destroyed our lives, our hopes and dreams as a family, and caused too much pain for me. How can you call yourself a Christian when there has been so much deceit, so many lies, all in the name of fame and money and social position. Where is God in all of this? You think He's put His stamp of approval on our family because Watson's is successful? Is that the litmus test? Look at us, John," The use of his first name feeling like a blade was run through him . "Look around you, and what do you see? A family in ruins. One dead wife and mother, a grandmother and mother-in-law dead from suicide, a building in shambles, and a longtime friend dead by his own hands. And the P.S. to all this? I don't even know who you are."

"Well, just so you know, Sax and I are getting married as soon as I'm able to get out of here. I'm not willing to risk losing the person I love most in my life by bringing him into a family business that has managed to corrupt the very soul and spirit of every person it has touched."

JD remained silent. As he turned to leave, he looked back at his daughter with the face of a man so crushed and defeated that for a split second, Laura almost let her rock-hard angry veneer crack open just enough to let a little bit of compassion escape.

"Someday, somehow, Laura, you'll be able to hear my heart." Silence followed as he left the room.

JD was like a father to me, and I was blown away hearing what Laura said had just transpired between her and her stepfather. I couldn't grasp it. To see Laura put through yet another drama was bordering on the edge of insanity. I had to quickly make a move; she could not remain in Peck's Beach now, and maybe not ever return. So I talked to my mother, "Auntie Mame," as we liked to call her, and she was in total agreement that it was best for us to get married and move into her apartment. Mom was spending much of the time in Peck's Beach with her boyfriend, and soon-to-be husband. She was learning the "back end " of real estate, was an excellent typist, and knew a great deal about how to handle an office after many years in the insurance business. Brian and Mom had met through mutual friends at a party on the island in the spring of '65, and after their first date, they'd known it was the beginning of something magical. My mother had a number of dating opportunities and knew a good thing when she saw it. Years of being a dating widow had taught her to separate the wheat from the chaff. Although more than several offers of marriage had been proposed, she'd never found the right man to spend the rest of her days with. Most of the men had either been mama's boys or too in love with themselves to prioritize adoring her. Besides, she had a wonderful group of girlfriends who found the time to enjoy each other and who loved to cut loose, have fun, and not take themselves too seriously. Mom had no desire to return to the dutiful wife roll, tied down to a controlling husband. She loved her independence too much.

I made arrangements for Laura to transfer to a rehab center in Bryn Mawr, PA. My life pushed the limits of busy, as I was going to school, chauffeuring Laura to rehab, running back and forth from Peck's Beach to work at Watson's, and generally taking care of my mother's apartment in Bryn Mawr. Laura's main job was to get well, to rehabilitate her body to where it had been the night I'd left her off in the parking lot of Watson's, which now seemed like a lifetime ago. Her physical healing was making headway, but the emotional side was so much slower. Laura had continual nightmares, screaming out in her sleep, "Save me, please! Someone save me! I'm trapped! I can't get out!"

In April 1965, we were married at Narberth Presbyterian Church in Lower Merion, PA, the moment Laura was well enough physically. It was very private, with only my best friend John and his wife, Noel, my close friends and some crew from the Big W, several of Laura's good buddies, Ella, and of course my mother and Brian. JD was not invited, per Laura's decree.

CHRISTMAS, 1966

Christmas Eve was winding down as our guests made their exit somewhere around midnight. Perfect timing, because I wanted to enjoy the two of us, logs on the fire, lights down low, and Johnny Mathis singing "Sleigh Bells Ring" on the vinyl 78 speed record player.

"I want you to open your stocking first, honey," I said as I took it down from the mantle hanger and handed it to her. Laura was sitting close to the Christmas tree, among all the presents I was about to give her, so I placed the stocking in her lap.

"Can't imagine what's in here," she said, shaking it to see if it made a sound she'd recognize.

"You'll see quickly enough; just reach in and find out," I said, which Laura did, retrieving a small wrapped gift box with a tag that read "I love you."

Laura tore into the gift like a little kid, opened the box, and then screamed in utter delight. Making no attempt to try it on, she leaped in my direction, throwing herself around me like a warm blanket, managing to get out the words "It's absolutely beautiful."

Feeling very satisfied with my choice of a 14K charm bracelet, something I knew she'd really love, because a woman can never have enough jewelry, I said, "The charms come later; I didn't have enough money left to buy any of those little gems."

"I love it just the way it is. You know how long I've wanted one. It's beautiful, Sax, and the fit is perfect."

She slipped on the bracelet and held her arm up toward my lips so I could kiss it like she was a princess, and I planted a tender kiss on her wrist. "You are so beautiful, my princess; how did I ever manage to steal you away from all the knights of the realm who were in hot pursuit?"

"It wasn't easy, my prince, but I'm so happy you did." Laura stood up, grabbed the stocking with my name on it, and settled alongside me and the Christmas tree. "Now, open your present, please! Enough about me."

I reached into my stocking and brought out a very small package, barely big enough to hold a piece of coal.

"Hmm…wonder what could be in such a tiny box? Good things come in little packages, they say."

"You'll never find out if you just stare at it, Kris Kringle; open the damn thing, will you?" Laura looked like she was about to explode if I dragged this out any further.

Laughing, I pulled a little box out of the stocking in slow motion, just to torture Laura a second or two longer.

Inside the box was a small wad of cotton with a gold charm buried between the layers. I must have had a very puzzled look on my face. At first, nothing registered. I didn't get it, and then it hit me. I was staring at a charm in the shape of baby booties. As I looked over at Laura, the look on her face expressed a thousand words, but I heard only three: "Merry Christmas, Daddy."

My hand could not stop shaking, and with a trembling voice, I said "This is a Christmas miracle!" I wrapped her in my arms, holding and kissing her, not wanting the moment to end.

"You've made me a very happy man, Laura Saxon. This is a Christmas made in heaven that I will never forget as long as I live, but I'm in shock. How did this happen?'

Laughing out loud, Laura said, "You need to ask? There was no star in the east, that's for sure, and if you'll recall, you assured me there was no chance I'd get pregnant just because I forgot one little birth control pill. So much for Sax the Prophet versus Russian roulette."

"I'm glad the bullet wasn't a blank, but I'm still in shock, honey. I love you so much, and by the way...how did you know to get a charm when there was no bracelet to attach a charm onto until just now?"

"Confession time...you inadvertently left the receipt in one of your jeans. You know how I always check the pockets first before putting your clothes in the washer, and voila!"

"You're a pretty good actress, honey, pulling off a surprised reaction like that; sure fooled me."

We reached for our wine glasses resting on the coffee table. "A toast to our Christmas baby and to the mother of my child." Both glasses were raised, and I took some big gulps of Chardonnay and several more after that. Laura took a few modest sips...no need to get high, as we were already drunk with joy!

The pregnancy was a good thing, on many levels, for Laura. Her life became centered on our baby. If a girl, it would be named Tiffany and if a boy, Christopher. No longer focused on her old demons, Laura was able to put the last few years behind her; at least, that was what she told me. That way, she didn't have to deal with her emotions right then. I worried a lot about when and how those emotions would surface once the baby arrived. But for now, all was well.

My dream ever since I was a kid was to have my own business. When I wound up at Watson's during my college years, I realized how much I loved the restaurant business. I quickly came to know how backbreaking the job was, the long hours and days without a break, but I also knew it was for only six months of the year in a seashore town. I figured I could manage to survive anything, knowing the goal would leave me free to do other things I'd never accomplish being anchored to a nine-to-five job. Watson's offered that kind of lifestyle amid wonderful surroundings on a sun-soaked, sand-laden, seven-mile barrier island along the southern Jersey Shore.

JD imparted to me a heavy dose of wisdom, both practical and spiritual, as well as a head full of knowledge about the restaurant business. We became very close, despite the situation with Laura. The break between JD and my wife was an unresolved issue, hanging in a state of suspension, always there, never discussed. I still hoped that once I received my MBA from Villanova in two years, I would be able to move into a management position at Watson's and become an integral part of the company. That was my long-range goal, but for the immediate future, I had to concentrate on school and the arrival of our baby.

Tiffany arrived with much fanfare after a long, protracted labor. Laura was fantastic and, following transition, pushed her out in eleven minutes. I was there to see it all; it was a rare event in the late sixties for fathers to be included as participant and coach.

It was a crazy time. We teamed it up in every way to balance a newborn, school, and, as time passed, a toddler. Once Tiffany got her wheels, meaning her ability to walk at nine months, the world was suddenly within her reach. Pots and pans, soap underneath kitchen cabinets, toilet paper rolls, you name it, she found it. But what a joy she was, what a treasure, and what a wonderful mother Laura was from the moment Tiffany was put to the breast. Was it possible to love our daughter more? I think not! But what was possible was another child someday. Laura and I had decided long before Tiffany showed up on the stage that we'd have at least two children. An only child was not our desire if we could help it, having too many generations on either side of our families where siblings were nowhere to be found, and we aimed to reverse the pattern, Lord willing!

When Tiffany was sixteen months old, she spiked a fever of 107 degrees, convulsed in my arms, and we rushed her to the emergency room. The doctors put her on an ice mattress for three days and were able to isolate the cause...E-coli sepsis, caused by deadly bacteria.

I begged God to save her life. There was no bartering with Him. Rather, I came as a pauper, broken in spirit, pleading for the life of our daughter. And then it hit me: could this be my "payback" for letting my friend almost die in the pool so many years ago?

With Laura in my arms, I blurted out, "Could this be my payback? Is Tiffany the sacrificial lamb?"

Laura whispered, "Sax, Tiffany's not the sacrificial lamb. What are you talking about? Only Jesus owns that title, and it's a good thing for all of us He does. But what's this 'payback' thinking of yours?"

"Laura, you know the story I told you long ago about me almost drowning in the Asteria's pool?"

"Not about to forget that one!"

"Well, it's not true." The words came out before I realized what I had just admitted. No taking it back now. I was shaking. I couldn't even look at Laura.

"You're scaring me, Sax. What are you saying?"

"I'm saying I only told you part of the story. Parts of it are true. The event did happen, but not how I made it sound. My close friend Peter and I had a fight over a girl I was dating. Peter never told me he was dating her behind my back, and she had even given him a friendship ring. I was furious. Then Peter got his hand stuck underwater in the intake grate. Actually, I never saw it happen, because I was swimming for the surface to get some air. I hung onto the pool's edge waiting for Peter to surface, but he didn't. I figured he may have come up at another spot opposite where I was, so I submerged my head in the water to check, eyes open, and there he was, still over the grate, thrashing from side to side like a fish on a hook. For a split second, which now seems like forever, I thought, Let him suffer a little, so I did nothing, nothing. Then I snapped out of it. I dove deep, grabbed hold of his hand, and yanked it with all the force I could bring to bear, and his hand came free. To me, it was a miracle the ring released its hold on the grate when it did.

"I screamed for help, the guards dove in, and within minutes, the medical team was there. Peter was unconscious, but he was revived by the pool lifeguard and taken to Shore Memorial Hospital. Lack of oxygen caused minor brain dysfunction, and, to this day, his spoken language is partially impaired, and it's tough for him to concentrate for long periods.

"I was the hero of the day. I saved his life. Little did anyone know that in that one second, I wanted to end his life. For that, I've been haunted with guilt and shame all these years, Laura. One precious second of anger and jealousy, and look where it's brought me...to my knees, begging the Lord not to take my daughter because of my hateful, hateful impulse to so quickly destroy another human being." The aching in my heart turned into one of those gut-wrenching cries, the kind where you can't breathe.

Laura grabbed hold of me, her arms wrapped around my entire frame to make sure I wouldn't come apart. The love and compassion in her eyes let me know one thing: "I hurt with you, too."

"Sax, if the Lord operated on the premise that paybacks were deserved, none of us would stand. He loves you, I love you, and our daughter will not pay the ultimate price because of you. Jesus took all our sins on Himself, so there's no need to carry the guilt honey. His love is unconditional, Sax. It's called Grace, a gift this side of heaven we'll never really be able to completely grasp."

I just looked at her and said, "Does that include forgiveness?" Without realizing it, I had dropped the bomb...the "forgiveness" word. It fell to the floor, exploding in total silence. Here we were. I could never forgive myself, and Laura could never extend forgiveness to her father. Pretty pathetic.

"It does include forgiveness," came the monotone response. I knew my wife; that flat affectation of hers always belied an emotion behind which is often found a deeper truth.

I gave her a hug, one with a heavy dose of desperation mixed in, and I whispered, "We sure have built a bunch of walls that need to come down." All the while, I was praying Laura would realize it was time to tear down her wall, the one with her father's name written all over it...time to play the forgiveness card.

Interestingly, Laura didn't follow through with a whisper to me. Communications stopped, and we retreated behind our personal walls for protection.

This I know for sure. There at the hospital, that heart-wrenching night, I tore down my wall, the one that kept me from forgiving myself, and for the very first time, I truly embraced God's forgiveness.

All night, sleeping on a cot next to Tiffany's bed, I knew what hell must have felt like. But the sun rose, and the fever fell. Had I been forgiven? The doctors said Tiffany had, as one put it, "made it through the dark side." And so had I.

It was the best Christmas ever. All the presents under the tree were just that, presents. All else paled when seen in the light of the precious gift of life so miraculously given to our daughter and to us.

CHAPTER 28

Looking back, I could never have foreseen how my future would turn out. I'd fallen in love with JD's daughter, and then she'd turned around and divorced her own father. I hadn't seen that coming, nor, of course, did Laura. She was left with no roots, no real family except Ella, whom she considered one of the most trusted, beloved, and truly genuine Christian persons she knew. And as for my part in all this, I was not about to lose a mentor, father figure, and friend, three things I considered of great value and worthy of holding on to. I was committed to figuring out how to circumvent Laura's deeply wounded spirit, wounded to the point that she extricated her father from her life.

I graduated from Villanova with an MBA and spent the next 9 months pounding the pavement trying to find a job while very grateful that Laura had money from her inheritance. If it hadn't been for that, we'd have been basically bankrupt financially. I was able to bring some money in by working at Watson's during the summer months to help JD over the hectic "height of the season" weekends. I'd stay on the third floor of the restaurant for an overnight and then shoot home late Sunday evening. Laura was reluctantly okay with the arrangement as long as she wasn't involved. She knew how important it was for me to keep my relationship with JD on solid ground. She was not at the point in her life to reconcile, and it was made even worse because we had a daughter that her grandfather was never allowed to see, let alone love in person. JD was always asking about her, and I'd show him pictures and update him on Tiffany's milestones. Caught in the middle, I was determined to be the link that helped bind these two together in any way possible, no matter how dire it looked. Someday, somehow, it was my greatest prayer and deepest hope that Laura would be able to forgive her father. JD waited for that moment to come, but

Laura made it very clear forgiveness was not even a shadow on the horizon. I longed for the miracle it would take.

I like to call it the "Boom Theory"...you're walking along the street one day, and "Boom!"...out of nowhere, you're hit on the head with an unknown object, thrown to the ground, and suddenly your life flashes before you as everything changes.

The message on our phone said, "Please come to Peck's Beach on Saturday, late afternoon... It's very important and something I believe you will be interested in hearing... We're away till then."

I tried calling my mother right back but to no avail. She knew how to hook me. She had my curiosity working overtime, so of course, I had to go to the shore, even though the timing could not have been worse. I was knee deep in prepping for a job interview in central Philly. I told Laura about the message and that I would go to McGuire's in the AM, that it must be pretty important. She just looked at me, shaking her head, and not in a positive way either. Not unexpectedly, I figured I'd go it alone.

Saturday came, my curiosity had not waned, and I took off for the island. No matter how many times I crossed over the causeway bridge to Peck's Beach, I was always flooded with childhood memories of summers lived without a care in the world, just thrilled to be headed for the beach. Fun in the sun and amusement rides at night, my youthful idea of heaven.

I pulled up in front of the beach cottage where my mother and Brian lived, the same place McGuire's Real Estate was located as well, perfectly perched at the ocean's edge. No wonder clients bought their homes from them. One look at the location was enough to encourage potential buyers to dream, and then to make the dream real, of owning property right along the beach.

McGuire's tag line, "A home at the shore is square footage for the soul," said it all.

I was greeted warmly by the receptionist and directed to the conference room. To my surprise, my mother, Brian, and Scooter were already seated and in deep conversation when I entered the room. All three stood up, with my mother coming right over and giving me a big hug. Brian was close behind her to shake my hand.

"Sax, you know Michael J., or Scooter, as we call him," Mom said with a smile.

"Sure, Mom, we've met on several occasions, but it's been a while."

Scooter shook my hand. "Nice to see you again, Sax."

I replied, "Nice to see me too," which made us all laugh, creating a relaxed atmosphere. Then I thought, Okay, where's the elephant in the room?

Brian took the lead when we sat down, explaining they'd wanted to meet me at the office because they had a proposal to offer. Scooter was leaving the organization to venture out as a real estate broker and start his own business in the Somers Point mainland area.

As I was trying to reprocess yet another one of my "boom theories," Brian said, "After much consideration and numerous interviews by qualified applicants, finding none that fit, your mother suggested you as a candidate. We decided to at least run it by you and see what your thoughts are. Hopefully, you will decide to take the offer, since we feel you'd be a wonderful asset as office manager. Scooter is willing to stay on for at least a month or two, depending on how fast you learn."

I was taken aback by the offer and expressed concern about my qualifications. My objections were quickly overridden by the fact that I already had a real estate license in escrow, obtained at the urging of my mother, to earn some spending money, though I'd hardly used it since my early college days. I could get the license out of escrow, and Scooter would be right there to help with the transition. My mother said she figured the timing was right, that I was job seeking anyway and this could be a great opportunity to get on the ground floor to manage a thriving business. My MBA factored into the equation, I'm almost certain.

Two thoughts ran simultaneously through my mind… One was negative: What will Laura's reaction be to all this? One was positive: If I accept, it will put me closer to JD and Watson's… The answer to the former thought was gravely in doubt; the latter thought made me smile.

"I'm really flattered by all the confidence you've shown in me and frankly blindsided by the offer. It's a bit overwhelming, but let me say I'm interested. However, first and foremost, I have to run this by Laura. It's a big decision, one that's life changing for us, so you'll understand my needing more time."

Brian said, "Sax, take whatever time you need. We understand completely. And while we're on the subject of life-changing events, your mother and I are in the early planning stages of sailing around the world. Hopefully, this winter, when business quiets down during the off-season, we'll set sail for three months for ports unknown. It's been a dream of mine for years, and you know how much we both love the sea. By then, you should have a good handle on managing McGuire's, especially with our team of professionals backing you."

"I can't wait" came my mother's response, and her look of delight flooded the space between her eyes and mine.

"Oh, I almost forgot," Brian continued. "The P.S. to all this is we sweetened the deal; you and Laura can have the apartment above the garage at no cost. It's a very spacious two-bedroom, as you know, and would be very adequate for your expanding family."

With a hint of satisfaction in my smile, I said, "I couldn't be happier to see you both sail across the Seven Seas. Hopefully, I can help make this part of your dream come true. Stay tuned, I'm off to consult with management. Give me until Monday."

On the drive home, I thought, What an opportunity has just been handed to me out of the blue…the boom theory working again. Just when I thought our lives were settling down to somewhere between chaotic and normal, I'm being given this chance to get involved with a business most people would fight to get. It pays to know the boss, I guess. But no, it went beyond nepotism. I felt a genuine belief by all parties concerned that I could not only do the job but was considered the best person for it.

I found an envelope under my car windshield wiper marked "Chris." It was from my mother; I knew her writing. Besides, she was now the only one who called me by my first name. I threw it on the front seat as I took off out of the driveway. Once the cruise control was on, I reached over and with my right hand, opened the letter, and began to read, carefully keeping two eyes on the road when needed.

To my dear son,

Please don't share this with Laura. It's just between you and me. I really wanted to offer you the management position, not only because I feel you are very capable, but also for the reason of helping to save your marriage. I know your first love is Laura—there's no question that is true—and your second love is that damn restaurant... why, I haven't a clue, but it's a fact, and not one I'll ever understand. I have also been aware of the conflict these two passions of yours have caused over the years, inflamed partially by Laura's refusal to make peace with her father. I know you like a book, my son, so I gambled on writing a chapter in that book of yours by bringing you in as part of McGuire's. If you decide to make the move, it will bring you and Laura back to where it all began. Maybe, just maybe, in the future, it will bring healing for you both and for Laura toward her father. That's my prayer for you, Chris, and for my very special daughter-in-law. If I know you, what may seem like lemons right now will be lemonade later down the road.

XOXO Auntie Mame

I was well aware what a risk it was for my mother to write what she had. It was out of love for me and for Laura, and she could not have been more right. If I took the job, it would get us back to the island with a chance, though a longshot, for healing. I'd known from the moment the position had been offered to me that I wanted to take it. The question was how Laura would react.

On arriving home, I barely got out of the car before Laura came out to meet me with "Well, what was all the mystery about? I've been playing guessing games with myself all day."

"Brian and my mother offered me a general management position because Scooter is leaving to start his own brokerage on the mainland."

The mystery was revealed and greeted with dead silence. "You're not kidding, are you!"

It wasn't a question. "Nope," I said.

"What did you tell them?"

"I said I'd have to talk it over with you first and I'd give them an answer by Monday, which they understood. Scooter would train me, staying on as long as it takes to bring me up to speed. Brian and Mother are planning a three-month round-the-world sailing adventure during slow season, a life's dream they never thought would come true. Oh, and I almost forgot…we can live in the garage apartment…free." My voice rose with a little too much excitement, so it wasn't difficult for Laura to see what side I came down on.

"Sax, you know how I vowed never to return to Peck's Beach, how much hurt and despair the very thought of the place holds for me."

"Honey, no one is more aware of that than I am, believe me. Here's my thinking: your father is only there five months. Then he leaves for California after Watson's closes. McGuire's is at the south end of the island, and during tourist season, your father is a hermit, working from sunrise until well after it has set and going home to hibernate until the next day, doing it all over again. I don't believe your lives are going to intersect."

"This is seriously high-risk stuff for me, Sax, and I just can't think what's best."

"Best for you or our family?" My remark hung out there like thick fog. I made no attempt to clear the air. "There's more to consider here. The money is excellent, the opportunity is equally good, and it's a wonderful town for our daughter to be raised in. Laura, if you'd be willing, let's at least give it a trial period of, let's say, six months and then re-evaluate. We can keep the apartment here in Philly, giving us a backup plan if the shit hits the fan. I'm convinced they really want me, so I'm confident I can sell the idea to Brian and Mother. Will you give it some thought?"

We walked into our place as we talked, making our way to the refrigerator to retrieve a bottle of wine. As we sat beside each other, Laura just looked at me with those beautiful emerald eyes of hers, leaned over, and kissed me, saying, "As someone wiser than I once said, 'Healing is a process, not an event.' I'm working on the process, but I'm far, far from overcoming the event. Sax, I know this is a great risk on both our parts. I don't have a crystal ball, and maybe I'm glad I don't. All I know is this...as you and I have always believed and as Ella has always imprinted on our minds, if we want to see faith in action, step out into the darkness and see if God is there. If He's true to His word to never leave us or forsake us, we'll know it then. I feel like we're taking that step, and if we say we live by faith and only give lip service to our beliefs, then we are just 'posers,' aren't we? So, with great trepidation and a very shaky faith, count the four of us in."

"The four of us? Are we bringing Ella with us too?"

"No, hopefully, our new, yet-to-be-born son!"

The Boom Theory struck again like lightning, twice that day. I was speechless, though for only a moment. Then I went crazy with joy.

CHAPTER 29

That night, I called Brian and Mother with my acceptance of their offer, but I was silent on the baby news front. It was killing me, but we thought it best to delay the good news until more time passed, since Laura was only six weeks pregnant.

They were thrilled I was coming on board. I made no mention of the contents of the windshield message when Mother got on the phone. I figured I'd talk to her about it later.

I spent an equal amount of time that week at McGuire's. Brian held an office meeting to let everyone know I was going to be their new office manager and to go over the various roles the staff were going to play during and after the transition. People generally don't like change; some staff members were surprised and a bit reluctant at first to embrace the new order of management. However, at the end of the "shock session," I got the feeling everyone was willing to jump on board and roll with the changes.

After the meeting broke up, I had the unique pleasure of being introduced to the top producer in the office—by the agent herself, come to think of it. Cindy Kaz, which, as she said was short for Kaczmarski. There was no holding back on her part. She came right up to me, big smile, tiny frame, and all. "Hi, I'm Cindy, and if all my clients looked like you, I'd never get any work done!!!"

I know I turned a little red.

My retort: "You're our biggest producer. Does that mean all your clients are ugly?" And with that, we both burst out laughing, still shaking hands like we were pumping water from a well!

She was the tonic I needed that day, and as it turned out, it was the beginning of a long-lasting friendship.

Not missing a beat, Cindy continued unabated, "I was on a sales call the other morning, driving my beast of a truck, the '59 Suburban, when, glancing out the window on my side, I saw a huge tire rolling free as a bird, making its way down the street, even passing me!

"I thought, I wonder whose tire that could be? At which point, my truck made a sharp, involuntary left hook into the opposing lane. Fortunately, no car was coming, and I made a three-point landing on the sidewalk...three point 'cause the tire was mine!!! Oh, and the tire smashed into a plumbing store's front window. Now, that's how my day started yesterday...how about yours?"

Oh, this job was going to be fun, no doubt about it.

I had known Scooter for quite some time, but only as a friend, not as management. I loved the guy. Who didn't? Given just his charisma alone, he was in the right career. Real estate fit his personality perfectly.

So, who was this charismatic soon-to-be cohort? I reminisced...Scooter Caldwell was in his late thirties, born with a silver spoon in his mouth, the youngest of three children of Main Line parents too busy to smell the wetlands at low tide. He had ADD... Actually, he had all the letters in between as well. You had to have a butterfly net to catch him. But when you did and he made eye contact, focusing clearly on the topic at hand, there was no one better at the profession of real estate than Scooter.

The nickname fit him like a glove: he scooted from one job to another, always on the run. It looked like he was spinning wheels all the time when, in fact, he was not.

As a kid in his early twenties, college wasn't his thing, so he fled to Peck's Beach to the dismay of his family, heading for fun in the sun...sailing, fishing, water skiing, surfing...surprising how those activities don't put food on the table or a roof over your head. When his father decided to extract the silver spoon, Scooter was forced to bunk with friends and sponge off anyone he could until he found gainful employment. With the summer ending and the tourists returning home, the island returned to quiet, as no one needed extra help to run their seasonal businesses.

After Scooter was forced into some major self-evaluation, he realized he was in a mess, both emotionally and monetarily. Act one of his life was not looking too promising until, as life sometimes does, things led to a way to escape. One of his surfing buddies had parents in town who owned a real estate company, and there was an opening for a front-end office clerk. One thing led to another, and Scooter secured the position, unqualified as he was. If his hand got stuck in a cookie jar, he could talk his way out of it, cookie still in hand.

ADD notwithstanding, the boy was smart. After a period of adjustment and confidence building on the owner's part, Scooter was encouraged to get his real estate license and started making some serious money. So he grabbed the golden ring and rode what would eventually become the crazy "merry-go-round" world of real estate. The rest was not hard to figure out.

After hopping around to various brokers in town, Scooter wound up at McGuire's, and it was there that he really found his niche. Accumulating wealth came easily, so he bought a big house on the bay and married Aston, not the girl next door, but the girl next to his desk at work.

They were as different as high and low tide: she went to college at Bryn Mawr; he went to the nearest bar! Her parents were the Armstrongs, middle class Main Line wannabes, non-professionals whose heritage never had the credentials to make the Blue Book. But Aston had the looks, the class, and the smarts to override any deficits in social norms, so when the opportunity presented itself, she had her hooks out for Scooter. She dropped a line, and he took the bait. Aston had always been a conformist, a people pleaser, but with Scooter, she could throw away all her inhibitions and cut loose; she wanted to catch the good life with all the security that went with it, and he surely seemed to hold the ticket for that ride.

Since I was going to dive head first into the world of real estate, I could not have picked a better place than Peck's Beach to start. As the original playground for the upper crust of Philadelphia's sailing society, this seven-mile barrier island was an ideal place to drop anchor. The open waters of Great Egg Harbor Bay provided the perfect conditions for sailing, yachting, fishing...comparable to none along the southern shores of South Jersey.

Over the years, the island had become a haven for summer vacationers. It attracted people from all parts of the country, due mainly to its three-mile boardwalk and pristine beaches stretching for seven miles along a coastline filled with all kinds of fish and sea sports. Add to that its accessibility to major East Coast metro areas, and you've got a major hit.

The island really came into its own around the mid-sixties. Celebrities are like magnets; they tend to follow one another from place to place, and having the Grace Kelly clan as a regular commodity in town definitely didn't hurt. Peck's Beach became the "in" place to go for fun in the sun, a strong competitor to Tinsel town.... Hollywood.

To prove the point, one Saturday in August, I was doing on-the-job training with Scooter when I told him I needed to make a fast stop at the Thirty-fourth Street

Acme Market to grab some food for dinner. We rushed in, along with a ton of Shoobies as well, totally forgetting what day it was...check-in day for renters...but it was too late to turn back. Scooter shot off in one direction, and I made a beeline for the canned goods aisle...bad move number two... It was packed, and I could hardly maneuver the cart around all the bodies in front of me. I heard a voice say, "Come on through. It's OK." With that, this woman very nicely accommodated me by leaning her body tight up against the canned goods as I slid my cart under her butt. With a "Thanks," I steered my way forward, and I saw a man with his cart coming straight toward me, flanked by what looked like a muscle bound bodyguard. Then it hit me: I was looking right at Prince Rainer. I swung my head around and realized I had just nailed Princess Grace up against the baked beans!!!

I wanted so badly to go back and tell her she was my idea of what a real-life princess would look like—in other words, make a drooling ass out of myself. Besides, no one was mobbing her as she floated around dressed in her classic turban headpiece and casual beach attire.

I met Scooter outside the market. He asked what took me so long. I said, "You wouldn't believe it."

He didn't!

So, the celebrities had landed. Hollywood loved the fact you could step out of your summer rental condo and put your toes right in the sand, all at a reasonable price compared to California. Plus you were within driving distance of Philadelphia, New York, or Washington, DC.

After the '62 storm, the town went through a renaissance; construction was in high gear, with architects redesigning how people lived in comparison to the generation before them. Duplexes became condos, doubling the tax base almost overnight, allowing for major municipal expansion and the usual waste of taxpayers' money, the plague of too few in control of too many bucks!

McGuire Realty cashed in on the island-wide expansion, selling and listing homes at a record pace. Amid all this activity, the rental business was thriving, up fifteen percent every year and going strong. And so was competition. Privately held real estate brokerages were all vying for the same ten square miles of land, a cutthroat business that only the committed and craftiest competitors had any chance of making a success of the business.

It was into that business atmosphere that I stepped, with Scooter at my side...hook, line, and sinker!

McGuire's...you can't even mention McGuire Realty without expanding on what that name encompasses...for starters, lunch at the Full Belly Deli, the local hangout for agents from all over the island. If you wanted to keep your finger on the pulse of Peck's Beach, this was where you wanted to be.

Stories were told and retold, exaggerated just enough to suck you in, and if you were observant enough, you'd see agents listening intently, as evidenced by long pauses between bites of pizza or steak sandwiches, not wanting to miss a word of the tale unfolding before them. Here's an example. One of the deli devotees said he called a summer rental client one day to remind her that her deposit was past due. He didn't want her to lose the rental vacation week for lack of payment.

When she answered the phone, he explained why he was calling, and she said rather casually, "Well, darlin', I'll tell you what. I'm in bed tryin' to make it now."

At his end of the phone, there was dead silence. Then, without missing a beat, the agent retorted, "Do you charge by the hour, or is it a flat fee?" The potential renter hung up, so he never got the answer. Not surprisingly, the deposit never showed up.

The deli erupted with laughter, and it only went to prove that real estate stories are stranger than life itself. It was a living, moving, real-life sitcom at the Full Belly Deli!

Then, not to be outdone, Scooter chimed in with this very entertaining gem. The D'Angelino family of ten from South Philly arrived at Maguire's on a Saturday to pick up keys for a vacation home they were renting for the week on the beach, price tag $5000. They showed up at 11 AM only to be told check-in time was not until 2 PM to accommodate the cleaning service, which needed time to get it ready for the next tenants.

This was not acceptable, as the family had brought all their perishable food with them for the entire stay. They had absolutely no plans to spend one dime for food on the island. They were very self-contained, bringing every piece of pasta, every ounce of sauce, from Mama's kitchen. There were containers on top of containers, all packed in ice and ready to thaw, boil, cook, and eat at a moment's notice. It was Italian cuisine on wheels, and they needed to roll the picnic right up to the freezers of their beautiful rental by the sea.

To be told they had to wait did not compute. All the food would defrost; it was a hot Fourth of July weekend, but Scooter held firm to the 2 PM check-in policy to the point where a fight almost ensued. Finally, a compromise was reached: they were allowed to go to the rental cottage, put their food in the freezer, and return at the official check-in time.

Returning right on schedule, the D'Angelinos discovered, to their horror, all the food was gone. Italian expletives can still be heard rumbling over the waves, ricocheting off the rocks of the jetty. Then there was a knock at the door, and it was Scooter. He was totally unaware of what had transpired because he was out showing properties to clients from Pittsburgh. Of course, one of the properties on his list to preview was the cottage by the sea, which now contained the infamous D'Angelino clan. When they opened the door, said, "Oh, hi. Glad you got in. We're here for dinner."

Before Scooter could laugh at his own joke, he had a fist in his face, and looking up from the ground, he realized they all failed to see the humor.

After much chaos, the mistake was uncovered. Scooter went around the back of the cottage and found a trashcan filled with most of the missing food. When the cleaners came in, they found the food in the freezer, and thew it out, thinking it was leftovers from the former tenants. At least, that's what they said. Scooter saved the day from total disaster by managing to get the cleaning crew to return the packages they had salvaged. After the dust settled from this fiasco, Scooter was invited to stay for dinner, so the day closed out with ten D'Angelinos and one frazzled real estate agent sitting around a huge dining room table and eating some of the best Italian food ever to cross Scooter's lips. Needless to say, the cleaning crew was fired. I came to learn there were many such stories in "America's Finest Resort to Drop Anchor!"

"Take care my soul, for what you strive to be, less the sight of focused desire neglects the following sea".

During the six-month trial period, Laura and I locked heads repeatedly when it came to Watson's. I was not willing to totally block out JD from my life, and Laura was not willing to forgive her father under any circumstances, creating a recipe for tight-roped tension.

"Laura, you and I are coming from totally opposite directions on this thing. My whole relationship with JD has been built on trust, on our connection through Watson's, and, more importantly, through you. You, however, have been confronted with a person you trusted with your life only to find out that person was not what he said he was. Your trust has been ruined, and your relationship with JD is laced with a whole bunch of baggage. I do understand the effect all this has had on you, please believe that. I can see it's effect, so I know right now forgiveness toward your father is not an option. That said, nothing is impossible, so I have always hoped reconciliation would happen. I want you free of this stone around your neck, Laura. It's weighing you down."

"I know you want freedom for me, Sax, and I want it too. I just can't bring myself to forgive JD until I feel it inside. I can't fake it. It's got to come from my heart, and I'm not there yet."

"Fair enough, but give me enough leeway so I can stay connected with JD... It's a matter of my heart as well."

Shortly after some fairly tense exchanges, we reached a compromise. The restaurant needed help on the management level, and I told JD that I was willing to assist in any way I could, taking into consideration that my time was limited by real estate and family life. I found that Scooter had trained me well, as I was able to implement a support team that allowed me more job flexibility. I carved out sections of time to assist JD, for which he was very grateful, and we co-managed problem solving the various issues facing the business.

With the passage of time, Laura and I realized that our self-imposed "trial period" proved to be very profitable. We both saw the value of living and working on the island, but especially Laura, having grown up in the town and graduating from one of the best high schools in the state. She realized how wonderful the island was to raise a family, to be able to enjoy the ocean and bay with all the activities available.

Coming back to Peck's Beach was an unimaginable blessing far beyond our ability to have projected. The commitment to return to Peck's Beach, step by step, proved a very good decision, made even more permanent after the birth of our second child.

Laura's water broke on Labor Day night, so we hurried between contractions to Shore Memorial Hospital. It was a good thing the hospital proximity was just over the bridge to the mainland, because we made it just in time, thanks in part to the speed I was traveling. Rushed into the delivery room, I coached her with every contraction. While the nurse and doctor worked quickly to get ready for the birth, Laura pushed like a champ, and our baby's head crowned and then the infant was gently delivered. Then I heard the best sound in all the world, the baby's first cry. That first sound said it all, "I'm here, and I'm ready for life!" I didn't give a damn whether it was a boy or girl. All I wanted to see were ten fingers, ten toes, and a healthy pink baby.

"It's a boy!" came loudly over the commotion. I was beaming, holding Laura tight as she started to cry. I turned to capture my first glimpse of Christopher while the doctor said, "What a healthy boy you have!" The nurse wrapped Christopher tightly in a blanket after gently drying him off, placing him in Laura's eager arms amid her tears of joy as well as exhaustion. The union merged into a family embrace. Shortly after, the nurse took our baby to be circumcised right there in the delivery room. The doctor believed in traumatizing a male newborn only once, relying on the presence of the baby's stress hormones from birth to continue to decrease the pain of the procedure. I was leaning over the warmer with my face and right hand very close to Christopher, whispering quiet words of comfort while the doctor cut off his foreskin. With eyes wide open, Christopher reached up with his tiny right hand and grabbed my forefinger, holding on for dear life. After only minutes on this earth, my son was reaching up to me for comfort! It was an unbelievable moment, a rare gift of father-son bonding, a moment I would never forget.

Taking things one step at a time, I was able to connect again with Watson's, the business I truly loved. It was a small crack in the door...a door that maybe someday Laura could walk through so that forgiveness and healing might take place for her and JD.

For the entire nine months Laura was pregnant, I spent most of my energy developing skills as office manager and selling real estate. Brian and Mom were able to get free for two- and three-day sailing adventures, because their goal, I eventually learned, was to slowly groom me to someday take over the company. But long before their goal became reality, they decided to sail off into their dream adventure...around the world in 120 days, and they planned their timing just right. Christopher had made his appearance, all nine pounds of him, just in time for them. Neither Mom nor Brian wanted to miss becoming grandparents for the second time in their lives.

We all threw them a huge "round the world" party at the yacht club, courtesy of McGuire Real Estate, and what a send-off it was! When it was time to take to the sea, I gave my mother a big hug, pulled her slightly away, and said, "Have a safe trip, Mom; I pray God will protect you both, and as old salts say, 'May you have fair winds and a following sea.'"

"Don't worry, Sax, I mean Chris," she replied, and we both laughed. "I feel really good about this trip, and we'll send you postcards at every port. And know this: McGuire's is in good hands with your involvement. And don't forget to kiss those chubby cheeks of our grandson every day. I'm missing him already and so glad we got to meet him before we sailed."

"Thanks so much, Mom. And be assured, Christopher will be smothered with kisses from you every chance we get."

We hugged again, and this time, Laura joined us, hugging Mom, wishing her a safe and fun trip. The guests worked their way to the dock and the connecting beach to wave goodbye. It was an absolutely gorgeous evening. The sun was setting as they got underway, the sails of their boat catching the golden light reflecting off the water. Brian and Mom waved wildly to all of us as the Fin and Tonic slowly maneuvered through the inlet. We cheered and waved back like we were witnessing a bride and groom leaving for their honeymoon, but in a way, it was just like that, sailing into a new life, being willing to take the risk rather than stay safely inside the harbor. The seas were calm, the water azure blue, and like a scene out of a movie, dolphins suddenly appeared doing a high-wire flying act as though on cue. Everyone had to run to the beach to get a final glimpse of the happy sailors, and Sax was able to barely see them on the stern of the boat, waving back again as they sailed toward the night's diminishing light.

Those promised postcards came sporadically from ports far and wide. Occasionally Laura and I got a phone call, so between the cards and the calls, we were able to track their progress around the globe. Days turned into months, and before we knew it, Mom and Brian were sailing into Great Egg Harbor Inlet, tying up at the yacht club, and then being greeted with a wonderful homecoming celebration. The adventure had lived up to their expectations, and their stories would be told repeatedly in the years to come. I was just grateful they'd survived to tell their tales!

CHAPTER 30

After our son was born, Laura decided to renew her nursing career, receiving her BSN degree in the early seventies. She was drawn to ER nursing but could not have possibly considered hospital nursing again if it weren't for Ella's help. Now in her seventies, Ella was beginning to slow down a little, but she was still blessed with plenty of energy, and with baby number two having made his entrance, Ella was on cloud nine when it came to caring for newborns. Good thing too, because she was going to need all the energy she could muster.

Following some disastrous economic years nationally, Watson's slowly recovered from the recession, thanks to a great Peck's Beach Tourist Department. The public relations program it generated was extremely effective, making sure visitors' needs were met and all were welcome. And when they came to play, they felt safe. Tourist traffic increased tenfold, and Watson's reaped the financial benefits as a result.

My relationship with JD deepened over these years, maybe in part to fill the void that his daughter's absence had left behind. JD never had a son, and I suspected I was about as close as anyone had ever come to fulfill that role. JD was a private man and didn't date much, maybe occasionally but never seriously. Other than the restaurant, his energy was directed to his church and the community at large. He was basically a lonely man. Watson's was his salvation from loneliness, and it kept him from inching toward the darker side of life. Laura, however, had no problem flirting with the darker side of her life, holding on tightly to resenting my attachment to JD and, by extension, Watson's...always a sore subject. Though seldom discussed, her anger lay just under the surface, much like a volcano gone dormant for way too long.

On Memorial Day weekend, the restaurant held its seasonal grand opening. After a long day preparing for Saturday's opening, JD took a much needed break and had an early dinner with friends at a restaurant on the bay in Somers Point. For May, the evening was unseasonably warm, a perfect time to put the top down on his convertible while coming over the causeway. The car radio was on, and his thoughts were a mile away, mostly centered on Watson's. There was no indication the drawbridge was going up; in fact, the bridge in front of him remained in place as he approached, but the other half of the bridge suddenly began to open independently. The usual bells were never heard, nor did the warning gates come down. There was no time to stop the car, even though he hit the brakes. The car careened into the water.

The captain of the sailboat Close to the Wind, which was poised to make its move through the bridge opening, had just returned from a sunset cruise. JD's car plunged into the bay about thirty feet in front of the boat. Another thirty seconds, and the car would have landed on the deck of the schooner, with a totally different outcome. Fortunately for him, JD's seat belt was not attached, so he was thrown free of the car.

At first, no one on the schooner had any idea what had just happened. The noise the car made as it hit water and the wake it caused rocked the sailboat so violently it began to take on water. All this happened in a matter of seconds. It was total chaos. Right after the initial shock, a cry for help, short and weak, echoed over the water beneath the bridge.

The crew's reactions were instant. One of the men dove in and was able to reach JD before he was pulled under from the swirling outflowing tide. By now, all hands were on deck, and they were able to bring him onboard. A ship-to-shore distress call was placed in seconds, while the crew made sure he was getting enough oxygen. Blankets were placed to keep him from going into shock. The Coast Guard responded very quickly, taking JD, unconscious and bleeding, aboard their cutter. They shot over to Somers Point Memorial Hospital, tying up at the dock outside the ER. There are no coincidences in life, they're orchestrated well in advance by a higher power. What are the chances Laura would be on duty. When they brought JD out of the Coast Guard Cutter on the stretcher, she had no idea who the patient was.

The medical personnel were barking orders while Laura was trying to move in closer to get a handle on the extent of the head injuries when suddenly getting a clear view of the man's face.

"This is my father!" she gasped.

The attending doctor said, "What, he's your father?"

"Yes!" she wailed.

"Back off, Laura. No way are you assisting with this case," he replied, as he respectfully but very firmly motioned her to step aside.

She did, but being unable to help at such a critical time really cut deeply. She had "backed off" her whole adult life from her father, so why should it hurt now? Why so different? Those words, "back off, back off," kept repeating in her head, finally beginning to resonate.

Like Ella had tried to tell her a hundred times, "Doesn't you see, child, mercy me, it ain't fittin' to carry all that bitterness around when your daddy loves you so much. It's gonna kill you inside with no good comin' from such feelings. Undeserved love is God's grace, a free gift poured out on you. The Lord's forgiven you, child, and He wants ya ta pass that same forgiveness right onto your daddy."

Somehow hearing those words "from the Spirit," as Ella liked to say, caused them to swirl in her head along with the vision of her badly injured father. It brought to life emotions, deep down emotions that she had not felt in years.

Laura successfully followed her father's progress during the night. It's interesting how circumstances often direct how our lives unfold. She was on the night shift until 7 AM. It was not her usual slot, but she was helping out a fellow nurse who was desperate for the night off.

JD's healing was slow, but Laura took charge of his aftercare management, and it was during this time that she was able to open up to him and he to her.

The thought that JD might die and that she'd never have the chance to at least listen to his side of the story started to sink in, and she knew this opportunity was never going to present itself again. If she were to make her move, now was the time.

"I know in my heart that I'm called, as a Christian and as Ella has always said, to forgive you regardless of whether I feel like it inside or not. But I need to hear your side of the story. Are you up for it?"

In a very weak voice, gathering as much strength as he could, JD took Laura's hand into his and said, "I've waited years to have you come and ask me that. Nothing would help me heal faster and make me happier."

Slowly, softly, with eyes half shut, JD began to retreat, in what seemed like slow motion, into his life long ago with Laura's mother, opening up and revealing all the deception Vi had thrown at him over the years. When he had finished, he looked beat, frail, and defeated.

Hands still held tightly together, Laura bent over him as he lay there, put her lips close to his ear, and whispered, "Dad, I forgive you." More unspoken words desperately wanted to be part of that whisper, but her tears drowned them out.

JD owed his survival to an amazing medical staff and to the quick actions of a number of professionals who'd just happened to be strategically placed that night to save his life. As he said later, "They were truly my guardian angels." His head injuries were the most dramatic, leaving him with memory loss, not critical, but enough that he became concerned about what his future would look like. So, after a considerable passage of time, JD decided it was best to sell the business, a fact he kept private. He was adamant about it, because he felt unable, physically and emotionally, to handle the essential daily management required. He took into account the fact that I was a huge help to him but was realistic enough to know I was divided in my attempt to juggle life between two very different jobs. It wasn't fair to expect me to drop everything and come on board to a seasonal business that took almost twenty-four-seven attention to operate.

The saving grace in all this was Chris Botta and her wonderful family. She had come on board as a waitress many years ago, bringing her daughter Florence and two sons, Sam and Joey. They made a great team working in the dining room and kitchen in the intervening years. Chris eventually became a pinch hitter for me when I got in the weeds trying to cope with two jobs. Chris was a natural when it came to hostessing and easily became part of Watson's. I don't know what I would have done without her.

Even with a great backup team, the energy, time, and commitment was overwhelming for JD to even think about, much less do physically. As a result, he quietly tested the waters with a few restaurateurs whom he could trust to keep their mouths shut. Not even Ella was aware of his decision, and it was a rarity for her to be excluded.

I knew nothing at all about JD's decision to sell until I found out at a real estate function from a tipsy restaurant owner, one whom JD would have expected to kept his lips sealed…proving the old adage "Loose lips sink ships."

I went to Ella privately and asked her if she had been privy to what that loose-tongued sailor had heard on the street about JD selling Watson's. She said she was out of the loop, but told me it made sense because JD was failing after his accident. It was time he made a move to lessen the pressure he felt and enjoy some quality of life while he was able.

I said nothing, but I knew exactly who would have been interested enough to explore the possibilities of a purchase. Placing strategically targeted phone calls with my business base, I was able to solve the mystery. It wasn't that difficult, considering it's a small town with too many realtors per capita.

The interested party contacted JD, striking a deal, and over the next month, JD never revealed that the pending sale of Watson's was under contract. The restaurant had been the focus of so much family unhappiness over the years. JD knew how much I loved Watson's and that I'd jump at the chance to buy it…a fact that, if accomplished, would have caused a serious split between Laura and me. Laura had forgiven her father, but she could not forget the pain her mother's actions had inflicted over the years, so JD believed his best option was to say nothing, get the place sold, and put it all behind him.

The settlement went well, or as well as JD could have expected. The buyer was a young restaurateur with no experience in food service on the scale of Watson's, so JD agreed to stay on as a consultant to help the new owner over the hump of the first season. Watson's was like fine food service on a treadmill, no stroll on the boardwalk, as they say in the business, and if you're not tuned in to that kind of pace, you'll get crushed, never knowing what hit you. In a fast-turnover business, if you're not savvy, you're the one who will turn over.

JD must have dreaded the drive to our apartment, knowing how tough it was going to be to break the news that Watson's would soon be history. The rain could only have enhanced his already depressed mood.

From my second-floor bedroom window, I saw JD slowly approached the front door... He paused for a second, and then I heard a knock. I came down the stairs as Laura opened the door. "Hey, Dad, come on in. What brings you out on this rainy night? You're usually knee deep in grease, closing up the joint!" The lightness in Laura's comment didn't brush away the look of concern on her father's face.

"Is everything okay? You look worried about something."

"I've got to tell you both something. Is Sax home?"

JD moved into the kitchen, and Laura followed as she called out for me. "Sax, your old boss is here." She walked to the refrigerator. "Dad, do you want a beer? I'm having a glass of wine."

"That sounds good right about now. Thanks."

Laura grabbed a beer and her wine, turned to the center island, where her father had pulled up a stool, and planted herself beside him—beer in a bottle for JD, her wine in a crystal glass she had refilled several times before the knock on the door.

I came in, sat down beside them, and asked, "What's up?"

With eyes cast downward and body language that revealed anxiety, JD slowly related why he had come to our house in the first place: to inform us that he had sold Watson's. I tried very hard to understand where he was coming from and even pitched a good defense about why I should have been the one to purchase Watson's despite JD's concerns to the contrary. After mutually shared feelings and more than a few tears, he'd finally realized what Watson's had come to mean to everyone in the family. The restaurant's near demise years ago was all behind them…old history, old bones, buried forever. Looking back now was just a bit too late…it served no purpose. The finality of it suddenly hit JD…he wanted to take it all back, but couldn't. I think he left the house feeling even more depressed, even though Laura and I had assured him that "All things work for good to those who love the Lord," a favorite Bible verse of his, easy to say but difficult to hold on to when you're in the midst of some tough life circumstances.

CHAPTER 31

As JD slowly drove away from the house, I stuffed my real feelings way down inside because it hurt too much to deal with them. I wondered how all this was going to play out.

Given the fact that Watson's was a landmark in town, it only seemed right to celebrate with a big bash in September as a way to say thank you for all the years of patronage.

It seemed the entire city turned out for this "major happening." The party started at Watson's for cocktails and hors d'oeuvres and then moved on to the Asteria Hotel for dinner and dancing in order to be able to accommodate all the people who had responded. Patrons from every station in life came forward to express the effect the ambiance of the restaurant had on their lives...marriages, births, engagements, weddings, funerals...every conceivable high or low point in life deserving of a celebration seemed to have taken place at Watson's.

JD stood up and made a heartfelt speech, a great accomplishment considering the limelight was not his forte, thanking everyone for what they'd meant to him over the years. He then asked if the new owner would please step forward. Jonathan Reilly got up and made his way to the podium. Guests applauded, and as JD started to introduce him, Jonathan cut him off.

"John, I am not what you think I am. I am who you say I am. I'm Jonathan, that's certain, but I'm not the new owner of Watson's; that title belongs to..."

"To me." The words rang out over the room as if riding on an arrow aimed straight at JD's heart. Everyone turned around in an attempt to find out who shot that "arrow."

I slowly weaved my way around the many tables of guests, heading toward the podium, as the place erupted with wild applause, shouts of "Bravo, bravo!" and "Amen, brother!" JD was stunned. He didn't see or hear anything or anyone else in the room but was totally focused on me, his son-in-law, making my way through the eruption of sound toward my "father," the person who had taught me so much about the values in life, about what really counted in the end, about hope, love, and faith.

Coming on strong right behind me was Laura, her face soaked with tears. She knew there was not a chance in hell she was going to sit there, watching this unbelievable moment pass by and not be part of it. She had held onto my secret in confidence from the moment she'd heard it.

After JD had initially dropped the bomb to us about selling Watson's, I confessed to Laura what I had done. She was well aware of my lifelong desire to own the restaurant, to save not only the business, but it's place in the historical fiber of the island. So I told her how my in-depth due diligence had revealed the notorious background of the group of men behind the deal struck with JD. Yes, the offer had been full price, but these guys had the reputation of buying property, managing the business for a year or two, and then tearing it down and building high-rise condos. The profits to be made were huge. Since the contract was still in attorney review, the realtor three-day waiting period imposed by the state, I was able to come in with my "straw buyer" and present an offer way above asking that JD could be a fool to turn down. The rest was easy. I used my mystery buyer at the settlement table to keep my personal ownership anonymous.

Laura had said to me, "It's all beginning to make sense now. When my father told us he had sold the islands land mark, you looked really sad, and I was amazed you weren't more vocal about objecting and expressing your disappointment."

I knew then what I had pulled off and it was all I could do to not tell JD then. I knew plans were in the works for a big celebration in the coming month, so I decided to wait. That was a tough thing to keep secret, that's for sure.

Nothing could keep Laura from wanting to be at the center of this monumental chapter in all our lives. She had come full circle by forgiving her father, and it felt wonderful, providing closure for her and a new beginning for me.

JD and I were hugging so hard when Laura joined us that she had difficulty wedging her way in, but once she did, the three of us held desperately to one another, stretching the moment out as long as we could.

What no one saw in all the commotion was Ella. She had been seated beside Laura and was now making a gallant effort to join our group hug but was struggling to get on her feet, let alone keep her balance. I caught a glimpse over JD's shoulder of her attempt to stand, so I broke rank for a second and scrambled back to assist her.

Gently lifting her up, I whispered, "Come, Ella darlin', let's join the love fest."

Her reply, "You know it too, darlin'?" After the look of joy I caught as she came to her feet, I knew I'd never forget the contentment evidenced on that beautiful face of hers.

"You are somethin' else, child," she said, and with that, she and I maneuvered our way to the podium, completing the team hug.

The evening celebration lingered on for hours, lighting up the ballroom of the gracious old Asteria Hotel, a throwback to days gone by. Funny how the past, so present in the ambiance of this stately "Lady by the Sea," seemed to step aside on that special evening to embrace the future of those among us who were so willing and open to receive redemption, healing, and love.

Laura and I danced well past midnight, reminding me of the Dunes till Dawn after-hours club outside Somers Point. It brought back memories of another time and place. But tonight was reserved for creating new memories, a time to move forward with great expectations. Let the past stay where it belonged. Laura and I had so much to be thankful for, so many blessings.

In the middle of a slow dance with Laura, I looked into those beautiful eyes of hers and said, "I've got an idea. Let's say our goodbyes and blow this popsicle stand. Come on, follow me." With that, I grabbed Laura's arm, and we made our escape—after much hugging and kissing of the man who'd made the evening possible, JD.

Laura, looking a little lost, said, "What are you up to? Where are we going at this hour?"

"You'll see," I replied as I opened the door for her and got her in my car. All pistons running, I aimed the car toward the south end of the island. The night was unusually warm for mid-September, a real plus for what I had in mind.

When I pulled up and parked where the beach and the road came to a dead end, Laura said, "You are a crazy man, Mr. Saxon. I'm in my party dress and heels."

"Well, kick off those heels and pull up that dress." I scooped up a blanket from the back seat, a bottle of Champagne, two plastic glasses, and then coming around to Laura's side of the car, I took hold of her hand and led her down a dune path that was very familiar from years ago. Nice to know some things never change.

We were both laughing at the absurdity of the "crazy man's" little plot to end a wonderful night at the very place it had all begun. I spread out the blanket and poured the Champagne as we knelt facing one another. "Here's a toast to us, honey; no, here's a toast to you, the true love of my life, the mother of our beautiful children.

I've never known where you end and I begin, because we wouldn't fully exist if we were separated. This, I know: we became one here among these dunes one moonlit night long ago, two very naive kids determined to hold onto their love for each other despite the odds. We made it, honey. We made it!

I caught the moonlight in her eyes as she started to whisper, but I gently put my two fingers against her lips, and then her words got lost in my kiss.

The feel of the ocean, the taste of champagne, it was magic once again, and we made love with no inhibitions. Sex without love is just sex... Sex with love is like whipped cream on top of ice cream. Our bodies and souls, hidden among the dunes, had come alive once more.

The next morning, I awoke in an empty bed. Laura had left a note saying she'd gone for a walk on the beach, one of her favorite things to do. I was really charged up and couldn't wait to get to Watson's. The restaurant was closing for the season, the last weekend in September, as usual. I wanted to be there to work with JD to finalize last-minute details with the staff. I had to pinch myself; was this really happening? Was this really my first day on the job as owner of Watson's...? Unbelievable.

Driving to the restaurant, the reality of last night's celebration finally started to sink in. Hopefully, the crew was running late and had not made breakfast yet... I loved the way they could whip up bacon and eggs like you never had before, turning simple into scrumptious... It was magic. I parked the car close to the building and went up the back steps, so familiar to me, and then paused. Flashbacks to my first day on the job came rushing in when I had, back then, also paused to think that life would never be the same once I opened that screen door. Little did I know then how prophetic that would turn out to be.

The pause was fleeting; reaching to open the door, it opened itself to reveal the face of my beautiful wife. Taken by surprise, I said, "When did you get here?"

"Shhhh."

"But?"

"Shhhhh."

That said, Laura very lovingly drew herself up as close as she could get to me, looked up, locked both arms around my neck, and whispered through lips pressing ever so gently against mine, "So glad you could make it!"

AUTHOR'S NOTE

It may take a village to raise a child, but it took me a lifetime of loving, laughing, crying and praying with family and friends to birth a book.

57158198R00157

Made in the USA
Columbia, SC
06 May 2019